Joseph R. Rosenberger

THE HEROIN CONNECTION

A Critic's Choice paperback
from Lorevan Publishing, Inc.
New York, New York

Reprinted by arrangement with The Author

ISBN: 1-55547-123-4

First Critic's Choice edition: 1986

From LOREVAN PUBLISHING, INC.

Critic's Choice Paperbacks
31 E. 28th Street
New York, New York 10016

Manufactured in the United States of America

*This book is dedicated
to
Perry and Pema
and
George and Dorothy*

CHAPTER ONE_____

IT'S a fine night for a removal. Skul drove the Corvette several hundred feet into the woods, parked between two walnut trees and turned off the lights and the engine. He reached into the compartment in the dash, took out a miniature night vision device, turned it on, and carefully scanned the area. He soon realized his big fear—that a couple might be parked and making love—had not matured. He had the woods all to himself. He got out of the car, leaving the door open. There was only the soft rustle of leaves, moved by the late summer breeze. He reached behind the driver's seat and, from a large cardboard box, took out two coiled lengths of nylon rope. Next to the box was the folded 12 foot aluminum ladder, which he also removed from the car. Then came the belt and special ballistic nylon holster filled with a .22 caliber Ruger Mk-1 auto-pistol, which had a noise suppressor built around the barrel. On one side of the belt was a black nylon magazine pouch containing three packets of C-4, each small brown package of high explosive, weighing 10 ounces, equipped with a detonator that could be triggered by remote control.

Unbuttoning his tweed jacket, Skul buckled the belt around his waist, then reached into the cardboard box and

removed two spare magazines for the Ruger; he also took
out a soft rubber full-face mask and a pair of thin leather
gloves, then tossed his brown leather touring cap onto the
front seat. After locking the door, he took one final survey
through the night vision scope. Satisfied that he was alone,
he dropped the device into his left coat pocket, picked up
the ladder in his right hand and started moving southeast,
accompanied by the music of crickets and a pale yellow
halfmoon.

The home of Salvatore Giulio Tuccinardo was only half
a mile away. All he had to do was go over the wall, sneak
past the guards, get inside the large house and put a .22
Hydra-Shok bullet into Don Salvatore's brain. Yeah—one
other thing. Get out of the house and outside of the
compound, without getting killed! While there were always uncertainties in even the best planned termination,
Skul was positive that, in this case, the target would be
very well guarded. Tuccinardo was one of the most notorious gangsters in the United States. As *Avvocato,* or chair-
man, of the Cosa Nostra's Grand Council, he practically
controlled all the six Mafia families in New York City—
*That spaghetti-bender will be better protected than the
President of this country!*

Thinking about the layout, Skul moved through the
heavily wooded area, now and then pausing to look through
the night vision scope. Agents of COBRA had secretly
obtained photo copies of files from the New York office of
the FBI. Skul was not only familiar with the arrangement
of the rooms in Don Salvatore's house, but he also knew
there were flaws in the security system. For one thing, the
house and grounds were too close to the wooded area. For
another, while there were two revolving tv cameras in
back of the house and in the front of the house, they
moved in only a half-circle. And that 180 degrees required
a full minute. Worse, there were dead spots, areas that the
four television monitoring cameras totally missed. One of

these dead places was the southwest corner of the 8 foot
decorative concrete wall that enclosed the compound. The
biggest flaw of all lay just outside that corner. Outside the
wall was an oak older than God, judging from its height—
over 100 feet—and thick trunk. Best of all was the large
branch that intruded over the wall for almost 10 feet, at a
height of 20 to 25 feet.

Skul covered the distance rapidly, stopping when he
could see the compound through the night vision scope and
estimated that he was only 400 feet from the north wall.
He had crept southwest, then straight south, and finally
east. Now, the southwest corner of the wall was only 150 feet
away.

Standing beside a maple, he again surveyed the forward
area through the battery-powered infrared scope, which
amplified available background light 500 hundred times
and had a 25mm/fl.4 lens. It was one of the best small
night vision devices sold by Law Enforcement Associates.
The area was clear.

The woods had thinned out, and for 125 feet the area by
the wall was open, except for the large oak that was 10
feet from the southwest corner, and a cluster of much
smaller trees in the vicinity of the oak. Nonetheless, Skul
did not underestimate the danger. It was always possible
that someone on the second floor of the large house was
keeping a watch on the entire area through a night vision
scope. Possible, but not very probable. Don Salvatore was
too secure in his power. After all, who would dare attack
him? The Feds would drive right up to the double gates in
front and ring the bell.

Four point six miles to the south was the small commu-
nity of Glen Cove. Eight miles southwest of Glen Cove,
Long Island, was the northeastern boundary of New York
City. Less than a mile away, Skeeter Ronson waited in
Hempstead Harbor with the motorboat. Skeeter was the
back-up man—totally reliable, always exactly where he was

supposed to be, and one tough, uncompromising son-of-a-bitch. Skul also suspected Skeeter was in charge of sudden retirement should the inside man screw up. His very presence inspired success.

More determined than ever to put Don Salvatore asleep forever, Skul made a final check of his equipment. The RC station that would detonate the C-4 was in an inside coat pocket. He took out the Ruger, sent a cartridge into the firing chamber, pushed on the safety, shoved the weapon back into the holster and made sure the flap was securely fastened. He didn't bother to check the .45 Pachmayr Modular pistol he carried in a right shoulder holster. The big weapon was always ready to be fired—just push off the safety.

He put the night vision scope into his coat pocket, made certain that the two coiled lengths of rope were securely strapped to his belt, and picked up the folding ladder, which was painted black to deflect light. He hurried forward, moving as silently as a shadow through the darkness, and wondered what Deborah Miles was doing. Skul frowned. It was a few minutes after midnight. No doubt she was in bed with Alexandr Yasakev, screwing up a storm with the Russian son-of-a-bitch!

A man for whom the process of double-think was normal, Skul, nonetheless, found himself the victim of conflicting emotions when he thought of the Doves, the female agents of COBRA, who were highly trained in "sex-pionage." They used sex the way the KGB's Swallows used sex; the way the Eagles, the male agents of COBRA, made use of conventional intelligence tradecraft.

To counterbalance his disgust with the "Patriotic Prostitutes" of COBRA (as Skul and the other Eagles called the Doves—but never to their faces), was the common sense logic that any method was permissible in fighting world Communism. In this silent but very real war one had to set aside morality and ethics, and never lose sight of the fact that to win, one had to be not only more intelligent than the enemy, but also more ruthless. On this basis, if a COBRA Dove could gain vital information by seducing some Russian scum bag, so be it. *But I don't have to respect her for it . . .*

Skul didn't waste a tenth of a second when he reached the huge oak. Unfolding the black aluminum ladder, he locked the sections, placed the ladder against the south side of the tree and climbed to the top, pausing long enough to tie a length of strong cord to the last rung. Keeping the other end of the cord in his hand, he pulled himself up to a branch several feet above his head. Taking in the cord, he pulled up the ladder, unlocked the sections and, using the cord, tied the four 3 foot lengths to a branch on the south side of the oak. Now the problem was how to reach the limb sticking out over the southwest corner of the wall.

Perched somewhat precariously, Skul took out the night vision scope and studied the tree. He quickly found that while the long limb was high enough from the top of the wall, there was still a very real danger from the smaller boughs, the offshoots that jutted downward from the big branch—one in particular. His weight on the end of the limb would cause the lowest offshoot to touch the alarm wire stretched lengthwise across the top center of the wall.

Skul carefully climbed upward until he reached another limb 8 feet above the large branch. He moved 10 feet out on the limb, leaves and tiny side branches slapping at him, and tied one end of the shorter nylon line around the branch and let the rest of it dangle downward. He then retraced his climb and returned to the bough he needed so badly.

He moved 3 feet outward on the limb, took out the NV scope, moved a few more feet, then looked at the offshoot branch which angled toward the top of the wall. The branch was now closer to the top of the wall. By the time he reached the nylon rope dangling from the branch over-head, the small offshoot bough was only 3 feet above the wall. Skul tied the rope securely around the large branch on which he was standing, then tested the limb. The branch moved only a fraction of an inch; the line was as tight as a piano wire. Just the same, the branch would bend when he moved toward its end, particularly when he descended to the ground, but it wouldn't bend 3 feet, not with the rope fastened to it.

Carefully, Skul crawled outward, inching himself along. Soon he had moved past the top of the wall and was in a position that placed him inside the compound. Again, he took out the night vision scope and studied the entire area inside the compound. Nothing. No one was in sight. Good! He was directly above the dead spot. Below, by the inside corner, there was pitch darkness.

Skul removed the longer length of coiled nylon rope from his belt, tied one end to the limb and played out the rest to the grass beneath the branch. He put on his leather gloves and was soon sliding down the line. The very lowest offshoot branch came within a foot of the top of the wall, but no lower. Then his feet were on the dew-wet grass.

From where he stood, he could see the swimming pool, the water shimmering from colored lights at the bottom. He could also see the south end tv monitoring camera mounted on a white metal post in front of the long patio, which was toward the west center of the large house. There was also a small light burning at the north end of the patio, its glow revealing part of the small guest house to the north.

Hidden within the darkness of the dead spot by the inside corner of the wall, Skul slipped on the rubber face mask, which was of the type sold by novelty houses, masks of Richard Nixon, President Reagan, Dirty Old Man, etc. Skul's mask was of Frankenstein.

Getting inside the house would be comparatively easy. Since both tv cameras were a good 20 feet away from the house, all he had to do was wait until the south end camera had turned its half circle to the north, then make a run for the southwest corner of the house. Not that there wouldn't be any danger. There were five guards—unless the FBI files were inaccurate. They would be on an enclosed sun porch on the north side of the house where the four tv screens for the tv cameras were located.

Skul pulled the Ruger with its built-in silencer, thumbed off the safety lever and waited, his eyes watching the south tv camera through the night vision scope. A few minutes later, he made the run that ended by the southwest corner of the large brick structure.

He moved rapidly, keeping within the darkness by the side of the house. A very large room jutted out not far from the west center, appearing as if it had been built and tacked on after the rest of the house had been completed. Don Salvatore had built it as a special meeting room, where he and the *caporegimes*—or underbosses—of his Mafia family could discuss business. Drapes were pulled over the small windows.

Moving north, Skul reached the southwest corner of the room that stuck outward. He crept along its west side, paused at the northwest corner and carefully looked around the edge. Now he could look down the full length of the patio—very clearly, too, because of the light at its north end. He also saw that the patio was no longer deserted. Ah, what luck! Two men had just come outside through the French doors, both carrying large flashlights. The shorter of the two men locked the doors while the other lighted a cigarette. The short man dropped the keys into a side-slat pocket of his windbreaker jacket and with the other man began to walk leisurely west. Skul knew that very quickly they would be within 10 feet of him.

To shoot or not to shoot was not the question. It was

only a matter of when. The "when" for Skul came when the taller man turned on his flashlight and began playing the beam on the ground.

Skul raised the Ruger and gently squeezed the trigger— *phyyyyt!* The .22 slug hit Tall Man in the left side of his chest, zipping in at a very steep angle. He let out a low "Uh!," jerked, and had not yet started to fall when there was another *phyyyyt!* Short Man's head jerked violently. The flashlight slipped from his hand. Skul's .22 projectile had speared through his left temple and had scrambled his brain. He fell a second after the other man crashed to the ground on his face.

Skul left the corner and raced over to the two dead dummies. He was not concerned whether the man hit in the chest was dead. Skul knew he was. A Hydra-Shok bullet does tremendous damage, even in small calibers such as a .22, the destruction coming from a lead post, or cone, set within the center of the hollow point bullet giving the projectile greater tearing power.

Skul took the keys from Short Man's jacket, realizing he was fully exposed to enemy fire. He didn't, however, have much of a choice. He couldn't leave the two corpses lying there in the light. He shoved the Ruger into its holster, grabbed the dead men by their collars and dragged them across the lawn to the darkness by the side of the house. Silently then, he moved to the French doors, the Ruger in his right hand. After trying the fourth key on the ring, he opened the doors, slipped inside and found himself in a sitting room with doors on the east and the south sides. Skul crept across the carpet to the south door, going over the layout of the house in his mind. He knew that beyond the south door was a hall that moved from east to west. Toward the center was the staircase that led to the second floor.

Skul gingerly cracked open the door and listened. Hearing nothing but the ticking of a grandfather clock at the east end of the hall, he left the sitting room, soon came to the stairs, and started upward to the second floor. He went up the stairs very fast, keeping his feet toward one end of each carpeted step to prevent it from creaking. He reached the top, looked around and listened. There was faint snoring coming from one room. The hall was short and, dimly lighted by a small blue bulb, stretched to the much longer main upstairs hall, on each side of which were bedrooms. Don Salvatore's bedroom was at the end of the hall to the west. Remembering the diagram obtained from FBI files, Skul recalled that the Don's room had the only door that fully faced the east, that faced the full length of the hall. The doors of the other bedrooms faced either the south or the north.

Skul made the turn from the short corridor and was halfway down the long hall, which was lighted by three small, blue bulbs, when all his good luck vanished like smoke in a tornado. The door to a bedroom on the north side opened and a woman—yawning and clad in a cream colored dressing gown—stepped into the hall. Behind her, through the open door came the glow from a lamp.

Skul froze! So did the woman when she saw him—a man with a pistol in his hand who had the face of *Frankenstein!* She let out a high pitched scream at the same time Skul pulled the trigger and a man—as bald as an orange and wearing only undershorts—started through the door. A bullet hole between her breasts and a silly look frozen on her face, the woman started to topple forward.

Phyyyyt! Skul fired a micro-moment later, simultaneously with the man jerking himself back into the bedroom and slamming the door, the .22 Hydra-Shok projectile striking the edge of the door and burying itself in the wood.

FAILURE! The word screamed in Skul's mind as he turned and raced down the hall. The wipe-out had been blown. Behind him were four loud reports as the man in the bedroom put four 9mm slugs through the door, the shots sounding thunderous in the shattered stillness. Certain that everyone in the house was now awake, Skul reached the short hall and headed for the steps to the first floor. Now that all the fat was sizzling in the fire, there wasn't any need for secrecy and silence. The only need was for escape. Accordingly, he pulled the .45 Pachmayr pistol and, with the big weapon in his left hand, started down the steps. He was halfway down when he saw the three other security men. One man was coming out of the door of the sitting room, a Smith and Wesson 9-millimeter automatic in his hand. The other two goons were only 20 feet from the bottom of the steps, to Skul's left. The gunsel with the thick head of curly black hair carried a MAC-Ingram submachine gun. The other joker's right hand was filled with a .357 Colt Python revolver.

Neither Vincent Fiorino nor Charley Sirignano were timid souls. For that matter, neither was Big Buster Umberto, the button man coming out of the sitting room. All three were "made-men," each having committed at least one murder to become a full-fledged member of the Mafia. Each was as tough as armor plate and utterly ruthless.

"KILL THE GODDAMNED MOTHERFUCKER!" yelled Charley Sirignano, the curly haired hood with the Ingram SMG. As Sirignano started to raise the Ingram, and Vinnie Fiorino threw up his Colt Python, Skul threw himself down on the stairs, snap-aimed, and pulled the triggers of both the Ruger and the Pachmayr Modular auto-pistol, the big booms of the .45 Pachmayr and Fiorino's .357 mag Colt sending echoes reverberating throughout the large house.

Sirignano never got a chance to fire the little Ingram chatter box. Skul's .22 projectile struck him directly below the nose. It zipped through his upper teeth, skimmed across the roof of his mouth, tore through his throat and came out the rear of his neck. As good as stone dead, the knees of the hood buckled.

Vinnie Fiorino's flat-nosed .357 magnum slug came so close to Skul's right shoulder that it ripped a line across his coat before it chomped into the wall. Fiorino had used up all his chances. The slob never even got the opportunity to see if his bullet had hit Frankenstein. He didn't because no sooner had he pulled the trigger of the Colt Python than Skul's .45 slug struck him in the forehead, an inch above the bridge of the nose. Fiorino might as well have had his head a foot from an exploding hand grenade. An ordinary .45 ACP bullet would have done enough damage, but a .45 Hydra-Shok projectile was pure TNT. It did more than shatter the frontal bone of Fiorino's skull. It exploded the entire top of his head, sending a shower of ripped apart brain, bone, flesh and blood all over the rug and the still warm corpse of Sirignano, who lay on his back, eyes open, a widening pool of thick red underneath his head and neck.

Big Buster Umberto, a cautious crud, had not fired a shot. From his position outside the door of the sitting room, he couldn't get a clear view of Skul. The banister and its numerous posts were in the way. Skul had the same disadvantage; nonetheless, he snapped off a quick shot with the Pachmayr, just to let Umberto know he was still alive and in good shape. The bullet banged into the wall a foot from the hood's head. That was more than enough for Big Buster whose creed was never face a man in the open if you can shoot him in the back or whack him out from the side. Shit! That was only common sense.

Umberto ducked back into the sitting room and ran through the east door into the study. He got down on one knee by the side of the door and pointed his 9mm S4W autoloader at the door of the sitting room. Now let the son-of-a-bitch come through that door!

It was the slight creaking above that warned Skul, who was getting to his feet. All in one motion he threw his body to the other side of the steps, spun, and brought up the Ruger and the Pachmayr Modular as two auto-pistols roared from the short hall at the top of the steps.

One of the men at the top of the stairs was Dominic "Little Blue Eyes" Anselmo, one of Don Salvatore's personal bodyguards. He and Joseph Bruno, the other bodyguard, always slept in the bedroom next to the Don's. Bruno was in the bedroom of the Don, crouched by the dresser, an UZI submachine gun in his hand, its stubby barrel pointed at the door. Don Salvatore and his wife Angela waited in a bulletproof closet with a steel door, which could only be unlocked from the inside.

The other man with Little Blue Eyes was Simon Rupert Rosenkrantz, an attorney who handled much of the Don's Family business. It was Rosenkrantz's wife Skul had put to sleep, and the attorney was determined to have his revenge on the assassin who had snuffed her. He should have stayed in bed!

Rosenkrantz's 9mm bullet and Little Blue Eyes' slug burned air through the space where Skul had been. By then it was too late. During that micro-moment, Skul's big Pachmayr Modular pistol roared and the Ruger whispered *phyyyyt-phyyyyt.*

The .45 Hydra-Shok slug stabbed Little Blue Eyes in the groin, with all the force of a runaway express train, the terrific impact doubling him over and pitching him back 6 feet. He was dead before his back slammed to the rug. The slug had torn through his lower intestines and shattered three vertebrae, cutting the spinal cord in the process. He hadn't even gotten a chance to mutter *"Scifosa . . . grinudo."*

One .22 Ruger projectile popped Rosenkrantz in the belly and gave him a second navel before tearing through his colon. The second bullet caught him under the right rib cage. It bored through his liver, cut through a rib and rocketed out his back. Unlike Little Blue Eyes, who had dropped his Llama Omni pistol, Rosenkrantz retained his hold on the Browning Hi-Power Automatic. Still wearing only undershorts, he half turned, his skinny legs doing a final tango. As he fell sideways, a spasm made his finger pull against the trigger. The Browning roared, a slug hitting the rug.

Angry with himself, Skul didn't hang around to see who else might storm into the short corridor and start tossing slugs at him. He hadn't forgotten the creep who had ducked back into the sitting room. Running the rest of the way down the stairs—one eye on the hall side door of the sitting room—Skul paused long enough to reach into the magazine pouch on his belt and take out one of the small packages of C-4. Switching on the detonator, he placed the packet on the rug next to the bottom step.

Most of the lights had been turned on upstairs, but the ground floor was still dark, not that it made any difference to Skul. Making a mental picture of the bottom floor, he knew that due east of the sitting room was the study. East of the study was the large dining room. The hood who had retreated had gone either through the French doors to the outside, or else he had used the east door and was in the study—*or he's waiting in the dining room!* Skul had only two choices: either go through the south door of the sitting room or the south door of the dining room.

Hearing shouts from the upstairs, Skul chose the latter route. He ran across the hall, flung open the door, darted in low, moved to his left and took refuge by a solid walnut china cabinet. In an instant, he had taken the remote control detonating station from his pocket and turned it on. When the light glowed green, he pushed the small red button.

BLAMMMMMMMMM! The 10 ounces of C-4 exploded with a roar that shook the entire house and made the chandelier over the dining room table sway back and forth. After the smoke cleared in the hall, a third of the staircase was gone and there was an 8 foot wide hole in the floor, the edges jagged with splintered flooring.

The C-4's going off completely unnerved Big Buster Umberto. He wasn't about to go up against a motherfucker who was blowing up the joint. He didn't stop to think that Skul must have left the stairs in order to blow them up, and might be in the dining room.

Fleeing the study, Big Buster used the east side door that opened into the dining room. His eyes were adjusted to the darkness, so the first thing he saw was Skul crouched by the china cabinet on the far side of the room. Umberto wasn't a coward, and he was very fast, but he wasn't a match for a master technician like Skul.

Muttering *"Bucco del culo!,"* Big Buster brought up his Smith and Wesson and fired. There was the crashing sound of another auto-pistol firing and a very brief crucifixion in his chest, then nothing—nothing at all.

Skul had been faster. From his position, he had been keeping a close watch on the door of the study and the door to the living room. He had moved to his right and fired a micro-second before Big Buster, who didn't move. He would never move again. Skul's .45 slug had turned his heart to bloody mush. He lay on his left side, a hole in his chest the size of an orange. All his 9mm slug had done was hit the china cabinet and shatter a lot of Angela Tuccinardo's dishes.

Skul first reloaded the Pachmayr and the Ruger. Then he sprinted across the dining room, tore through the study, raced through the sitting room and left the house via the French doors. He saw that another of his fears had been realized: scores of lights had been turned on and much of the outside was as bright as high noon. At least he didn't have to worry about the Feds parked down the road. They kept a constant watch on the Don's house but Skul knew they weren't a problem. FBI agents would not come gang-busting in, not until they had gone through the proper legal procedures. That's why the Federal Bureau of Investigation was so ineffective in fighting not only organized crime but also foreign dirty-tricks and espionage; the Bureau had to operate within legal channels. COBRA did not; neither did agents of COBRA—which is why the ultra-secret organization was formed.

COBRA was a "black operations" bureau that officially didn't exist. It was so secret even the Central Intelligence Agency and the National Security Agency were unaware of it. The Defense Intelligence Agency—the intelligence branches of the Army, Navy, and Air Force—didn't even suspect the existence of COBRA. Neither did INR, the State Department's Bureau of Intelligence and Research; and of course the FBI was in the dark.

However, there were 5 high officials in the National Security Agency who did know that some kind of highly covert organization existed and that, in a sense, it was connected with NSA. They didn't know its *name*, or *why* it existed, or *what* its agents did. They only knew it existed—it *was*. They knew because operational funds for COBRA were channelled through the various departments of NSA, this system making it impossible for Congress and other traditional branches of government to monitor COBRA, since Congress could not butt into NSA with its silly and useless investigations.

Why NSA? Officially, NSA's field was cryptography. In reality, NSA was a vast army of specialists who received, analyzed and sifted secret information gathered by electronically equipped ships, spy planes and satellites. It was NSA that uncovered such top secret information as the locations of Soviet missile bases and confidential Soviet policies discussed in private conversations.

It was because of NSA's size and complexity that money for COBRA was "lost" within its various departments, funds that eventually made their way to the desk of Jonas Farley Barron, the Director of the *Counter-Subversion Operations Bureau of Resistance and Action*—COBRA.

Skul reasoned there was little danger from the police of

Glen Cove. They wished Don Salvatore would leave the planet. If anyone reported the explosion and the sounds of guns firing at the estate, the local police would think it was mob warfare and not show up until the shooting was over.

By then, I'll be long gone!

With all the lights on in the yard, getting out of the area would not be easy. Skul realized he could not leave the way he had come in, by going up the nylon line to the big limb, and then climbing down the oak. No way. And he had to anticipate gunsels coming after him.

Grateful that the guest house was dark—*No one is in it*—he moved south, going the opposite way to the direction he had used when he had first approached the house. He ran past the patio, thinking again of COBRA and how valuable the small but highly efficient intelligence organization was. COBRA did what other Government agencies could not do: *it got the job done by any means available.* If an individual or a group—foreign or American—was a threat to the people of the United States, and other government agencies, such as the FBI, CIA or the Drug Enforcement Agency, couldn't legally, ethically or morally eradicate the danger, COBRA stepped in with its 250 highly trained agents.

Sixty-five of these agents were women. While the girls used conventional methods of tradecraft, they also employed sex. They used sex for blackmail, sex to gain information, and sex to gain entry into groups and organizations off limits to male agents; and when a COBRA Dove used sex as a weapon, she had more techniques at her disposal than could be found in the *Kama Sutra!*

Skul came to the special meeting room that jutted out from the west side of the house. He raced past it and was between the swimming pool and the remainder of the house when several lights in the meeting room came on. He reached the southwest corner of the house—his first goal—and carefully looked around the edge up the southside of the house. He wasn't too surprised at what he saw. Three men were creeping along the south side, heading toward him—one in pajamas, slippers, and a green cotton bathroom, one fully dressed, and a big goon, so hairy he resembled an ape, decked out only in a T-shirt and shorts. He was barefooted. All three were armed: Pajamas and Slippers carrying a MAC-Ingram submachine gun, the other two holding pistols. It was the gunsel with the chopper-box that worried Skul. An Ingram could vomit slugs with all the speed of a Vegas slot machine eating silver dollars.

Skul knew he had to take the chance. If he pulled back around the corner, the hoods would box him in and prevent him from reaching the southwest corner of the wall. Skul did the only logical thing possible: he moved into the open and threw himself to the grass, firing both pistols as he went down, at the same time that the creep with the chatterbox got off a long burst. Behind Pajamas and Slippers and his Ingram, the two other jokers brought up their pieces.

A stream of 9mm hollow point Ingram projectiles passed over Skul's head and back. One bullet came within an inch of hitting his left ear lobe. A second slug streaked half an inch from his right temple. A third projectile burned air even closer to the top of his head, so close it almost zipped through his hair.

The little Ingram was still snarling angrily, exhausting the remainder of its magazine, only this time the projectiles were shooting upward at a steep angle toward the sky. Skul's .45 slug from the Pachmayr Modular had smacked Pajamas and Slippers high in the chest and smashed him backward. Dead on his feet, he was falling to his back, his finger frozen in death on the trigger.

Albert Bucerelli, the fully dressed dummy with the 9mm Beretta, and the ape, Daniel "Momo" Mustone, figured they couldn't miss Skul, who was prone on the ground on his stomach. A split second before Mustone fired his Arminex Trifire autoloader—and he was a fraction ahead of Bucerelli—Skul rolled over on his back, brought up both weapons over his shoulders and, mentally aiming, pulled each trigger twice.

Mustone's .38-super slug thudded into the ground a foot to Skul's right where his head would have been if he hadn't rolled over. Bucerelli's 9mm hollow point projectile popped the turf even closer to Skul. And Skul also missed, but only with one .22 caliber slug. It passed within a foot of Bucerelli's left, went through a window and buried itself in the east wall of the dining room. The other .22 bullet tore into Bucerelli's throat, turned his Adam's apple into jelly and tore out the back of his neck. With blood spurting from his throat and his arms flapping like broken chicken wings, he started to go down. So did Momo Mustone. Skul's slug had stabbed him in the knob of the left humerus—the shoulder bone—and the terrific impact and ripping quality of the Hydra-Shok bullet had torn off the arm. Skul, rolling back over on his stomach, had to give the big bastard credit. Blood spurting from his torn shoulder, from his veins and arteries, Mustone was still trying to bring up his Arminex Trifire and get off another round when Skul shoved him into hell with another .45 slug in the chest.

Skul jumped to his feet, hurried back to the shadows at the southwest corner of the house and pulled out a package of C-4. He turned on the detonator attached to the explosive, measured the distance to the inside of the wall's southwest corner—*It's almost 60 feet!*—and threw the package. He was down on his knees and taking out the remote control station when he heard someone, far to the north, yell, *"THE SON OF A BITCH IS ON THE EAST SIDE!"* and saw 3 men coming around from the west wall of the meeting room. Two of the hoods carried flashlights and revolvers. The third man had what appeared to be an assault rifle.

I'm running out of luck! Desperately hoping the C-4 was against the wall, Skul got down flat, turned his head toward the house and pressed the red button of the remote control station.

BLAMMMMMMM! There was a brief but bright flash of fire, and shattered concrete blocks dissolved, small chunks flying through the air. Pieces hit Skul on the legs and back, the largest the size of a marble. The C-4 had blasted a 7 foot wide opening in the wall, and smoke still curled from the edges of the broken blocks.

The three hoods to the north, stunned momentarily by the unexpected explosion, pulled up short, making easy targets. The joker with the assault rifle went down first, a .45 Hydra-Shok slug having torn through his chest. Before the other two knew what was happening, they died, one with a .45 slug through his groin, the other with two .22 projectiles that struck him in the face and torn off the back of his head.

Do it! Run for it! Skul tore across the yard toward the gap in the wall, his feet pounding the grass. Then he was tearing through the opening and *outside* the wall. Ahead was the darkened woods and safety. He paused, pulled out the last package of C-4 from the ammo pouch, turned on the detonator and dropped the explosive into a pile of concrete chunks. He'd blow the packet when he was 500 feet into the woods.

Taking out the night vision scope, Skul headed northwest. Now, to reach the Corvette, get away from the area and head back to New York City.

Bitterness flowed through his mind.

I've failed!

He thought again of Deborah Miles . . .

CHAPTER TWO⎯⎯⎯⎯⎯⎯⎯⎯⎯

FEELING the male juices stirring in his loins, Alexandr Yasakev looked at Deborah Miles with all the enthusiasm and expectation of a 6 year old child on Christmas Eve. *To have her naked in bed! To possess that lovely body—my God!* This was only his second date with the beautiful redhead, and he was certain that tonight he would—to use an American term—*score*. She had certainly given him enough hints, saying how she missed the "feel" of a man late at night. And it was she who had suggested they go to his apartment.

A good thing, too, that she was cooperating this night, thought Yasakev. The Date Right Escort Service charged 300 dollars an hour, and already he had spent a small forture on time not to mention, dinner, drinks, the theater, cab fare and tips. Yasakev shuddered when he thought of how he had acquired the money by juggling the books of his government's mission to the United Nations. Should Moscow ever learn of his duplicity, he would end up in the Gulag with a life sentence.

"Let's sit down on the couch, Miss Miles," Yasakev suggested. He smiled and handed the young woman a glass of wine. "Or we can go out on the balcony and look over the city. But I suppose the city at night would not interest you, since you've lived in New York most of your life.''

"Call me Debbie," she said softly, giving the Russian maritime specialist an inviting smile.

She turned and walked toward the ratchet-arm sofa, confident that he was watching her buttocks move up and down through the long dress she was wearing.

"Fine, fine—Debbie." Yasakev, hoping his erecting member wouldn't be obvious, sat down next to her. She sipped the red Bordeaux, her pretty face turned toward him.

She was tall and statuesque, the natural color of her hair a Titian-red. Her eyes were gray, and she had long, naturally curved eyelashes. Her high forehead, arched eyebrows, narrow temples and slender nose gave her an aristocratic appearance. Her skin, smooth and light, was obviously well cared for and flawless. Another asset was her full mouth, which really didn't need lipstick to appear desirable.

It was her breasts that excited Yasakev. They were full and round rather than pointed. Her slim waist accented lush hips which tapered gracefully into long shapely legs, both in the thighs and calves.

It wasn't that she was outstandingly beautiful, or had the glamour one associates with a movie queen. Nor was her figure of startling proportions. It was something more, something intangible and indefinable, something that hovered in the air when she was in the vicinity and communicated itself to every male from twelve to ninety. Some women have it. Some women don't. Deborah Miles had it; far more than her share.

Yasakev suddenly felt a slick line of perspiration form on his upper lip. The room had become uncomfortably warm and he realized he could no longer control his erection. He crossed his legs to hold his rigid staff in place and reflected that, when she had moved to the sofa, her buttocks had been so frankly suggestive that it had been difficult for him to resist the temptation of pinching them.

Debbie almost felt sorry for the Russian pig. She knew she had excited him to the point of no return. To help titilate him even more, she scooted closer to him and pushed out her breasts, watching his eyes dart hungrily to her bosom, half of which was exposed in the low-cut dress. She could see that he wanted her so badly he was already tasting her.

No, definitely not. Don't ask him about his job at the United Nations. Any mention of that would instantly put him on guard. Any Soviet diplomat was always extremely cautious.

"Tell me, Alexandr, have you traveled much?" Debbie asked innocently. "I haven't. Oh, I've been to Mexico and Canada, but that's not really seeing much of the world."

"Yes, dear. I've been posted to several countries as a representative of my government." Yasakev paused and cleared his throat, his eyes moving to her ample breasts and devouring the outline of her nipples against the thin material of her dress. "I have been in your country for several years. I believe I told you—Debbie—I'm the Secretary of the IMO at the United Nations. That's the International Maritime Organization."

"Oh, that does sound exciting!" She pretended great interest, positive that she had—even on the first date— given him the impression that she was a rattlebrain in everything except what a woman does best. "It deals with ships, doesn't it? I don't know anything about boats." She uttered a little laugh. "All I know is that they float on the water."

Yasakev nodded tolerantly. "The IMO gives advisory and consultative help to promote international cooperation in maritime navigation and to encourage the highest standards of safety and navigation." Keeping his legs tightly crossed, he put his left arm behind her, spreading it along the back of the sofa, and moved closer to her. "Let's talk about you. I don't want to bore you with stuffy details about IMO. Do you have other employment, or do you work only for the escort service. The reason I ask is that living in New York is expensive."

Debbie leaned forward, placed her glass on the cocktail table, reached for her small handbag and took out a pack of Virginia Slims. So that's how he intended to get her into bed, by offering to pay her. She felt disappointed. She had hoped for a smoother approach from Yasakev. Did he think she was only a high class whore? Of course he did. Why else would she be working for the Date Right Escort Service?

On the other hand, what else did he have to offer, if not money? He was an ordinary looking man. In his late forties, thin, with a long, scholarly-looking face and thick brown hair heavily tinged with gray at the temples, Yasakev was not a ladies man. Seduction to him would be as alien as Bibles in the Kremlin!

The nice part about the setup was that he had a wife and four children back in Mama Russia. He was a perfect patsy for a blackmail scheme. Once she lured him to *her* apartment cameras could record all the action.

Debbie and Unit-1 of COBRA had developed quite a bit of information about Alexandr Yasakev. For example, Debbie was positive this apartment was not his, that he only "borrowed" it for his dates with her. The apartment was at 54th Street, on Sutton Place, a very exclusive section of New York. The Soviet Union was not about to pay 4,000 to 6,000 dollars a month rent on an apartment for a minor official. Yasakev actually shared a small apartment with another minor Soviet official on West Street, in the SoHo section in southwest Manhattan where the rent was only 1,750 dollars a month.

Quick to pick up the large black onyx lghter from the

cocktail table and touch its flame to the tip of Debbie's cigarette, Yasakev deliberately pressed his left thigh against her leg and said, "I might add that if you do have two jobs, you certainly hold up well. You always appear so fresh and relaxed."

Debbie exhaled smoke, smiled, and let him have it. "Thank you, Alexandr. It's very simple. You see, a good-time girl who sleeps all day can always look infinitely better than a woman who earns her living working long hours in an office."

She reasoned that her bluntness would give him an opening—*I know he's not all that shy*. If she had to be more explicit, she would come right out and say, "I'll go to bed with you for money!"

Yasakev had gotten the message, her words exciting him even more; yet he pretended ignorance—for only one reason. He had only 600 dollars with him and he wasn't sure if that was enough to buy her . . . special services. Even so, he remained trapped in a quandary; wanting her desperately yet not wanting to spend the money, even if he did have enough. He was also afraid that there might be something in the bedroom that would tip her off that the apartment was not his.

Yasakev both surprised and disgusted Debbie by replying in his flawless English, "I see. Then you work only for the escort agency. It is pleasant work." Seeing her quizzical look he took another tact. "I suppose you meet a lot of interesting men, Americans with lots of money?"

Sensing Yasakev was stuggling up to the Main Event, Debbie vaguely wondered if Jon Skul would meet with success on Long Island. She would have bet her night's wages he would, that Salvatore Tuccinardo would be stone dead before she left the apartment, unless Yasakev was a tiger (*I don't think that's too likely*) and kept her for the night—*if he ever gets in gear and gets started!*

Alexandr Yasakev was the weak link in the KGB's spy

apparatus—code-named *Fast-Drop*—operating in New York. It was more than his weakness for female flesh; it was he who knew the names of all Soviet vessels, as well as the names of ships from other European Communist nations, that at times brought processed heroin into the United States. Not infrequently, the drug was unprocessed morphine.

For almost 3 years, the Soviet KGB had been smuggling heroin into the United States. Much of it was brought on U.S. soil by Soviet diplomats stationed at the United Nations. Their luggage could not be searched by U.S. Customs officials as they were allowed to pass through with diplomatic immunity.

The KGB was not buying the heroin. The Soviets didn't have to. After all, the so-called brave soldiers of the Red Army had conquered three-fourths of Afghanistan, the largest producer of poppy seeds in the world. Not even the Golden Triangle in Southeast Asia could match Afghan production.

Both the FBI and the CIA, working independently of each other, had learned that the KGB, in turn, was giving the heroin away; giving it gratis to the Tuccinardo Mafia Family. Don Tuccinardo and his animals were selling the horse very cheaply to Wilbur "Dynamite" Jackson, who headed the most powerful Black mob in Harlem. Jackson and his net-work of apes were then retailing the drug to distributors, who supplied middle men. From the middlemen the heroin found its sneaky way to regular pushers all over the country, some of whom even had access to military installations.

The Central Intelligence Agency had been powerless to act. The heroin was being brought into and distributed in the United States. Therefore, the matter was an internal one, and as such under the jurisdiction of the Federal Bureau of Investigation. But the best the FBI had to offer had not been good enough. United States law demanded proof, and the KGB and the Tuccinardo mob were too clever. Try as the Bureau might and had, it could not trap KGB officers in the act of turning over the heroin to Don Salvatore's boys.

Finally the very highest Authority in America had enough and called in COBRA. Jonas Farley Barron had assembled 10 of his best operatives, 8 Eagles and 2 Doves, and had placed the Unit under the command of Jonathan Victor Skul. Barron had given Skul only one order: Defuse the Soviet spy net-work in New York and stop the KGB from bringing heroin into the United States.

"Skul, I don't care how you do it," Barron had said. "Just do it—and do it fast!"

The operation had been ciphered *BLUE TANGO*.

Thinking of Jonathan Skul, Debbie inwardly grimaced. She had not gotten along with him from the first time they had met, 3 months earlier. He was such a goddamn prude; had the morals of the Pope. She knew it was Skul who had come up with the Patriotic Prostitutes tag-line for the Doves.

COBRA wanted its agents who worked together to have confidence in each other. For that reason, members of a Unit read each other's files.

Skul's talents and abilities were considerable. He was not only an ex-Green Beret, having served in Vietnam, he was also ex-CIA. Highly educated, fluent in 8 languages with a special gift for dialects, he possessed a Ph.D in abnormal psychology from the University of Chicago. He was divorced, but had no children. There was a note in his dossier stating he had been raised as an orphan—his parents having perished in a freak car accident when he was 4 years old—and that Skul had a special soft-spot for homeless children and was known to donate liberally to worthy orphanages. His hobbies were astronomy and clock repair, avocations which further honed the edge of an already precise mind.

On the violence side of business no one was better. A firm believer in the successful end of a mission always justified the means, Skul was expert in weapons, explosives, electronics and communications. Physically, he had trained his body as a lethal weapon and his raw strength and endurance were awesome. He didn't smoke, but he was a prodigious drinker!

What puzzled Debbie was why Skul had gotten into trouble while in the Covert Section of the CIA. How could a stable professional like Skul, with a GS-11 rating, pull such a goof that, according to the notation in his file, he was given the choice of either resigning or getting fired? Could it have been his drinking? The file didn't reflect the fact that he had been specifically selected for COBRA and as a part of his recruitment it was necessary to appear he was a rogue Company man. His dossier was clean even though it contained a myriad of conflicting traits capped off by a plethora of unanswered questions. The man was an enigma to the outside observer. To COBRA he was the foundation on which it could build an efficient and effective force against world injustice and the threat of Communism.

The first day, when she realized Skul disliked her and Ann Brandon, the other Dove in the Unit, Debbie had bluntly asked him why, pointing out that she and Ann were highly trained—"Or we wouldn't be here. We wouldn't have been chosen."

Skul had been equally as unceremonious, and had not made any excuses.

"Sure, I'll tell you. I don't like women who obtain information by letting agents of the other side crawl up between their legs," he had told her in a cold voice. "As far as I'm concerned, all the Doves in COBRA are nothing more than super horny broads using the guise of 'patriotism' to get all the sex they want—and not giving a damn from whom they get it!"

Debbie, who didn't believe in arguing with a fool, had not tried to change his opinion. She had only said, "You're free to think what you want. Fortunately, you're not the head of COBRA. Barron is. Remember that!"

Debbie gave Alexandr a long, searching look, knowing that she was going to have to take the initiative. He had a sort of vacant look in his eyes. She didn't realize he was thinking of France and how French whores acted. Pay a French whore, she'll walk you to a cheap flophouse, and the first thing you can be sure of is that you owe money for the rent. Having paid the proprietor and the whore, you may then remove your clothes and get onto the bed, but no matter how fast you are, the girl will always be down to her garter-belt and stockings before you! Always! The fastest prostitutes in the world are in France—Alexandr Yasakev was convinced of it . . . *da!*

"Alexandr, honey, I can always find a man with lots of money," Debbie said softly. She put her slim left hand on his shoulder and let a hurt look cross her face and express itself in her low, sultry voice. "I suggested we come to your apartment because I thought you wanted me as much as I wanted you! You do want me, don't you?"

His mouth fell open, and for a moment he stared at her, seeing that below the roots of her red hair on her neck, the creamy white skin glowed with incredible softness. With a sort of choking sound, Yasakev reached out clumsily and took her in his arms, his thin lips going to her neck. He was so excited that he began to babble words of passion and endearment in Russian. He slobbered on her neck and ear, at the same time trying to get his right hand under her dress to fondle her legs.

Breathing heavily, his hands trembling, he leaned back and, with one arm around her slim waist, began to fumble with the front of her dress. Debbie didn't help him, nor did she resist. Finally, he succeeded, and her beautiful breasts were freed from their prison. Trembling, he gaped at her hard, pink nipples the size of strawberries. Then, still sounding as if he might be strangling, he leaned forward to take one of the succulent berries between his lips. Almost feeling sorry for him, Debbie stopped him gently by pressing against his chest with her palms.

"No, sweetheart, not here in the living room," she whispered tenderly. "It's not nice. Let's go into the bedroom . . ."

CHAPTER THREE_____

KARSTEN Lindley Hayes switched off the television set and sat back down on the hassock. No one spoke. The newscast, devoted almost exclusively to the "Massacre at the Long Island home of Salvatore Tuccinardo, reputed to be a leading Mafia chieftain," had said it all.

Finally, Douglas Almaine tapped ash from his small cigar and said, "Well, Jon, you missed the Don but you left one hellava body count out there. You know for someone who screwed up royally you have a wide streak of luck. You even missed a ride back with Skeeter."

Henry Kowitt, on the recliner, commented in his gruff voice. "We'll never get another chance at whacking out the son-of-a-bitch. From now on, his security will be tighter than a virgin."

Debbie Miles sat in an armchair drinking tea and nervously chain smoking. Dressed in cream colored gabardine slacks and an ivory colored silk blouse with long sleeves, she kept her eyes on Jon Skul. He had placed the hairpiece he had worn to Glen Cove on a foam head and was carefully brushing the genuine black hair. His neatness was one of the things Debbie liked about him—and that was about all she liked.

Debbie's mind wandered. Actually, there were several things she liked about Skul, not the least of which was his slim, athletic build. He moved with the smooth, sensuous, animal grace of a man totally in control. Debbie never tired of watching his strong featured face, searching his deep set hazel eyes for clues to his private thoughts. He certainly wasn't handsome but she thought he was good looking and very sexy. She watched his long, slim hands caress the wig form and almost shuddered at the thought of his touch on her. The sound of his voice snapped her back to full attention. Unconsciously she pushed her hair back behind her left ear as if waving a daydream out of her mind.

"The point is, I failed to remove Don Salvatore," Skul said tonelessly. "Failure is precisely that—failure." He picked up the wig and the foam head from the small table, walked across the room, and carefully placed them in a storage trunk.

"Ah, yes. We have to put our failures into the proper perspective," Kowitt said briskly, the mid-morning sun falling on his cocoa colored skin. "According to the tv reports, the woman who was killed was Ethel Rosenkrantz, the wife of the criminal lawyer. If she and her husband hadn't walked out of the bedroom when they did, you'd have been able to take out the Don."

Karsten Hayes nodded thoughtfully. "As the ancient Romans would have said, 'Exceptio probat regulam de rebus non exceptis'—an exception proves the rule as to things not expected."

"Yow-suh, boss! You sure snuffed dem white folks up ta big hause!" joked Kowitt. "You sure 'nuf did!"

In no mood to listen to either Hayes' historical citations or Kowitt's obsequious Steppin' Fetch It routine, Skul strode over to the small bar and filled a waterglass a fourth full of blackberry brandy. On top of the brandy he poured lime soda.

"Deborah, may I assume you didn't spare us any details in your report?"

He stirred the soda and the brandy, his back to Debbie and the others in the living room.

"My report was complete," she replied evenly. "Alexandr Yasakev is hooked; all we have to do is reel him in. We have another date scheduled for the nineteenth, 9 days from now. That gives us more than enough time to set up the two-way mirror, the cameras and the recording equipment. I'm certain I can get him to my apartment. I'm positive he'll cave in and cooperate once we show him the photos and he hears the tapes."

Doug Almaine's chuckle sounded obscene. Like the other men present, he found Debbie's serious attitude amusing. A former CIA case officer, Almaine, of medium height and muscular, had wavy black hair, an easy smile, and a passion for chemistry. To a stranger, he appeared to be a man of curious innocence with a tolerant view of mankind. The truth was another matter. His extreme Right Wing attitudes made Hitler look like a Liberal!

Debbie glared at Almaine, wishing he had kept silent. All he had done was give Skul an opening to say something insulting about "nymphos screwing for Uncle Sam!"

With the glass in his hand, Skul turned from the bar and started back across the room, his eyes on Debbie. "How can you be so positive about Yasakev?"

Debbie didn't enjoy telling him, but she knew she had to.

"Because he's a timid man." She hesitated. "I had to take the first step, or we'd still be sitting there in Guy Davidson's apartment." Her eyes flashed a warning. "And don't say what you're thinking! It's too early in the day for any of your snide prudish remarks—so *don't!*"

Skul stopped in the middle of the room and said, "I don't consider his timidity about women and sex indicative that he'd cooperate readily in any blackmail attempt. I think he will cooperate because of his wife and children back in the Soviet Union.''

Hayes commented: "How he performed during the sexual act could give evidence as to how much iron he might have in his spine.''

"Only up to a point," Skul reminded him, dropping down to the couch. "A lot of factors are involved. A man can be bashful about getting a woman into bed, he might even perform poorly, but still be crazy-brave in other areas.''

Debbie shrugged. "He performed like a bull!" Without thinking, she added drily, "Even if he wasn't built like one!''

Skul shrugged his broad shoulders and surprised Debbie by not making a derogatory retort. "First we have to get photographs and a recording of his doing with you what comes naturally. In the meanwhile, we're not going to sit around and cut out paper dolls.'' He took several long swallows from the glass, then looked from face to face. "Any suggestions?''

"We can't expect Ann to come up with anything in the near future," Debbie said. She finished pouring tea into her cup from a silver pot on a side table next to her chair. "Russians may like having sex with good looking Black women, but she hasn't had a nibble.''

Almaine laughed heartily. "A 'nibble?' Was that pun intentional, Debbie?''

"You know damn good and well what I meant," she snapped. "I don't even know if any other Russians are using Date Right. And remember, Ann isn't the only Black chick working at Date Right. A lot of Blacks sign on because they know they're in demand. The only other girls that get to pick and choose are the Orientals. And stow your cheap remarks, Kowitt. The point is you can't always persuade Hooten to pair you up with your choice— besides you don't always get a look-see in advance. We lucked out with Yasakev when we learned he was partial to naturally grown redheads.''

Henry Kowitt edged forward in his seat, genuinely curious about what Debbie was saying. "What about Alice Hooten—any information on how she's managed to stay in business so long? What about her connections? After all she's running a glorified whorehouse and servicing over half the delegates to the U.N.''

Six feet four inches tall and weighing 242 pounds, Kowitt kept his head shaved and a Smith and Wesson .44 Magnum revolver always handy, even taking the big weapon to bed with him. He was an expert in weapons and in underwater operations, and at one time had been a Master Sergeant in the 101st Air-Assault Division. After leaving the military, he had considered entering the Episcopalian priesthood. Instead, he had joined COBRA.

Debbie's eyes narrowed slightly. "Hooten is an ex-call girl and one sharp cookie," she said. "I know the primary function of the escort service is as supplier of high class sex for mostly 'visiting firemen.' Of course, there are some men, who only want a girl for the evening because they hate dining alone, or simply enjoy the company of a pretty, well-groomed woman. It does something for their ego.''

"None of that explains how she manages to keep the police away," Kowitt said. "The Vice Squad has to know what's going on.''

"She's paying them off," Debbie said. "We all know how things get done in New York. Besides, at her rates there's more than enough to go around. Only the greedy ones get closed down.''

"That's the truth," spoke up Doug Almaine. "After the sun goes down, you could carry off this entire town. New York is the largest moving con game in the States. All any player needs is grease for the wheels.''

Listening to Debbie and the others talk, Jon Skul silently thumbed through his mental filing cabinet. There wasn't a single clue to connect him to the *gang-related shoot-out* at Don Salvatore's estate on Long Island. He had to consider the danger not only from the Organized Crime Division of the New York City Police, but also from the FBI. The FBI didn't know that COBRA existed, and would treat members of Unit-1 as criminals if the Bureau should, for some reason, suspect them of breaking some Federal law. Not very likely.

Unit-1 had two bases in New York. This apartment on West 23rd Street, in Chelsea, was in an area characterized by incongruous architecture and a group of heterogeneous residents. There were some charming tree lined streets and superb brownstones, but they could be surrounded by dirty restaurants and tough looking punks. Like the rents, which varied from very cheap to very expensive, the caliber of the residents varied from very dangerous to very chic.

The second apartment was northwest in the Lincoln Center area, stretching from Central Park West to Broadway, from 59th Street to 72nd Street. This was a more sophisticated area than downtown but no less of a melting pot. The 8 room apartment west of Central Park on 64th Street was home base for the 5 members.

Alister Bates was the youngest Eagle in the Unit-1 nest. Only 27 years old, the sleepy looking Bates was an expert in locks and security systems.

William Holbrook was a big jawed, fierce eyed man with a well formed physique and a ruddy complexion. He had been a Green Beret team leader and had developed an unbridled style. Holbrook could drive any kind of vehicle that rolled on the highway, through the water or through the air.

Christopher Shinns' ability as a sneak thief and burglar was fantastic. He was a pleasant man, who was impatient with minds that did not race along as fast as his own.

Barry Bob Arden had held the rank of major with SEAD—

Suppression of Enemy Air Defense, which was part of the U.S. Marines Integrated Fire and Air Support System. Average looking and wiry, Arden had an analytical mind, tenacious will, and was a combat specialist. His job at the apartment was communications.

Finally, there was *Ann Marie Brandon*, a very attractive Black girl who was three-fourths white—a quadroon who never slept in a bed unless she was with a man. Whenever she was alone she slept in a chair because statistics proved the most people died in bed.

Skul's eyes moved surreptitiously to Deborah Areta Miles. Damn, she confused the hell out of him. He hated to admit it but secretly he thought she was one fantastic woman. As with all his agents he was thoroughly familiar with her background—a masters in parapsychology from the University of Southern California; age 26; a fast study with almost photographic recall; motivated through personal tragedy; utterly ruthless and uncompromising in her commitment to suppress the spread of Communism. In fact, she had an almost pathological hatred of anything left wing. In 1982, her father, a military attache to the U.S. Embassy in Rome, was kidnapped, brutally tortured, then savagely murdered by Italy's Red Brigade terrorists. Debbie had been assigned the unpleasant task of identifying what was left of her father's body. Skul knew she would never forgive or forget the ideological source of her father's murderers. He understood the motivation but had trouble with accepting her choice of weapon—sex! Skul thought of some of the neatly typed notations in her file—at least she was somewhat choosey and didn't spread her legs for just anyone. Debbie knew she had a powerful weapon at her command and Skul hated to admit she used it well.

Despising weakness of any kind, Skul felt like gritting his teeth in anger every time he was forced to admit that he felt desire for the attractive redhead.

Get her out of your mind, stupid! You have a job to do!

"I asked for suggestions," he said mildly, yet firmly, to the group. "Where's your imagination?"

"Well now, Jon, where's your own imagination?" Hayes said casually. "After all, you're the boss-man."

Skul took another drink from the glass, then moved his tongue around in his mouth, savoring the brandy and lime soda.

"Ah, that's a good point, Professor," Skul admitted, looking at Hayes, who, at age 71, was the eldest of the ten Unit-1 members. Retired from Harvard, where he had been a full professor of Ancient History, Hayes was a trim man, with a pencil thin mustache, a jaunty smile and a lazy, easy manner. Always fastidiously dressed, he was the sort of fellow who was inevitably described as dapper.

Hayes had joined COBRA to break the monotony of his retirement. He was the base agent. His job was mainly communications and all-around handyman. A gourmet cook—his speciality was Cantonese dishes, a cuisine Skul detested—he enjoyed fixing meals and the distraction of fussing. Oddly enough, he was afraid of firearms, disliked all forms of violence, and was convinced that the Third World and its liberal sympathizers were wrecking American society. In Hayes' eyes, both groups were the "World's Modern Vandals."

Skul said with an amused smile, "My imagination is working in high gear. That's why Henry and I and Doug are going up to Harlem and terminate Wilbur Jackson. We're going to blame it on Don Salvatore's boys and start a gang war between those two camps of dirt-bags."

"You're nuts!" Almaine said emphatically. "That's crazier than your attempt to snuff Tuccinardo. Two white dudes going into Harlem is a one-way ticket down suicide alley, even if they do take a Black with them."

"Doug is right, Jon," Debbie said. "How do you think you could get close to Dynamite Jackson. Three of you—2 whiteys and a Bro—in his *Cotton Candy Club*, you'd be lucky to even get in, much less out—alive!''

Henry Kowitt kept tapping the fingers of his left hand against his high forehead. ''There is also the small matter of escaping the police should we be lucky enough to snuff Jackson. I'm not anxious for a high-speed chase through the streets of Harlem—and don't tell me how good Bill Holbrook is behind a wheel! There are limitations for even a good git-driver like Bill.''

Hayes, oblivious to what was being discussed, began one of his diatribes on the ruination of American society. ''The welfare system engenders a breeding frenzy—the more babies the more money—and there's no consideration given to how this population explosion is going to be absorbed into the system The fact is they're not—they rot on the fringes, supported by our taxes. And then they express their gratitude by mugging us, robbing our homes and raping our women. Then those damned knee-jerk liberal journalists tell us to show them compassion; give them a second chance. Bullcrap. I'm all for rounding the bastards up . . .''

''Professor, please. Let's not get going on a subject that takes us in circles,'' Skul said patiently.

''Very well,'' Hayes said, not the least bit insulted. ''Have you thought about hitting the target at a distance, with a scoped sniper rifle fitted with a silencer? That would be ideal.''

''And far too complicated,'' Skul said. ''Jackson lives in *Cotton Candy*, and there aren't any available buildings for a successful ambush, not even around the club's parking lot.''

Skul finished his drink, got up, walked over to the bar and picked up the bottle of brandy. Then he turned to the others. ''One of you get the special map of New York. We'll spread it out on the counter in the kitchen.''

Once in the kitchen, while Skul poured more brandy

into his glass and Debbie moved the Mr. Coffee maker, Doug Almaine spread out a large, detailed map of Manhattan and the Bronx. All of them gathered around the counter—on both sides—and Skul, first taking a long drink, placed his finger on a heavy red circle.

"Here's Jackson's *Cotton Candy Club* on Lenox Avenue," he said. "You'll notice that the parking lot is north of the building."

"Uh huh, so what else is new?" Kowitt gave Skul a quick glance, then tapped the map. "And here's Harlem Houses housing project, and right here is Harlem Hospital, so what? What are you getting at?"

"Let's say we blow up Jackson, get out of the club and get to the parking lot," Skul said. "Once in the parking lot and pull out, we'll only be two blocks south of 138th Street. We'll drive to the Harlem Hospital parking lot—the hospital is only a block north of the club—switch cars, go back onto Lenox and drive to 138th. It leads straight to the Madison Avenue Bridge. We'll cross the Harlem River into the Mott Haven district of the Bronx and be in the clear."

"God damnit! That section of the Bronx is damn near as bad as Harlem!" growled Almaine. He fumbled in his shirt pocket for a small cigar.

"The South Bronx looks like Lebanon with sunshine," Kowitt said.

A smile slid over Debbie's pretty face. "I didn't know God's last name was 'Damnit!' "

Skul gave her a patronizing look and tipped the rim of the glass to his mouth. Then he looked at Kowitt, who was saying, "It could work. But who's going to drive the second car to Harlem Hospital? It can't be one of you whiteys." He snickered and deliberately slipped into Black dialect. "De black bros dey love to see whitey all alone in a set of wheels. Like man, it would be throat-cuttin' time!"

Skul put his empty glass on the counter. "Professor, old buddy, contact Barron on the URC and tell him to send us a Black agent, but don't give Barron any details, not unless he orders you to."

Hayes stroked his mustache. "Why not? Any message that goes out on the URC is double-scrambled, and since we frequency-hop, anyone listening in would hear only meaningless static."

"I know, but I want tight security just the same," Skul said. He didn't want to admit that he was superstitious and felt that sending even scrambled information frequency-hopped was the same as announcing it to the world. "Tell Barron to send the agent as quickly as possible to the 64th Street address. Code recognition on his part *Blue Easter*. On ours *Red Fourth of July*."

"Professor, tell Barron to make sure that the dude he sends isn't gun-shy," Kowitt said and moved a big hand over the dome of his shaved head. "There are plenty of mean niggers in Harlem, and Jackson's bunch is the meanest of all!"

Debbie leveled an all business look at Skul. "Jon, what kind of a time-frame do you have in mind?"

Skul pulled the cork from the bottle of brandy, and fixed his Presbyterian stare on Debbie. "Within 10 days, they'll be lowering that big black boob into his new 6 foot home and pulling the grass over his head—unless they cremate him!"

CHAPTER FOUR_____

A WHITE MAN had to be an idiot or have a death wish to go into the *Cotton Candy*. The club was more than one of the prominent nite spots in Harlem; it was also the headquarters of Wilbur Dynamite Jackson, the mobster who controlled all the rackets in Harlem—the *hos* and their pimps, the narcotics, the loan-sharking and the numbers. Jackson's kingdom was Harlem; a hell for most who lived there, a heaven for the ones who didn't, and a paradise for parasites like Jackson and his goons who had grown rich from exploiting human weakness and Black misery.

Harlem was dangerous for even an honest Black man, but it was positively a walk on the tightrope of suicide for a white man, even if his companion was Black. Life in Harlem breeds a very dangerous arrogance and a very special kind of strength, both cemented with bitterness and pain, both cleverly hidden by a pseudo-happiness, a gaiety that is only a psychological weapon to beat back the truth, the reality of living conditions, in which everyone is born poor, lives broke, and dies in debt. And with all this misery, there is a burning hatred for and a fierce jealousy of *Whitey*.

Skul had not minimized the danger, and he knew his

being with Henry Kowitt was not really any kind of security, for in the *Cotton Candy Club*, whites were as welcome as Jews in Iran. It wasn't that there weren't any whites at the club, but the comparatively few white men and whores were regulars. More important they worked for Jackson, and were known to his hoods. Jon Skul and Henry Kowitt were total strangers. Worse, they were dangerous looking strangers.

The September sun had gone to bed and the real Harlem, the Harlem of the Night, had awakened. The sleeping dead had risen. They had shaken their bones and deserted their tombs to strut on Lenox Avenue. Now the hos would walk their beat, looking for johns while their high sidin' mack men kept their eyes on them and told each other lies. Drugs would be sold in doorways, in alleys and in washrooms. Now, with the darkness, it was time for stick-ups, rapes and muggings, or a building or 3 torched for the insurance.

At 9:15, Skul and Kowitt parked their blue Cadillac in the parking lot of the *Cotton Candy Club*, got out, locked the car and walked into the club. They weren't concerned about anyone's trying to steal their set of expensive wheels. Try to open any of the doors, the hood or the trunk and several loud sirens would start screaming.

Earlier that afternoon, Chris Shinns had stolen the caddy from a parking garage—of all places—and had fitted the vehicle with phony license plates supplied by Jonas Barron, who had sent the plates with "Little" Davy Wickewire, the new Black COBRA Eagle who had driven up from Baltimore. Wickewire first made contact with Norman Skeeter Ronson, Barron's liaison in New York City; then he had gone to the 64th Street address for a meeting with Jon Skul.

"Little" Davy was 6 feet 6 inches and weighed 280 pounds, every ounce solid muscle. An ex-Marine, he was not a stranger to danger and had a very high efficiency rating. He had changed his last name from Brown to Wickewire after he had been discharged from the Marines because, "There must be a million niggers named Brown. Besides, I like the name Wickewire. It has a nice ring to it."

Skul and Kowitt went straight to the bar, to the left of the large dance floor, and, feeling the curious and hostile stares on their backs, ordered drinks—whiskey for Skul, brandy for Kowitt. In the mirror behind the bar, they could see they were being scrutinized—weighed, measured, and taken apart—particularly by four sets of eyes belonging to four men sitting at a table a short distance away. With them was Candy Barr, the club's leading stripper. The four jokers—high-hair, touch-muscled, tough-faced and in expensive suits—were some of Dynamite Jackson's goons. To Jon Skul, they were just apes disguised as human beings.

One of the three bartenders served the drinks, glaring at Skul and Kowitt and deliberately spilling some of Skul's drink.

Skul looked straight at the bartender, a fat-faced, mean-looking man with saucer-sized lips and a short but wide scar on the bottom of his left cheek.

"Fella, I pay for a full drink, I expect a full drink. Get me another—*now*!"

There was that special something in Skul's quiet tone; there was an even greater warning in his cold eyes. The bartender considered. What the fuck! Why start trouble. Anyhow, Louie and the others would find out who they were and what they wanted.

The plan was basically very simple: go in, terminate Wilbur Jackson, dash to the parking lot and escape. The key to the lock of success was neither speed nor surprise, but a violence of a kind never experienced—and certainly never anticipated—by Jackson and his crowd of creeping scum.

Jackson was not the ordinary Black mobster. He was not the bastard product of a welfare mammy, nor was his father one of maybe a dozen fly-by-night blackbirds for whom life had been reduced to the ordinary pleasures of eating, drinking and fucking. His father—a dentist—and mother were actually married and lived in Paterson, New Jersey. One of three children, Wilbur Jackson was a college graduate. He hadn't, however, used his degree to make an honest living. Instead, he had migrated to New York City and become a numbers runner in Harlem. Sixteen years later, at the age of 44, he was the king-pin of all the Harlem rackets, wielding a power that even the Mafia respected.

His looks were very deceptive—he had an almost sweet face—but Jackson had acquired his nickname "Dynamite" because of his explosive temper. Jon Skul did not underestimate Jackson. He was a shrewd and clever business man who was guided by well developed street-smarts.

Jackson's office was upstairs at the end of a hall, off which were 15 small rooms where white and Black prostitutes took their customers for straight and french jobs. Next to Jackson's office there was another room where he and his friends played poker. Trapping the son-of-a-bitch would be easy. There was a door between the office and the poker room, a plain wooden door. The hall doors to the office and poker room were also wood, but sheet metal steel doors could be closed over them from the inside. Skul wasn't worried. The Composition-4 explosive would send the doors flying.

After sundown, Jackson was either in his office or in the next room playing stud poker, one of his great loves. His other two passions were fucking Oriental sluts and playing auditory voyeur by listening to conversations at the long bar of the *Cotton Candy*. Accordingly, there were half a dozen microphones hidden underneath the top of the bar.

It was not even a problem of how to get within killing

range of Jackson. A man with a lot of ego, it was not very likely that he would come downstairs and talk to them. It was almost a certainty that, when he found out what they had to tell him, he would have them brought to his office. This meant that Skul and Kowitt would be searched by the hoods and relieved of their weapons. Skul carried not only his .45 Pachmayr Modular, but also a backup 9mm SIG-Sauer D.A. auto-pistol. Kowitt had two pieces in shoulder holster leather, his S & W .44 Magnum, and a S & W Bodyguard hammerless revolver. Worse, the hoods would discover the two knotted nylon escape-lines and the four packages of C-4 buckled to the calves of Skul and Kowitt. No way! They couldn't permit themselves to be searched.

In planning the hit, Skul had said, "First we'll try to get that piece of garbage to come down to us."

"An exercise in futility," Kowitt had opined. "That nigger never goes to anybody."

"Then we'll go up and get him."

"You'll have to put to sleep a lot of innocent bystanders," Debbie had offered.

"There aren't any *innocent bystanders* in the *Cotton Candy*," Skul had reminded her. "They're all trash. And Henry and I aren't going to do anything. Remember, it's Don Salvatore and his mob who will be held responsible. The Don's removing a chapter from the book of the man who tried to kill him—Dynamite's hit-boy. The Don is only returning the favor." A sly, mean smile spread over Skul's mugged face.

Skul and Kowitt were halfway through their drinks when the 4 hoods left their table and strutted over to them. Two took positions one on each side of Skul and Kowitt. The other 2 crumbs stood behind them.

The man with the massive shoulders and a nose so wide you could park a wagon in each nostril pushed close to Skul and growled, "Honkys ain't welcome here 'less they's invited. That goes for honky cops as well!'' His voice sounded as if he were speaking from the bottom of a barrel.

"Neither are Uncle Toms who come in with white trash,'' said the hood standing behind Kowitt. He had the build of a dump truck and the face of a road map that someone had shit on. He put walnut-colored hands on his hips and stared at the back of Kowitt's head.

Skul, watching the 4 thugs in the mirror, as well as the bartenders, turned to Kowitt and chuckled. "I suppose these jokers think they're bad cats, huh? Remind me to be nervous the second Tuesday of next week.''

Kowitt grinned, showing big teeth. "Yeah, if I weren't in a good mood, I'd kick the piss out of these niggers and shove their pieces down their throats. I'd enjoy watching them crap iron.''

The 4 triggermen hesitated. While they hadn't expected timidity, neither had they expected answers that could only be interpreted as *We're bad and we're looking for trouble!*

Jackson's hoods sensed the 2 strangers weren't cops, and they sure as hell weren't two dummies who would walk in and risk getting the hell beat out of them by mouthing spit-in-the-face insults, not unless they had a reason, not unless they knew exactly what they were doing. So who in hell were the salt and pepper jokers and what the fuck did they want?

"Maybe they came over to buy us a drink,'' Skul said lightly, his eyes, looking at the hoods via the mirror, laughing.

"Man, we ain't gonna buy you a fuckin' thing, 'cept maybe a short funeral!'' sneered the man standing to the side of Kowitt. His big tub face was decorated with a short goatee, and his dark eyes had the look of an alert fox as they roamed up and down Kowitt and Skul, both of whom were dressed in 800 dollar silk suits. It was obvious that the bulges in their armpits weren't small loaves of bread.

"We think you both's a couple of jiveass motherfuckers!" said the man standing by the side of Skul. Of medium height, but not too broad, he wore a green and red turban and had on a pair of Foster Grants. "We don't like jiveass motherfuckers. Suppose you git the fuck outta here while you can still walk."

Kowitt finished his drink, got off the stool and turned around. He wasn't smiling. Skul, who had finished his whiskey, slid off the stool, but remained facing the bar. The four hoods just stood there, one man with his hand in his right coat pocket. Skul's eyes roamed over the 4 ebony faces, his gaze, his very manner, daring the hoods, taunting them.

Skul snapped his fingers at the bartender at this section of the bar. He pointed to the two empty glasses. "Give us a refill."

The man didn't argue. He poured the drinks, picked up the sawbuck on the bar in front of Skul and moved off.

Neither Skul nor Kowitt had failed to notice how the bar had suddenly emptied . . . how the other drinkers, one by one, had quietly edged away, in the manner of birds sensing a coming disaster and flying away before it could strike. The main floor had become quiet, the Black crows and their johns subdued, watching and waiting. In the pool-room adjoining the lounge, the dudes had stopped their snooker and eight-ball. They waited, prepared to drop at the sound of gunfire if the discussion at the bar came to that—all except 6 men. They were members of the Jackson mob.

Nor had Skul and Kowitt missed another fact: that the bottom of the stairs was only 30 feet to their left.

Skul picked up his drink and turned to face the goon with the massive shoulders and the wide brim blue hat on his pumpkin-shaped head.

"We came to this dump to see your boss Jackson,"

Skul said evenly in a low voice. "We have information he'll appreciate."

The bedbug with the Foster Grants and the turban—he was the creep with his hand in his coat pocket—sneered. "That's a fuckin' joke! What kind of information could you possibly have that would interest Mr. Jackson?"

"That's our business—and his," Skul said firmly. He sipped his drink, set to explode into action if need be.

"I'm Louis Thomas; you may have heard of me," said Foster Grants, an edge to his voice. "Anything you got for Mr. Jackson, you kin tell me. I'll see he gets the information."

"If what you crumbs got is important enough, we'll take you guys up to see the boss," spit out the tub-faced freak with the goatee, "after we take away the iron you're carryin.' "

"You talk like a man with a brick in his butt," Skul said with a snicker. "We didn't come here to let the help shove us around."

"No dice," Kowitt growled. "Nobody lifts our pieces."

"Jackson can come down here and talk to us," Skul smirked at Thomas. "You run up there and tell him that Don Salvatore is putting out a contract on him. This afternoon, me and Typhoon here turned down 15 grand a piece to hit Jackson."

Skul's words had the effect of an invisible bomb exploding. So startled were the hoods that their mouths almost fell open. Thomas jerked the pistol from his coat pocket, a cute little .380 Beretta. He became all the more angry when Skul looked at the pistol and grinned.

"Move, you cocksucker!" Thomas snarled. "You and this dumb nigger are gonna go up them stairs and talk to the boss whether you want to or not. Acey, get his guns. Boomer, take the heat from the other motherfucker."

Acey, the big faced goof with the short goatee, stepped in close, reached out and tried to jerk open Skul's coat. At the same time, Boomer, the piece of low trash built like a truck, attempted to put his hand under the suit coat of Henry Kowitt. It was the worst mistake that Acey and Boomer could have made.

Skul erupted into action. First, he stepped slightly to his right, having spotted the reflection of the bartender in Thomas' Foster Grants. He ducked in time, and the blackjack swung harmlessly past him. All in the same motion, Skul's right hand shot out; the fingers fastened around Thomas' thick wrist, and he pushed the Beretta up and away from him. The automatic went off with a loud crack, the .380 flatnose slug zinging into the mirror behind the bar. At the same time, Skul twisted the wrist and snap-kicked Thomas in the crotch, the tip of his foot a battering ram that wrecked the man's entire sex department. Thomas gasped horribly. His hand opened and the Beretta fell to the floor. Again it went off, but where the slug went was anyone's guess.

Jon Skul had slammed Thomas so incredibly fast that Acey, whose hands had only been inches from Jon's coat, became a complete victim of the totally unexpected. He had company. Dump truck and Blue Hat had also been caught off guard. Before they could fully realize what was happening, Skul's right leg came down and his left leg came up, and so did his right hand! With one chain-lightning motion, he kneed Acey viciously in the belly, and, with his right hand, chopped him across the side of the neck.

By now, Thomas was in a very bad way. With great gurgling gasps, he had sunk to his knees, his eyes two bugged black marbles almost jumping out of their sockets behind the dark glasses. His thick-lipped mouth opened and closed like a catfish out of water as his hands clutched his mashed-to-mush testicles.

Boomer joined him and Acey in agony. Henry Kowitt let him have a lightning left strike to the throat, a bunched-finger Nukite stab that caught him straight in the Adam's apple. Boomer didn't know it, but he was only minutes from death. His trachea and esophagus had been mashed together and he was choking to death.

Snarling, "Stupid nigger!," Kowitt then went to work on Blue Hat as Skul turned his attention to the saucer-lipped bartender, who didn't have the sense to leave well enough alone.

The bartender was stupid in more ways than one. He didn't know how to use a sap with a strap. Instead of putting only his hand through the strap at the end of the blackjack, and wrapping the strap around his thumb—so that if someone grabbed the sap it would easily slip off—he had put the strap around his wrist.

Now, the damn fool leaned across the bar and swung the sap in a wide arc, aiming at the back of Skul's head. Old pro that he was, Skul had anticipated such a dumb move.

The goon with the massive shoulders and the blue hat was convinced he had the upper hand over Kowitt. He jerked out—of all things—an old style broom-handled Mauser pistol from underneath his green, orange, and yellow plaid sports coat. If he had been truly experienced, Blue Hat could have easily burned Kowitt. He should have stepped back, hung loose, and waited for the right moment. He didn't. He let fear kick hell out of common sense. He moved closer, became more nervous, and permitted over-anxiousness to guide his moves. He erred thinking the big Kowitt would be slow and awkward.

As slow and as awkward as chain-lightning, Kowitt executed a high right Savate kick, thinking it was all as dull and boring as Rocky's fourth fight. The end of his foot connected solidly with Blue Hat's wrist, the blow snapping not only the bone but knocking Blue Hat's arm back. The Mauser exploded with a roar, the 7.63mm slug shooting up into the ceiling! Then the antique German weapon fell to the floor and skidded toward a line of red and black leather booths that were quickly emptying.

Dodging the 7 inch long blackjack, Skul grabbed it with his left hand as the sap arced to one side of his head, and pulled forward with all his might jerking the startled bartender over the bar. The dummy's lips flopped up and down like two small pancakes, as he did his best to free himself from the blackjack. The dummy was dead meat and didn't know it. Skul broke his neck with a terrific sword-ridge hand chop.

By this time, all the booths had fled, having come to the conclusion that getting juiced in the middle of a shooting gallery wasn't the safest way to spend an evening. Most of the men in the poolroom were of the same opinion, the exceptions were Fred "Screwboy" Willbanks and 5 other Jackson enforcers. A sadistic psychopath who could have given lessons in brutality to Stalin, Screwboy, along with the other gunsels, had been watching the show at the bar from the poolroom, and had almost fainted from surprise when he saw Skul and Kowitt kayo four of Jackson's best headhunters.

"Let's waste those two motherfuckers!" Screwboy yelled in rage. He jerked a huge .357 Highway Patrolman Magnum from a shoulder holster, and began shoving aside fleeing patrons running across the big dance floor. The other 5 fanned out behind him and began moving toward the bar.

When Louie Thomas' Beretta had gone off the first time, the report had stirred up a nest of black hornets upstairs—not only Wilbur Jackson and the 5 hoods who had been playing stud poker, but also half-a-dozen whores who had been testing mattresses with their tricks. The whores and the johns sat up and looked around in alarm; gunfire and their kind of sex had never been partners.

While Williams and his hoods jumped up from the table and rushed out into the hall, Screwboy and the other men

started toward the bar. Skul pulled his Pachmayr Modular
.45, and Kowitt filled his right hand with his S&W .44
Magnum revolver. Kowitt, his mouth fixed in a snarl,
went over to Blue Hat, who was crawling on his knees
toward the Mauser, and jerked him up by his collar. He
jammed the muzzle of the .44 Magnum against the man's
spine and said with a slight laugh, "Breathe extra hard,
nigger, and I'll part your backbone with a slug."

Terrified, one hand flopping around on his shattered
wrist, Blue Hat cried, "Man, don't shoot! Don't! I aint
gonna give you no trouble!"

During those few brief moments, Skul saw Screwboy
and the other hoods trying to get across the dance floor.
Glancing toward the stairs, he also saw the hoods in the
hallway. No mistake about it. One of the apes was the Big
Boss Nigger himself—Wilbur Dynamite Jackson.

Skul raised the Pachmayr Modular pistol and fired, the
two shots sounding like the roar of a mini-cannon. He
didn't miss. Three of the hoods in the open hall went
down, one of the Hydra-Shok .45 projectiles going all the
way through one man's groin and smacking the crumb
behind him. Jackson and the two other gunmen darted
back into the room next to the office.

Skul and Kowitt realized that before they raced up the
stairs, they would have to whack out most of the gunsels
coming at them from across the dance floor. On the steps
they would be clear targets.

Joe Whitecliff—Blue Hat—knowing that slugs were about
to start flying, had become the most frightened hoodlum
on the Eastern Seaboard. "Man, don't shoot!" he kept
saying over and over like a broken record. Ignoring his
cries, Henry Kowitt jerked Blue Hat in front of him,
pulled him backward by the collar, placed his left foot in
the small of the man's back, then propelled him like a
rocket toward Screwboy Willbanks, who by now had reached

the end of the dance floor and was raising his .357 Magnum revolver.

Simultaneously, Jon Skul pulled his SIG-Sauer D.A. pistol, dived to the side of a booth and got down on one knee.

"M-Man—d-don't!" Blue Hat yelled at Screwboy. "Don't go up 'side my haid with that piece! Don't . . ."

Screwboy's finger had already begun squeezing the trigger, and it couldn't back up. The Magnum boomed! The 185-grain slug slammed into Blue Hat's chest, bored out his back and stabbed at a steep angle into the front of the bar. Blue Hat didn't even scream. Knocked back by the punch of the big bullet, he crumped to the floor, his eyes rolling back in his head.

Kowitt fired as he pulled his Bodyguard hammerless and as Skul began tossing hot metal with his two auto-pistols.

"UHH!" Screwboy grunted, started to double over, and began a fast 1-2-3-4 backward tango. The big flat-nosed bullet went all the way through his body, streaked across the room and went through a bass drum on the band stand.

A .39 bullet streaked close to the right side of Skul's head. Other slugs came close to Kowitt, who was jumping behind the end of the bar. He was just in time to see the 2 remaining bartenders pulling weapons from underneath the bar. One man was swinging a sawed-off shotgun. The other crud was bringing up a .380 Bersa semiautomatic pistol.

Kowitt fired as he threw himself to the walk-slats behind the bar. The .44 Magnum slug exploded the head of the man with the shotgun. The other bartender fired, but his .380 slug stabbed air over Kowitt's body. Henry's .38 "Bodyguard" bullet smacked him in the mouth, tore through his tongue and bored a neat little bloody tunnel in his throat and through the back of his neck. Gurgling blood, he flopped to his back, his body heaving tremendous jerks.

The other gunmen should have fled and would have if

they had known Jon Skul was one of the world's deadliest in-fighters. There was only one other man as talented, and possibly more adept at quick-killing, that shadowy and legendary figure known as the *Death Merchant*.

Slim "Preach" Simmons took one of Skul's .45 projectiles in his right hip as he tried to dart between overturned tables and reach a potted palm. The terrific impact picked him up before it knocked him, dying, to the floor, his body slumping against Cliffie Banks, who was the next to die.

The moon-faced moron caught one of Skul's 9mm SIG-Sauer hollow points in the throat at the same time that Kowitt let him have a .44 mag projectile in the belly. The huge FP .44 tore away his colon, and the 9mm piece of swaged metal clipped his right internal jugular vein. Spraying out a fountain of thick red, Banks spun and crashed to the floor, almost in front of Lester Hawkins, who was having second thoughts about remaining in the one-sided shootout. He was turning to retreat when Skul's 9mm slug stabbed him below the left ear lobe and—horizontally—zipped all the way through his throat. Down he went, the final darkness rushing to meet him.

Freddie Blackburn, the last hood, had used his think-tank—so he thought. Several minutes earlier, he had grabbed Candy Barr and was using the screaming dancer as a shield, thinking that he could fire around her and that Skul and Kowitt wouldn't shoot a woman. He was swinging his Walther P-38 toward Skul when Jon triggered his Pachmayr Modular and Henry Kowitt fired his Magnum revolver.

Skul's .45 Hydra-Shok slug tore between Candy Barr's breasts, bored through her body and smacked Blackburn in the lower chest—only a millisecond before Kowitt's bullet tore through her stomach and stabbed Blackburn in the gut. Barr and Blackburn were 99 per cent dead by the time they crumpled to the floor.

Skul shoved a fresh magazine into the Pachmayr Modular as Kowitt took time out to reload his .44 mag revolver. Skul then pulled up his pant legs and unbuckled the two packages of C-4, each of which, wrapped in oily brown paper, weighed 13-ounces and was fitted with a remote control detonator. He dropped one of the packets into his coat pocket.

With the other small brown package in his left hand and the big autoloader in his right hand, he called out to Kowitt, "You OK, Mr. Oscar?"

"All the way, Mr. Meyer," Kowitt answered.

They raced up the stairs to the open hall, Skul stopping only long enough to place a package of C-4 on the third step from the top. He and Kowitt then sprinted past all the doors to the end of the hall. They were now only 15 feet north of the door to Wilbur Jackson's office.

"Henry, unbuckle your stuff," Skul said, taking out the RC station. "We'll blow both doors."

"We'd better do it fast," Kowitt said. "The cops have to be on their way . . ."

Skul opened the lid and flipped the ON switch. 1-2-3. The light glowed green. He pressed the red button.

BLAMMMMMM! The detonation sounded as though the foundation of the world was being shattered. But it was only 10 feet of the steps and 16 feet of the flooring being blown apart, some of the rubble even showering down on Skul and Kowitt, 60 feet away.

"Cover me," Skul said, pleased with how the operation was going. Wilbur Dynamite Jackson was trapped—*Unless the son-of-a-bitch wants to go through a window and drop 50 feet to the ground below!*

Kowitt beside him, Skul hurried forward and placed a package of C-4 against the bottom front of Jackson's office door while Kowitt pressed one against the door of the room adjoining the office. Then they ran down the hall, moving around the 3 corpses of the hoods, and stopped at the other end, 20 feet south of the smoking maw where the top of the stairs and a portion of the hall had been.

"On the count of three," Skul said, thinking that lately he had been blowing hell out of a lot of stairways. He placed the remote control station on the floor and pushed the tips of his fingers into his ears. He glanced at Kowitt to make sure that he was prepared to neutralize the pressure. *Go!* He pressed down with his left knee on the protruding red button of the RC station; at the same time, he and Kowitt yelled.

BLAMMMMMMM-BLAMMMMMMMM! Part of the hall flooring and both doors disappeared in a huge flash of fire and ball of smoke. The gray-black smoke was still thick and trying to make up its mind which way to drift when Skul and Kowitt picked up their four weapons and charged down the hall.

Dynamite Jackson and the 2 gunsels with him had not expected any explosions. After the 3 enforcers had been gunned down in the hall, Jackson, Brown and Clipps had darted back into the room used for poker, and had locked the steel sheeting over the wooden door. They had rushed into the office, and while Jojo Brown locked the wooden door between the two rooms, Jackson swung the steel sheet over the hall door to his office and locked it.

Jackson and the two gunsels crouched down behind his desk, Jackson having taken a Sterling Mark-6 carbine from a closet. The magazine of the weapon held 34 9mm cartridges and could only be fired on semi-automatic.

The explosion that had shattered the steps had also shaken the confidence of Jackson and the 2 hoods. The next 2 blasts did far more than just physical damage. The steel door of the poker room was blown inward with such terrific force that—hitting the east wall on its top edge—it gouged into the wall 6 inches before crashing flat to the floor.

It was the worst day of Wilbur Jackson's life. It had to

be. It was the last day of his life. The steel door protecting Jackson's office was ripped from its hinges as though they were made of tissue paper. The 480 pound door rocketed across the room, and, still in a halfway perpendicular position, slammed into the front of Jackson's executive desk, hitting it with such power that it shoved the massive piece of furniture a foot toward one of the windows. The steel door then tipped and crashed down on the desk, its underside narrowly missing the head of George Clipps. JoJo Brown had ducked and in doing so had sat down flat on his arse. Jackson had reflexively fallen to his right side. Terrified—they had never faced such a violent enemy— and cursing in frustration, they were scrambling to their feet, their ears ringing from the explosions, when Jon Skul stormed in low through the shattered opening where the office door had been, and Henry Kowitt streaked through the smoking hole next door.

George Clipps, crawling out from behind the desk to the right of Skul, never even saw the deadly COBRA agent. He never felt any pain, either, from the .45 Hydra-Shok projectile that smacked him in the right temple and, exploding the top of his head, scattered most of his gray matter against the desk and on the rug.

There was another loud report as Kowitt blasted the lock on the door between the office and the adjoining room— then a whole series of rapid shots. JoJo Brown had been the first to get to his feet and with his .44 Charter Arms Bulldog was trying to aim down on the weaving, ducking, dodging Skul.

Wilbur Jackson used another tactic. He fell back to his right side and tossed 4 9mm projectiles at Skul from the Sterling carbine. At the time, Skul had been darting to his right. JoJo's .44 slug came within half an inch of the left side of Skul's neck. Two of Jackson's 9mm projectiles were wide misses. The third came within a foot of Skul's hip. The fourth piece of metal cut across the bottom of

Skul's left arm. The bullet ripped through his silk suit and his light blue linen shirt sleeve and came so close to his flesh that it made Skul jump and left a blue-black burn mark on the outside of his elbow.

Life ended for JoJo Brown. Skul fired and so did Kowitt, who had kicked in the connecting door. Skul's .45 slug smacked Brown in the center of the chest at the same time that Kowitt's bullet stabbed him in the left rib cage. No human being ever died faster. JoJo went down with 2 giant holes in his torso, blood gushing from both of them.

Eight feet from the desk, Jon Skul dropped to the rug on his stomach. He did so because, when he had come into the office, he had noticed that the desk did not rest flush on the floor, but was supported by six short, massive legs, one at each corner and 2 in the left and the right centers. Each leg was between 6 and 7 inches long.

Holding the Pachmayr Modular in both hands, Skul placed the pistol on its side on the rug and pulled the trigger 3 times, spacing the slugs. Wilbur Jackson screamed in shock and agony when the first .45 smacked him in the left kneecap and tore off his lower leg. His cry of crucifixion was extremely short. The second projectile stung him in the groin. The third exploded his lower left chest.

"Get the lights," Skul said, getting to his feet.

Kowitt hurried to the light switch, tossing Skul his nylon line on the way. Skul, taking out his own 55 foot length of thin line from his left rear pant pocket, went around the side of the desk and looked down at Wilbur Dynamite Jackson whose fuse had been pulled permanently. Just to make sure, Skul stepped back, pointed the Pachmayr Modular and pulled the trigger. There was a big roar and a plopping sound, as if someone had hit a watermelon with a sledge hammer. The dead mobster's head flew apart, pieces of bone and brain splattering in all directions.

Having plunged the office into darkness, Henry Kowitt

ran to one of the windows, opened it, and looked out. The window faced the alley only 25 feet from the rear of the building. The alley was dark. Kowitt pulled a pair of leather gloves from his coat pocket and turned to Skul, who had thrown the ends of the two lines over the front of the desk, had pulled them across the bottom between the legs, and was now tying the ends to the lines.

"The parking lot will be one fine confused mess," Kowitt said gleefully, shoving cartridges into the cylinder of his .44 mag revolver. "We won't even be noticed."

Finished with securing the second nylon line, Skul took the last package of explosive from his right coat pocket, turned on the detonator and tossed the C-4 to the floor in front of the desk. He then began to play out the 2 lines and toss them through the open window.

He put on a pair of leather gloves, and said matter of factly, "Let's go and get us some fresh air. This place smells like a whore house with dirty wallpaper."

He swung a leg through the open window.

Once Skul and Kowitt had slid down the lines and were on the ground, they hurried past a row of garbage cans and crept to the northwest corner of the building. Soon they were mingling with and lost among bystanders who had gathered and were milling around in front of the *Cotton Candy* and in the southeastern part of the parking lot.

Four police cars and 2 SWAT vans were in front, SWAT members in position. Each of them wore an armored vest, combat helmet with face shield, and carried a Colt AR-15 assault rifle.

Not wanting anyone to notice them, Skul and Kowitt took their time going to the Cadillac. Within 10 minutes they reached the car and got in. Skul took out the remote control station and remarked as Kowitt started the engine, "We made it just in time. Half a dozen SWATs are starting to move along the north side. Let's give them something to worry about.''

Holding the station in his lap, he turned it on and pressed the red button. There was another muffled *BURR-RRUUUUMMMM,* the explosion shaking the building. Some female bystanders uttered little screams, and the cops halted and got down, none knowing what to do. Had the terrorist gunmen left the building or were they still inside?

In a short while, the caddy was moving north on Lenox Avenue, the pace slow because of the traffic.

''In another 3 hours, we should be in the safe house in Mount Vernon,'' Skul remarked, ''I think within the next week, we'll move everything from both West 23rd and 64th Streets to Mount Vernon. It's not good security to hole up in apartments too long. There are too many people coming and going.''

Henry Kowitt sounded intense. ''And you still intend to hit the Russians?''

''It's the last thing Borsirev would expect.''

''If he is head of the KGB apparatus here in New York?''

''We have to believe that the CIA is right, that Borsirev is the top Ruskie,'' Skul said. ''Ahhh, we're almost there.''

He and Kowitt both saw the sign to the right: HARLEM HOSPITAL AHEAD. TURN RIGHT.

CHAPTER FIVE_____

THE white sound generator hummed in the bubble room, which was not shaped like a bubble but was composed of sheets of thick, clear plastic and was nothing more than a small, square room within a larger room. A fanatic for security, Mikhail Pavel Borsirev considered the safe room absolutely necessary. The American CIA was very good. NSA was even better.

Andrei Gouzenko tapped ash from his Lucky Strike. "I don't feel there is any direct danger to us," he said in excellent English to Borsirev and Shumaev. "It's obvious that someone—some organization—is attempting to start a gang war between the Jackson mob and that *chernozhopki* Salvatore Tuccinardo and his barbarians. None of that involves the Soviet Union, much less the KGB."

"All we can do for the moment is surmise, and at the same time set up a scenario of possibilities that, if they became reality, would be detrimental to our Otdel," Sergei Shumaev ventured. In contrast to Major Gouzenko, who was thickset, rather debonair, and handsome in a rugged sort of way, Shumaev resembled a long-faced American farmer all dressed up in his Sunday-go-to-meeting clothes. "My opinion is no matter what happens, the New York police and the FBI can't tie any of it to us, to the Soviet Union. The Jackson mob doesn't even know we exist, and Salvatore Tuccinardo can't tell anyone he's receiving heroin from us. He would implicate himself. We know how their system works. The Mafia never tells the police anything.''

Colonel Borsirev, frowning, studied Shumaev thoughtfully, feeling that his analysis was logical. Nonetheless, Borsirev was not satisfied. He could not afford to be. As head of the New York KGB Otdel, or network, all responsibility for success or failure fell on his shoulders. His main worry was the KGB did not have even one hint as to who had tried to kill Salvatore Tuccinardo and who had succeeded in terminating Wilbur Jackson nine days ago. Tuccinardo had a lot of lines of information in the New York Police Department, and not even the police believed the Jackson mob had tried to kill him. Neither did the police, including the federal FBI, believe Tuccinardo had sent executioners to kill Wilbur Jackson.

According to Tuccinardo's spies in the police department, the police—and the FBI as well—were working on the theory that one of the other families in the area was responsible. Don Salvatore was convinced that the authorities were wrong.

''None of the other families would try to knock me off and muscle in,'' he had said to Colonel Borsirev. ''The way Uncle Sugar and his Feds are constantly trying to indict us, none of the other Dons would try anything that could and would result in going to the mattresses—a war. They'd have nothing to gain and everything to lose. Hell, they hate all this publicity the same way I do!''

His arms folded, Borsirev leaned back in the bucket-type clear plastic chair and crossed his legs.

''We have to assume that the people responsible are freelance contract agents working for the CIA,'' said Borsirev. ''There isn't any specific security measure we can use to protect ourselves, other than extreme overall security, particularly in reference to the shipment of processed cocaine coming in on the *Boris Gudinov*. The problem is how to get 2 English tons of heroin off the vessel and in the hands of Tuccinardo. However, the problem is minor.''

"We can always use divers," Shumaev said casually. "One diver can easily carry 22 kilograms of heroin in a sealed watertight container. Ten divers could transport the heroin from the vessel to a dockside warehouse in a single night. The divers could come up through a trapdoor in the floor.''

"Yes, and Don Salvatore has an interest in one of the warehouses in the dock area," admitted Borsirev.

Major Gouzenko fingered his small, neatly-trimmed mustache. "As I said, I don't believe there is any direct danger to us, not yet. The situation could develop differently if we're correct about that fool Alexandr Yasakev and four other Comrades. If . . .''

"Well now, Andrei. We can't blame them for wanting to fuck good looking American women!" interrupted Borsirev with a loud laugh. His voice then became hard and ruthless. "We can blame Yasakev and the others for stupidity. And we can accuse Yasakev of theft and of being a traitor. Our agent in the Maritime Commission is still not certain, but she thinks he has stolen between 5 and 7 thousand American.''

"We can't expose him to the United Nations," Shumaev said bitterly. "It would be a reflection on the Motherland. After all, he is a Soviet citizen.''

"I'm leaving the decision to the Center in *Moskova*," said Borsirev. "The Center might feel exposing him would prove how honest and moral the Soviet Union is. Then again, the Center might decide to recall the son-of-a-bitch and try him in secrecy. At the moment, what matters is the two American women, Deborah Miles and Ann Marie Brandon.''

''Assuming they are a part of the network conspiring against us,'' added Shumaev tonelessly.

Borsirev nodded vigorously. ''Exactly. We can conclude that Yasakev is the target of Deborah Miles and that Brandon is a standby agent, hoping she can attract some Soviet official from the U.N. who might use the services of the dating organization.''

''Yes, but it's still supposition on our part,'' Gouzenko reminded him.

''It's not supposition that Miles is misrepresenting herself. Our people trailed her to an apartment on West 23rd Street. The apartment is listed under the name of 'Jarvis Sinclair.' Miles is posing as 'Mavis Sinclair.' Either as his sister or his wife. We don't know which. And there are men who come and go!'' A realist who never rationalized and who went out of his way to knock down his own operational theories, Borsirev added, ''But whoever heard of American Intelligence being so obvious, operating from a public apartment house? It doesn't make any sense.''

Sergei Shumaev slowly rubbed the end of his long chin. ''Colonel, it is not uncommon for American prostitutes and their pimps to use a variety of fictitious names—only you don't believe the two women are whores.''

''Why not put men on the Brandon woman and see what kind of alias she's using?'' suggested Captain Shumaev.

''I believe that Miles and Brandon are somehow connected with American Intelligence,'' acknowledged Borsirev, a little annoyed at Shumaev; yet he knew that Sergei was only playing the role of devil's advocate. ''The hole in the theory is that the CIA has never used sex in any of its operations, which is not to say that a freelancer wouldn't.''

''Could it be we're trying to complicate something that is basically very simple? After all, what could Alexandr Yasakev reveal to the Miles woman? He knows absolutely nothing about the heroin we've been bringing into the United States.''

"But they—whoever 'they' are—don't know he doesn't have anything of value,'' pointed out Borsirev. "Worse, if the women are enemy agents, it would indicate that the Americans have learned what we are doing, or at least suspect we're smuggling drugs into this rotten nation.''

He then looked calmly at Shumaev. "There isn't any point in wasting time to find out where Brandon lives or what kind of name she might be using. The fact that Miles took Yasakev to an apartment is evidence enough or me that shortly the Americans will attempt to blackmail him. No doubt they photographed and recorded every sexual act he and Miles performed. They'll offer him a choice of either working for them or having his foolishness revealed to our Embassy in Washington. I'm sure of it.''

"A blackmail attempt would be proof that the Americans are aware of what we in the *Kah Gay Beh* are doing here in New York,'' admitted Sergei Shumaev, speaking the Russian letters for KGB.

"Now you see why Deborah Miles is interested in that fool Yasakev!'' Borsirev spoke with confidence and assurance. "The Americans would automatically think of two ways we would bring the drugs into the country, diplomatic couriers and by ships of our merchant fleet. As the Secretary of the IMO, he would know in advance the names of Soviet vessels coming to New York.'' He paused and smiled. "The damn fool Americans probably also think that Yasakev has information about the drugs. I think it's time we teach them a lesson.''

He shifted about uneasily in the plastic chair. In response to his last remark, he had expected interest on the part of Gouzenko and Shumaev. Instead, Andrei Gouzenko said, "Colonel, did Salvatore Tuccinardo's last message give any information about what the American BATF learned from the samples of wood and other material they took from his home and from the *Cotton Candy Club*?''

''The explosive used is a common American military explosive,'' Borsirev said, concealing his annoyance and impatience. ''It's of the type we use, the type which Americans can 'Samtex.' The American explosive is known as Composition-4. It's composed of 77 per cent RDX and 5 per cent TNT. Composition-4 was also used in the attack on Tuccinardo's home.''

''I don't see how we can take executive action against the Americans,'' said Sergei Shumaev. ''With the damned FBI always watching every move most of our people make. And we can't completely eliminate the possibility that it might be professional CIA we're fighting right here in New York. The CIA could have changed its policy.''

''We'll first wait and see if Deborah Miles attempts to blackmail Yasakev,'' Borsirev explained. ''Tomorrow, we'll have a talk with that idiot and let him know that we have full information about his activities with Miles, as well as his appropriating funds for his own personal use. Once the blackmail attempt is made, we'll have proof that my theory is right.''

Major Gouzenko locked his hands behind his head and smiled. ''I'm sure Yasakev will give us his full-fill cooperation.''

Captain Shumaev did not find Gouzenko's remark amusing. He looked at Borsirev. ''What does Yasakev have to do with 'blood-wet-work' against these barbaric Americans?''

A glint of satisfaction came into his boss' dark eyes. ''We'll kidnap Miles and the man who calls himself Jarvis Sinclair,'' announced Colonel Borsirev. ''Or rather some of Tuccinardo's hoodlums will kidnap the 2 and turn them over to some of our wet-work specialists who will take them to the *Boris Gudinov*. The vessel will dock in 5 days.

By then, the Americans should have put their proposal to Alexandr Yasakev.''

Taking a pack of Kent Golden Lights from his shirt pocket, Borsirev began pulling off the cellophane, looking from Shumaev to Gouzenko, waiting for them to tell him what they thought of the scheme. Shumaev appeared to be thinking, to be calculating the risks. Major Gouzenko, looking worried, pursed his lips and made a face.

''You disagree, Andrei,'' said Borsirev, his face retaining a mask-like rigidity as he spoke. ''Why?''

The spy chief didn't look like an officer in the KGB. A slight man with a receding hairline and a receding chin, Borsirev appeared as innocuous as an 80 year old retired nun. Only Borsirev was 46 and as ''inoffensive'' as a piranha which had not eaten in a week. In his 21 years as an officer in the KGB, he had been stationed in 12 different countries, yet not once had he ever been suspected or questioned by police.

''I was thinking of the extreme violence used against Tuccinardo and that savage Jackson,'' Gouzenko said pensively. ''Whoever they are, they could take extreme measures against Yasakev. But I would imagine the Center back home couldn't care about him. That leaves only the people in this building.''

Colonel Borsirev paused in lighting his Kent and looked oddly at Gouzenko. Sergei Shumaev frowned and blinked very rapidly at Gouzenko.

Borsirev smiled knowingly. ''Surely, you're not suggesting they would attack us here at AMTORG?''

''I was thinking it is a possibility,'' Gouzenko said with disarming directness. ''We are dealing with extremely aggressive agents. They go directly to the target and utilize whatever means is at hand to accomplish their purpose. They are ruthless, determined and clever.''

''I agree,'' Borsirev said, his tone faintly mocking. ''I also think you're letting your imagination race wild. Our government has a 50 year lease on this office building. Accordingly, we have our own guards and security system. We're very well protected.''

"There is also the new laser system in the lobby," Shumaev said quickly. "It's worked perfectly ever since it was installed in December of 1985.''

"Andrei, you're also forgetting that the people who killed that black ape Jackson and attacked Tuccinardo are more than ruthless,'' Borsirev said gently. "They are also very smart. It took intelligent planning, exquisite training and professional teamwork to attack the estate and the *Cotton Candy*, then escape without being seen. I admit we're up against experts. We can, however, outwit them.''

Major Gouzenko did not bother to press the matter. To have done so would not have served any worthwhile purpose. In case he was wrong, it was better to keep his fears to himself. Another worry he had was the possibility of American Intelligence closing in and his spending the next 5 or 6 years in prison before he was traded for an American agent serving time in the Soviet Union, or in one of the satellite countries.

Soviet diplomats at the Embassy in Washington and at the Consulate in San Francisco were immune to prosecution. So were Soviet diplomats posted to the Soviet Mission at the United Nations. Should any of them be exposed as spies, they could only be declared *persona non grata* and kicked out of the country.

Soviet nationals who were not protected by diplomatic status were up for grabs. Gouzenko, Shumaev, and Borsirev were in the non-diplomatic category. Gouzenko was supposedly a correspondent for TASS, the Soviet news agency. Captain Sergei Shumaev was ostensibly a reporter for *Izvestia*. A minor official in AMTORG—the Soviet trading corporation—was Colonel Borsirev's cover. Should they be exposed as agents of the KGB, they could be tried and sentenced to an American federal penitentiary.

Sergei Shumaev spoke up, "Colonel, what assurance do we have that Tuccinardo will agree to arrange the kidnap of the woman and Jarvis Sinclair and then turn them over to us? He is not a man to be bossed, and we can't threaten him."

Borsirev smirked. "That damned animal will be only too happy to comply with our request, especially after we 'prove' to him that Deborah Miles and Jarvis Sinclair are members of the group responsible for the attack on his estate."

Shumaev and Gouzenko's expressions indicated skepticism.

"Tuccinardo is a ruthless barbarian and a vindictive bastard," Shumaev intoned. "He might just order his gunmen to kill Miles and Sinclair. What could we do about it?"

Borsirev's smile was sinister. "For one thing, we will threaten to cut off the supply of heroin. Just to make sure we do obtain possession of Miles and Sinclair, I'm going to send 3 of our *illegals* with the gunmen who go after those two." He got to his feet. "And now is a good time to get started."

Gouzenko and Shumaev followed their Chief from the bubble room, both feeling a vague fear.

Or was it a premonition?

CHAPTER SIX

"**C**ACCHIO, Sal! We should never have become involved with those godless Russians," Peter Dellacrote said in a hoarse voice, just above a whisper. "Look what it's gotten us—nothing but a hard look from Uncle Sugar and a lot of publicity. Now this! They wanting us to grab a couple outta apartment house! You should have refused!"

His face remaining calm, Salvatore Tuccinardo didn't reply. He continued to rock back and forth in the ancient cane rocking chair.

Joey "Gags" Maselli, the *sottocapo* of the mob, sipped his whiskey and soda and waited. Elegantly dressed, he looked more like a Wall Street broker than a Wall Street broker. A stranger would never have suspected he was the underboss of the Tuccinardo Family.

"We've also made about 26 million bucks from the H those Russian *cornuto* gave us," Tuccinardo said at length, his face as dark as the sky before a storm, "and we don't have to worry about the Feds. The FBI and IRS can't tie us in with Jackson or the Russians. Another thing"—he stabbed a bony finger at Dellacrote—"Jackson's boys don't believe we're responsible for the hit on him. We ain't going to have no trouble with them, either!"

Maselli said, "Rumor has it that Willie Dunn's taken over the Jackson mob. Shit! Tomorrow we'll hear it was some other burrhead. They'll be knocking each other off left and right for control of the rackets in Harlem."

Tuccinardo's laugh was low and calculating. "Joey, you and Pete put your heads together before you came in here. Out with it." He looked at Dellacrote sitting on the leather couch in the special meeting room. "What are you gonna try to convice me of?"

Dellacrote's thick, pale lips twisted into a smile. "You know the answer to that, Sal. My counsel to you is to break it off with the Russians while there is still time. The entire situation is getting out of hand. We all know that dealing with the Jackson mob, now that Dynamite is dead, is impossible."

Tuccinardo stopped rocking. "And you, Joey. You agree?"

"Yes, I do, Don Salvatore," Maselli said solemnly. "As I see it, the trouble our Family is having could make Don Rossi and some of the other families get ideas. Rossi would love to ease us out of the deals we got going at Kennedy and La Guardia, and for several years that *cazzo* Barbizo has been eying what we got on the docks in Lower Manhattan. Right now, we don't need no trouble from nobody, Don Salvatore."

"Even 2 tons of horse aint worth the risk," whispered Dellacrote. It was not that he was a naturally soft-spoken man—he had no choice but to speak in a voice that was just above a whisper. Twenty-one years earlier, he had almost been strangled to death with a rope, and the close encounter with death had damaged his vocal cords.

Tall, thin, and as grim-looking as the director of a funeral home, Dellacrote had grown up with Tuccinardo in New York's Little Italy, and was the mob's *consigliere*, although he was a year younger than Salvatore, who was sixty-seven. What bothered Dellacrote was why, in view of recent developments, Sal was willing to take such chances. It wasn't because he was stupid. Tuccinardo had started out as a triggerman with the old Luciano mob, and had used his smarts to rise steadily in the underworld, in spite of all his enemies. Most of his enemies were dead— Genovese, Gambino, Anastasia, Evola, Lucchese. All rotting away in their tombs. But Don Salvatore remained— stronger than ever.

"You're right—both of you," Tuccinardo said, surprising Dellacrote and Maselli. "Like I said, the Feds can't connect us in no way with either the Jackson mob and the Russians—not yet anyway. But if something went wrong in the future, the whole mess could blow up in our faces. We . . ."

"But if . . ."

"Silencio, Peter." Tuccinardo held up a restraining hand. "We can't ignore what has happened. The Feds gotta suspect we got a deal going with the Russians, or they wouldn't have tried to hit me. They wouldn't be trying to start a war between us and the Jackson burrheads. So now's the time to conclude our business with those Russian sons-a-bitches." He looked hard at Dellacrote. "What's wrong with you? You look like a high school boy who can't get a hard-on with his girl!"

"I don't like questions there aren't answers for," replied Dellacrote. "I mean, I don't think it's the Feds in back of all the trouble. Uncle Sugar and his straight-laced boys don't work that way!"

The Don frowned. "You heard what Borsirev said! Those two—what are their names, again?"

"Deborah Miles and Jarvis Sinclair," supplied Joey Maselli.

"They're supposed to be 2 of the members of the outfit behind all the shootings—not that we believe the Russians. Probably that pair is dangerous to the Russians for some reason, and they want them out of the way, or taken back to the Soviet Union. Why else would Borsirev want them hauled aboard a Soviet freighter?''

"What about the 2 tons of H, Sal? You mean we're going to keep the horse and double-cross the Russians?'' asked Dellacrote after a moment of shocked immobility.

"Why not,'' admitted Tuccinardo. "What can the Russians do about it. Send a couple of mechanics to try and hit us? So what? A lot of people would like to see us cold cuts and out of the way.''

Dellacrote slowly shook his head. "I don't think the Russians would send any of their specialists. They're more crooked than a politician in Alabama, but they're practical. They wouldn't risk everything just for revenge. They'll chalk up our grab to experience.''

Joseph Maselli said, "Don Salvatore, is that why you agreed to kidnap Deborah Miles and Jarvis Sinclair—to keep Borsirev and the other Russians off guard?''

"What better way to fool them?'' Tuccinardo said enthusiastically. "I don't want them to think we're having doubts about our arrangement with them. They'll know soon enough, but not until we move the heroin out of the warehouse. Joey, did you make all the necessary arrangements for tomorrow?''

"Sure. Grabbing them two won't be no problem,'' Maselli said smugly. "Me and 6 of the guys will take the van and meet the Russians on Eighth Street. It's a snap. The only thing I don't like about the grab is them 2 Russians who'll be coming with us. How in fuck can you trust men who don't believe in no god!''

"Joey, you're sure you and your men know what the man and the woman look like?'' asked Tuccinardo in a fatherly tone.

"We sure do, Don Salvatore. We got their photographs.'' He gave a loud snicker. "It sure comes in handy to have private detectives on the payroll, don't it?''

"Joey, don't become over confident about this deal,''

Tuccinardo warned in a cold voice. "I think Borsirev lied about the man and the woman. I don't believe they're part of the group who tried to kill me. But we can't be sure. Borsirev might have spoken the truth. If he did, the man and the woman could be extremely dangerous."

"Don Salvatore, I always assume any opposition is dangerous," Maselli said with a self-satisfied smile. "I'm taking Big-Nose Sam and Phil the Plumber with me. You know how good they are. They're 2 of the best mechanics in any mob. Don't worry, Don Salvatore. The *Boris Gudinov* docks this afternoon. By tomorrow afternoon, Miles and Sinclair will be on board her."

Don Salvatore nodded, then looked at his old friend Dellacrote whom he trusted completely—but not stupidly so. He trusted Peter because he knew he was not interested in power. All he wanted was a comfortable life and freedom to collect his expensive miniatures.

"Why the long face, Peter?" asked Tuccinardo. "You yourself said that Borsirev isn't likely to send any gunmen after us—and 2 tons of horse is easily worth a 100 million dollars on the streets, even after it's stepped on. What the hell is wrong now? Joey Gags and the others know their job. They won't have no trouble grabbing those two."

"I don't like your going aboard the Russian ship 3 days from now." Dellacrote rubbed a hand across the top of his bald head. "I think it's too risky, too damn dangerous."

"We'll use the same old dodge to duck the FBI snoops," said Tuccinardo with a relaxed sigh. "As usual, they tail us into Manhattan, right up to the front door of the house on Mulberry Street. They'll assume I'm inside and wait until I come out. That's been the routine for years. They don't know about the passage to the garage down the street. But I think your concern is the Russians."

Dellacrote made a face. "Sal, once you're on board, who's to say you'll come off? I don't see how our getting the 2 tons of horse from the ship to the warehouse is so complicated that Borsirev has to explain all of it to you in person? No, Sal. I don't like it.''

Tuccinardo's eyes twinkled at his friend affectionately. ''Borsirev's reason makes sense. The FBI is trailing him and other Russians all over the place. He feels it easier for me to come to him than for him to come to us. You know the city. You know how easy it is to tail anyone from the U.N. or the AMTORG building, or from the apartment house on East 59th where most of the Russians live.'' He laughed. ''Surely you don't think that Borsirev wants to ship me off to the Soviet Union?''

''Pete, if they wanted to knock off Don Salvatore, they wouldn't have to lure him to no ship to do it,'' spoke up Maselli. ''Hell, them KGB guys are almost as good as we are. They use all kinds of tricky weapons and methods.''

''Then you're going to the ship on Wednesday?'' Dellacrote said to Tuccinardo, sounding more forlorn than ever.

''Peter, you worry too much.'' Smiling slightly, the Don pulled an old fashioned watch from his vest, opened and looked at it. He closed the watch, returned it to his pocket and stood up.

''It's time for Mass,'' he said.

CHAPTER SEVEN

IF lack of opportunity is nothing more than lack of purpose and direction, Jonathan Skul had any number of opportunities. No man in New York had greater resoluion and determination. During the past few weeks, he and the other members of Unit-1 had gone into the shadows: they had moved from the two apartments in Manhattan.

The move had been a slow and tedious process. Skeeter Ronson, COBRA's front man, had not rented furnished apartments. The furniture in such apartments could have been bugged in advance. How do you rip apart a couch, or a mattress, and look for a hidden transmitter, and not explain to the owner of the place? Ronson, therefore, had furnished the apartments.

The two moves could have been swift and uncomplicated if Skul had called in professional movers. To do so would have endangered security. In case anyone was keeping the two apartments under surveillance, it would have been very easy to tag-tail a lumbering moving van to the new station in Mount Vernon, northeast of New York—an estate off Pelham Parkway.

Skul used another method. He had Doug Almaine rent a U-HAUL 3 ton truck. With the help of Kowitt and Hayes,

Skul and Almaine then moved one or two pieces of furniture every day, sometimes at 7 o'clock at night, other times at high noon or 6 in the morning. Using one of the 3 freight elevators, they carried the furniture out the rear of the Benington Arms. Alister Bates and the other four members of Unit-1 used the same technique to move from the Hideaway, the apartment house on 64th Street.

Jon Skul had been busy in another direction: developing information pertaining to AMTORG, headquartered in a building on First Avenue. Planning his operation around the mathematical logic that a straight line is the shortest distance between 2 points, Skul had made up his mind to go to the prime source of information: Mikhail Pavel Borsirev, who was the assistant public relations man at the Soviet trading corporation.

Months earlier, COBRA operatives had secretly photographed ultra secret CIA files and had learned that the Agency had put its finger on the KGB's *Rezident*—Chief of Station—in New York City. It was the meek-looking Borsirev. It was he who directed the entire Soviet *Apparat*, or network. It was also Borsirev who would have complete information about the heroin being smuggled into the United States. Or one of his assistants would possess the data: dates, places, methods of delivery. These 2 men were Andrei Gouzenko and Sergei Shumaev, both of whom were posing as journalists.

Jon Skul intended to accomplish the impossible as well as the improbable—kidnap the KGB spy chief and force him to tell everything he knew. The idea was not popular with all the members of Unit-1.

Alister Bates was all gung-ho. "I can open any of the locks. With a K-kit, I can even work the coded and the electric locks."

Debbie Miles and Ann Brandon did not give an opinion. They were not qualified in E.O.M.—Extreme Operational Methods.

"A remarkable exercise in tempting Dame Fortune," stated Hayes in his academic manner.

Barry Glen Arden, the ex-SEAD officer, was more than qualified to give an opinion. A specialist in combating terrorists, he was automatically an expert in the use of terrorist tactics.

"Jon, your scheme is entirely too dangerous," he said. "We might be able to get to the Russian pig and net him, but getting out of the building with him, and out of the area is another matter. The odds would be way against us. I should say by at least a factor of 75 per cent. Look at the map, then tell me differently."

Skul was forced to agree. All along he had known it would be impossible to blackbag the KGB chief inside the AMTORG building. Security was too tight. Worse, the area outside the building was too open. Pursuit would not be difficult.

Grab Borsirev on his way to work, or on the way home from AMTORG? This would be even worse. Sometimes, the KGB chief used a taxi. Other times he rode to work or returned home with another Russian who drove a blue Honda Accord. There were those times that Mikhail Borsirev drove his own vehicle, a Datsun Sentra.

Net him on a busy street, in the heart of traffic? Not very likely!

That left only the Armatage, the six story apartment house where AMTORG employees, and some diplomats from the Soviet Mission to the U.N. lived with their families. The Soviet Union had a 25 year lease on the apartment house. Forever suspicious of (and feeling inferior to) Americans, the Russians even imported their own people for building maintenance. The 2 doormen on duty were Russians. After midnight, when the doormen were not on duty, there were then 3 guards on duty in the small lobby. At all times, day and night, 365 days a year, there were 2 men on duty at the service entrance. Any delivery man was carefully scrutinized. If the delivery could not be left at the service entrance, a guard accompanied the messenger to the designated apartment.

By stealing secrets from the CIA, COBRA had learned also that 3 Russinas were always on duty in the basement. One of them—on both shifts—was an engineer who took care of the heating plant and maintained the 3 elevators.

The decorative bars on the windows of the first 2 floors was more proof of how fearful the Russians were of intruders.

There was one big vital difference between the AMTORG building and The Armatage on East 59th Street. The area surrounding the apartment complex did not contain a lot of open space, increasing the possibilities for rapid escape. A BMT subway station was close by; so was the Queensboro Bridge. Three blocks to the west was Central Park. In only minutes after they left the aprtment house, Skul and his men and their captive could be lost in the depths of the park and then have 3 directions of escape—straight across to the west side; south to midtown; or north to Harlem.

"We could grab the son-of-a-bitch from The Armatage," Barry Arden said. "It could work. As I see it, the real problem would be how to get in."

"And how to finger Borsirev, or Gouzenko, or Shumaev," inserted Skul. "We can only narrow it down. We do know from CIA files that they almost never go out at night."

Debbie Miles expressed doubts in another direction.

"Jon, what makes you think that a professional career KGB officer like Borsirev is going to talk? I'm thinking of a time-frame. He could be a fanatic. You might pull his fingernails out one by one, and he still might not tell you what you want to know."

A faint smile blossomed on Skul's face. "Borsirev will be only to happy to give us the information we want. If possible, I intend to grab his wife as well. He'll either make like a parrot or witness her execution.''

''You're not joking are you?'' Debbie Miles knew that he wasn't.

''I'd blow up my own mother, if whacking her out was necessary to stop the KGB from flooding this country with heroin. Don't get preachy about brutality. Think of the thousands and thousands of American lives being destroyed by their drugs each year. It's not only the people who stick a needle in their arm or snort snow. I also mean their victims, the people who are robbed and often murdered because of the drug user's need for money.'' Skul was breathing hard. ''Just what the hell did you think you signed up for—a picnic? These men are scum, sub-human. They deal in death and make no mistake, if they got their hands on your ass they'd burn you first, then ask questions.''

Karsten Hayes tilted back his head and began to scratch his throat.

''If the Russians had any sense, they'd know that they don't have to import drugs to wreck American society. Our own knee-jerk liberabls have already started the process, opening our borders to every piece of Third World trash who wants in. All we need now is for the jack-ass voters to elect some lame-brained dove president, no pun intended my dear. That's all we'd need, a dumb liberal son-of-a-bitch to cut defense spending and hand out more freebie welfare checks.''

''Kar, you forgot to include the ACLU,'' said William Holbrook. ''Their always crying about the poor criminal and how he is treated injustly. Naturally, they ignore the victim. Why in hell do you think they take so many free of charge cases involving rapists, murderers, and other human scum? It shouldn't be a surprise to anyone.''

Debbie Miles finished lighting her Virginia Slims and blew smoke in the direction of Hayes. ''I suggest we get back to business and stop wasting time.''

"I hope we do better than we did with Yasakev," muttered Ann Brandon. "It's a good thing we didn't return to Date Right, all things considered. No telling what the KGB might have done."

"The time to go into The Armatage is about 2 in the morning," Skul said, thinking about the remark Brandon had made. The KGB might know something was not quite right, but Borsirev would not know how his apparatus had been penetrated. To his surprise Skul was also happy for Debbie and Ann. Both girls were relieved that their "duties" with Date Right Escort Service were behind them. They had simply not returned. There wasn't any way that Alice Hooten, the owner, could contact them because the telephones at the 2 apartments had been disconnected.

Debbie had also terminated her association with Alexandr Yasakev. She had not had any difficulty in luring the Russian to the special apartment. Two cameras, one with infrared lens, had photographed every act, every position. A recorder had captured every moan and cry and a sigh of passion, every word that had passed between Debbie and the Russian.

And the entire blackmail scheme had backfired!

"Watch it, Phil!" Joey Maselli said sharply to Philip Sirignano who was driving the caddy Eldorado, and who had just shot ahead of another vehicle. "We don't want the cops giving us a ticket and remembering we was in this part of town, not with what's going down."

"You should have listened to me," growled Phil the Plumber. Built like an ape and as ugly as mortal sin, he made a clicking sound of disapproval with his tongue. "If we had turned off on Riverside Drive like I wanted to, we'd be making better time. We lost any Feds who might be trailing us back at Central Park."

"Stop bumping your gums and just be careful," Maselli said from the rear seat. He turned and looked out the window. He could not be positive, but through the other traffic, he thought he saw the Mercury Sable that Big Nose Sam Bianco was driving. With Sam was Max-Emil Grosbinarger, the only non-Sicilian in the group. One of the most expert assassins in the country, Grosbinarger was an "associate" of the mob. He had been called in from Massachusetts as extra security.

Carlo Oddo and Charlie "Lemmons" Aloi were in the third vehicle, an old United Parcel Service van painted a light blue. On both sides, in white letters trimmed in black, were JERRICO AUTO PARTS. In the rear of the van were the 2 Russians. Average looking guys, neither one looked like a leg-breaker.

Pete Dellacrote had warned Joey: *Listen, those Russians are probably members of the KGB, the Soviet secret police. Be careful of them. All you have to do is turn Miles and Sinclair over to them. The 2 Russians will then use the van to take them to wherever they're going with them.*

For any number of reasons, Joey Gags wasn't enthused about the kidnap job, and would have cancelled the deal if the decision had been his. For one thing, he and the other guys didn't even know the real names of the pair in the apartment on Payson Avenue, and the 2 dudes with them. Hell, not even Don Salvatore and his *consigliere* knew who they really were or what they were!

As a rule, you always knew the name of a joker who had had the big-X put on him, and you had some idea why you were going to whack him out. He had either crossed someone or had become a threat to the organization. It was different with Miles and Sinclair. They were unknowns, but apparently very dangerous. They weren't scheduled to be whacked out, either. They were to be kidnaped and turned over to the 2 Russians. The 2 dudes with them, however, were to be scratched. Yeah, but why did it take 7 bone-crushers—all made-men!—to put the grab on only 2 people, one of them even a doll?

The other guys had the same question bouncing around in their heads. Seven guys to snatch 2 people! It didn't make sense. Hell, 2 headhunters and a good wheel-man could have done the job easily. But *seven*! And who in fuck were the 2 "civilians" coming along?

Joey Gags couldn't tell the boys the full facts. He had only said, "Look, take it from me: those 2 are very dangerous. They're part of the group that attacked Don Salvatore's home and whacked out Dynamite Jackson."

Of course, now that the word was that there were 2 others with Sinclair and Miles, maybe 7 guys were necessary. The 2 extra jokers would make a difference. They would have to be made history in order to snatch Miles and Sinclair.

"God damn!" Phil the Plumber spit out when the raindrops hit the windshield. "That's all we need—rain!" He turned on the windshield wipers.

"The rain might not make any difference," said Dominic Macaterri, who was in the front seat next to Phil. "I mean whether or not the rain slows us down. The 4 of them might not even be there. First, we're supposed to go to a joint on West 23rd and grab those two. Next thing you know, we find they had vanished." He turned his big head to the left and said over his shoulder, "Tell me, Joey. How in fuck can you move an apartment full of furniture without anyone seeing it? I thought those private eyes were keeping an eye on the damn place?"

"They was," Joey said half-heartedly, wishing he was in Miami. "What happened is the fuckin' dumbells only watched the front of the damned building. That slick fucker Sinclair pulled a fast one. What he and the others did, they moved a piece or two out each day—out the back."

"That's what I meant, we can't be sure they'll be where they're supposed to be on Payson Avenue by the time we get there," Macaterri said with a snort. "I never did have faith in private dicks. They're lice, all of them, always slinking around and sticking their noses into people's business.''

"Dom has a point, Joey,'' chimed in Phil the Plumber. "It's been over an hour and a half since those private eye dummies called and said they'd located Miles and Sinclair in a dump on Payson Avenue. How in hell do you know they'll be there, huh?''

"I don't, but it's the best shot we've got at them,'' Joey said acidly. "Don't give me no shit about it. I only follow orders.''

Joey Sags looked out the window at the rain. It was only a light summer shower. Crap! It hadn't been private investigators who had tipped off Don Salvatore. It had been the Russians. How had they known where Miles and Sinclair were? The motherfuckin' KGB, that's how! Christ Almighty! How could God let such damned atheists exist?

Joey thought of the 3 cold pieces hidden in the back seat. Two of the hand guns were Llama .45 pistols. The third, an odd-looking weapon, was a 9mm Goncz High-Tech Long Pistol. The damn thing had a 32 shot magazine. All 3 weapons were equipped with silencers and had been stolen from the home of a wealthy man in New Rochelle. Joey felt like laughing when he thought of the slob. The dummy would have a lot of explaining to do when the cops confronted him with the weapons.

Any thoughts of mirth and amusement vanished when Joey recalled the hit—Paul Castellano had been gunned down and turned into history. Not even Don Salvatore knew why Big Paul had been whacked out. According to the newspapers, Castellano, the "alleged" head of the Gambino family, and Thomas Bilotti, his chauffeur and bodyguard, had been shot repeatedly by 4 hitmen as they walked from a car to a restaurant in midtown Manhattan.

Don Salvatore had been furious. Hits were always approved by the Commission, and to whack out a member of the Commission was never done. If a Commission member, always a Don, got out of hand somehow, he was ordered to step down. He "retired," as in the case of Joe Bonanno, who thought he was bigger than he was.

Who had hit Big Paul? It was well known that powerful factions within his own mob hated his guts and wanted him out. Could they have knocked him off? Or could it have been the mysterious assassins who had snuffed Dynamite Jackson and had tried to whamo Don Salvatore?

"It wasn't the new guys on the block," Don Salvatore had reasoned. "Only 2 guys walked into the *Cotton Candy* and whacked out Jackson—and they took on damn near half his mob to do it! They sure as hell wouldn't need 3 or 4 hitmen to knock off Big Paul. His own people blasted him."

Or had they?

Dominic Macatteri announced from the front seat. "We're getting close. Inwood Hill Park is just ahead. I'll make a left on Dyckman, then turn off on Payson."

"Okay. We'll first size up the building them 4 is in," Joey said. "Park half a block away, on the same side of the street, if you can."

It began to rain harder . . .

CHAPTER EIGHT

PLEASED with the job that William Holbrook had done, Jon Skul surveyed the wall where the mirror, with its world time clock, had been. The two-way mirror had rested over a 14 inch square opening, the opposite end of the aperture in the wall of the apartment next door. The high speed camera that had recorded the love making between Debbie Miles and Alexandr Yasakev had been in the compartment in the 13.6 inch wide wall, the lens pointing at the queen-size bed. Only now there wasn't any camera. There weren't any openings, either. Holbrook had placed a small section of wallboarding over each opening, and had carefully plastered them over.

Skul, his back to Debbie, smiled in satisfaction. "All we have to do is come back tomorrow and paint this wall," he said. "The job shouldn't take over an hour, once we start. We can put a tarp on the floor to protect the rug."

Debbie, sitting on the end of the bed, shrugged. "I don't see why we had to go to the trouble of sealing the openings. COBRA owns this building, and this apartment and the next one are never rented to outsiders."

"Orders!" Skul said promptly. "Barron is an extremely

cautious man—and not because of the KGB. Borsirev and the other Russians now know that this apartment belongs to U.S. Intelligence—or at least was used by U.S. Intelligence. But the KGB is not about to show up here. This is the last place in New York they'd come to."

He turned around, and Debbie, clad only in white shorts and a white halter, lay back on the bed and stretched luxuriously with all the grace of a cat. She opened her legs, bent at the knees.

Skul pretended not to notice her delectable posturings; yet he could not refrain from making a sarcastic remark about Alexandr Yasakev, suspecting that he would no doubt get into an argument with her.

"Don't tell me you're thinking about the 'good times' you spent with Yasakev a week ago," he said irritably. "No insult intended."

He didn't get the answer he expected, nor did he get a blast of Debbie's explosive temper.

She gave a little laugh and put her arms underneath her head.

"You sound like a jealous husband! Are you?" *I couldn't be that wrong! I know he wants me!*

"Am I what?" Skul stared down at her.

"Jealous?"

Skul smiled in amusement, a fake smile to cover his inner embarrassment "Don't be ridiculous," he lied. "I was only thinking of how we failed with Yasakev. Frankly, he made me feel like an idiot." *And so do you!*

Debbie sat up, wondering if she had miscalculated. She was positive she hadn't. Her instincts about men were too sharp, too on target. True, Jon Skul was a bundle of contradictions. He loved music but didn't dance because—she suspected—he was too self-conscious on a dance floor. He was a neat freak, who had the habit of running his knuckles over a piece of furniture and then running for a dust cloth. Other than his drinking too much, he had a habit that made Debbie grit her teeth: he often listened to symphony music through headphones connected to a cassette player in his pocket—all the while carrying on a conversation with whomever else might be present. And he was obviously a moral prude. But even male Puritans were subject to an erection of the horn with which all men buck. Skul couldn't be that much of a mid-Victorian!

On the other hand, as dedicated as he was to business, he might have been thinking about the failure that Unit-1 had had with Alexandr Yasakev. Several days after she had rolled in the hay with the Russian, he and she had again returned to the apartment, only this time, Skul had been present with several dozen 8 by 10 glossies showing Yasakev and Debbie engaged in any number of sexual acts, including fellatio and cunnilingus.

When Skul informed the Russian that if he didn't cooperate, "We'll send copies and a tape recording to the Soviet Embassy in Washington and to various United Nations' offices," Yasakev had coolly told him to "Do what you will. I could not care less. Goodbye!"

Yasakev, although nervous, walked calmly from the apartment, leaving behind him a stunned Debbie Miles and Jon Skull.

I should have seduced him then!

There could be only one answer for Yasakev's strange behavior: the KGB suspected what was going to happen and had ordered Yasakev to tell the Americans to go to hell!

"Mikhail Borsirev wasn't very smart," Skul had told the other members of Unit-1. "Or he would have ordered Yasakev to cooperate. That way the KGB could have given us false and misleading data. OR—Borsirev considered such a game to dangerous. Either way, we've failed . . ." *And Debbie wasted a lot of time fucking!*

Skul had not mailed the incriminating photographs and tape to the Soviet Embassy or to U.N. offices. Why bother? Such a revelation about the extra-marital love-life of an official of the U.N.,'s International Maritime Organization would not have excited anyone. Not really. A lot of the members of delegations to the U.N. shacked up with call girls, especially the African and the Oriental delegates who went ape over big teated blonds.

Feeling rather foolish, Debbie slid off the bed and stood up when Doug Almaine and Bill Holbrook came into the bedroom.

"What do you think?" asked Holbrook, looking at Skul. He glanced at the wall. "It was the best I could do."

"A good job," Skul said. "All that's left to do is paint the wall. We'll do that tomorrow. After we paint it, no one will be able to tell where the opening was. We'll do the same with the wall in the room next door."

"Why not paint them today?" asked Doug Almaine. "It's only about 2, and I recall our passing a paint store only a few blocks from here. Besides, tomorrow . . ."

Holbrook studied the other walls of the bedroom, which were of a light blue color. "We're going to have to find a shade that matches the 3 other walls. If we're not careful, we're going to have one wall mismatched, unless we paint all 4 walls."

"A little off color won't make that much difference," Skul said without thinking it over. "I can tell you right now, we're not going to paint all 4 walls. Anyhow, let's get out of here, We have a lot of last minute planning to do before tomorrow night."

"All right," Holbrook said. "Wait till I wash my hands." He walked into the bathroom.

"I wish we had more answers about that apartment house where Borsirev and the other Russians lived," remarked Almaine.

Skul looked toward the window. "Sometimes it's better to ask some questions than to think you know all the answers."

*   *   *

Joey "Gags" Maselli and the 2 hoods with him saw the small apartment house sandwiched between 2 general office buildings. Although there were stores on the ground floors of the office buildings, there were only 3 doors to the lobby of the apartment house, which was 5 stories tall.

The remainder of the east side of Payson Avenue consisted of small businesses—clothing stores, repair shops, a coffee shop. There was a J.C. Penny catalog store and, strangely enough, 6 doors away, a Sears catalog store.

There were no businesses on the west side of Payson. It was open and faced the southeast section of Inwood Hill Park. Half a mile to the north, the narrow Harlem River flowed west into the much wider (and dirtier) Hudson River. On the north side of the Harlem River, New York County ended and Bronx County began.

Phil the Plumber parked the Eldorado half a block south of the apartment house. In the back, Joey Gags removed a portion of the seat and reached for the 3 weapons.

"At least the damned rain has stopped," growled Dominic Macaterri.

To the north, Big Nose Sam Bianco eased the Mercury into a slot only a few doors from the apartment house.

"This neighborhood is too quiet to suit me," said Max-Emil Grosbinarger, opening a black attache case. "Even people on the sidewalks act like they have all day to get where they're going. It's safer to make hits where there are crowds."

Bianco looked at Grosbinarger, who was screwing a foot-long silencer onto the extra-long barrel of an 18-shot 9mm Steyr auto-pistol.

"Look, this ain't no hit," Bianco said, sounding annoyed. "I mean it is but it ain't. I mean we're going to knock off 2 of the jokers, but we're going to put the grab on the woman and the guy named Sinclair. You've seen

Sinclair's picture. He's the big good-looking guy. So don't get trigger happy. We gotta take him alive.''

"Never do I forget a face. I know what Sinclair looks like," Grosbinarger said quietly. "I trust that Philip Sirignano has received the same advice."

Bianco, who didn't like Grosbinarger, frowned and watched the stone killer return the Steyr and silencer to the attache case. "Well, you can't blame the Plumber for wanting revenge. The 4 in that apartment house are part of the group responsible for his brother's death. Charley was OK. He was a stand-up guy.''

"All I can say is that the van had better be in the alley," Grosbinarger said. "You got your piece ready?''

Bianco patted the left side of his coat. "Let's go. And don't worry about Phil the Plumber. He's a pro . . .''

Carlo Oddo had parked the UPS van in the alley in back of one of the office buildings. Then he and Charlie "Lemmons" Aloi and the 2 Russians got out. Carlo started walking north in the alley. Lemmons and the 2 KGB illegals, all 3 dressed in blue coveralls, began to pretend the van was having engine trouble. Aloi, a beefy, ugly man in his forties, had a G.E. UHF walkie-talkie in a leather case on a belt around his waist. Joey Gags had already called and asked if the van was in position.

Walking leisurely, Joey Gags and his 2 companions closed in on the apartment house. Down the street, only a few doors from the entrance, they could see Big Nose Sam Bianco and the dapper, sharp-featured Max-Emil Grosbinarger standing in front of *Nick's Novelty Emporium*, killing time by watching a battery powered mobile in the window.

"That god-damned Grosbinarger gives me the creeps," Dominic Macaterri muttered. "The son-of-a-bitch wouldn't get excited if he dropped dead and found himself sitting on the devil's lap.''

Joey Gags agreed. "Yeah, he's a stone killer all right.

The little fucker reminds me of a roadrunner going to a Mick wake. What do you think of him, Phil?''

"The hell with that damned kraut-head. I'm only interested in them 4 we're going after. I'm going to enjoy whacking out the 2 extra dudes."

"Just make sure it's only the two extra you burn," warned Joey gags. "You ain't going to bring back your brother by fucking up the show and getting yourself into trouble with Don Salvatore. OK. We're almost there. All we have to do is go up to the fourth floor and get them."

Moments later, Joey Gags and the 2 other Mafiosi had opened the doors and were walking into the lobby. Big Nose Sam Bianco and Max-Emil Grosbinarger, carrying the attache case, were only 15 feet behind them. From the north, walking briskly, came Carlo Oddo.

After double-checking to make sure that both apartments were securely locked, Jon Skul and the 3 other members of Unit-1 took one of the elevators down to the lobby. Although the life they lived kept them constantly on the alert, none were expecting trouble.

No human agency could have planned it with such micro-second precision. Joey, Dominic, and Phil had just stepped into the front of the lobby as the elevator doors slid open and Skul and his people stepped out. Both groups had not advanced 6 feet toward each other when the 3 mobsters recognized Debbie Miles and ''Jarvis Sinclair.''

In less time than it takes to inhale half a breath, Skul detected the biggest kind of trouble. So did Miles, Almaine and Holbrook, the tipoff being the startled and fearful recognition popping out on the faces of the 3 gangsters.

The silenced weapons that the hoods carried had been jammed into their waistbands, and could not be pulled out very easily. The Goncz High-Tech Pistol was particularly cumbersome. It had a long barrel to begin with. With the silencer attached, the weapon was so long that its muzzle, resting against the front of Joey Gags' left leg, was 4 inches below his penis.

The 3 hoods had not expected to pull their silenced pieces until they were on the fourth floor and approaching apartment 413. Nevertheless, they were far from helpless when they recognized "Sinclair" and Miles, heard Sinclair hiss, "Hit men!" and saw his right hand streak underneath his red and blue sport coat.

Debbie Miles was armed with a 9mm H & K "squeeze" pistol—for all the good it did her. It was in her handbag. Knowing she could not unzip the bag and pull the weapon in time, she dove to her left, and hit the floor. To her right, Skul—in a crouch and sidestepping to his left—pulled his Pachmayr Modular pistol with fantastic speed and thumbed off the safety at the same time that Doug Almaine and William Holbrook went for their own irons.

The 3 goons were not slow. Joey Gags had jerked a .357 mag Arminius revolver from a right shoulder holster and was swinging the 2 inch barrel toward Skul when Skul's Pachmayr Modular roared like a mini-cannon, and a Hydra-Shok .45 slug slammed into the center of Joey's chest. The bullet bored through his sternum, cut through his esophagus and sped out his back, narrowly missing Big Nose Sam Bianco who, with Max-Emil Grosbinarger, was pushing open a door and entering the lobby.

Phil the Plumber and Dominic Macaterri were every bit as fast as Doug Almaine and Bill Holbrook—Phil was a fraction of a second luckier.

Almaine made only one slight mistake as he pulled his Colt Officers .45: he tried to move too fast to his right at the same time. He was about to pull the trigger when Phil the Plumber's flat-nosed .45 Llama bullet banged him high in the chest and knocked him back toward the 3 elevators.

The lobby exploded with gunfire. Bill Holbrook triggered his SIG-Sauer at almost the same instant that Dominic Macaterri fired his S&W Airweight revolver. Holbrook's piece of 9mm metal caught Macaterri in the solar plexus and forced him backward in pain and shock, making him wonder if dying was like this—a roaring in the head and the world going dark.

Macaterri's 38 HP bullet had gone through Holbrook's right lung and had been stopped by a back rib. Choking on the blood bubbling up in his throat, Holbrook did his best to put another slug into Macaterri. He never got the chance. Phil the Plumber's Llama .45 roared, and the big slug chopped into Holbrook's left side, the impact knocking him sideways to the black and white checkered floor.

Only 10 seconds had passed; yet during that very brief lapse of time, Skul had spotted Sam Bianco and Max-Emil Grosbinarger coming through the doors into the lobby, pistols in their hands. Knowing he could not help Debbie, who had rolled over on her side and was desperately trying to open her handbag, he jumped back to an open elevator that—to his left—was next to the one out of which he and the others had just stepped. As he did so, he tossed off a quick shot at Phil the Plumber, who was dropping to the floor and getting off a round with his Llama, the roars of the 2 autoloaders echoing back and forth in the lobby. Skul's bullet came within half an inch of the top of Phil's head. Phil's slug streaked into the elevator and hit the stainless steel hand rail on the back wall and, with a shrieking scream, ricochetted to the floor.

The control button panel was to the right. Darting inside the elevator, Skul flattened himself against the right wall, punched the number two button with the forefinger of his left hand, and, simultaneously, crossed his right arm over his left arm, twisted his right hand slightly and fired 2 more rounds to prevent any of the gunmen from racing to the left wall of the lobby and getting into a position from which they could see him pasted to the right wall of the elevator.

The elevator doors closed. The last Skul saw of Debbie, her right hand was reaching into her handbag. A giant mushroom cloud of self-condemnation exploded in his mind at the thought of leaving her. Yet he knew he could not save her life by getting himself killed. More important to Skul was his awareness that *she* realized it—and he wondered: why hadn't the hood with the face of a stepped-on cabbage already killed her?

Skul did some rapid thinking. He had recognized the notorious Joey Gags Maselli, and knew it wasn't by accident that Joey and the other hoods had come to the apartment building. The damned KGB! Borsirev had sent some of Don Salvatore's gunmen to knock them off. Either that or—*Kidnap Debbie?*

Far more pressing at the moment was escape, not only from the three gunsels, but from the police. The shots had been loud enough to have been heard all the way to police headquarters, a fact the hoods would also realize. Skul reasoned that it was not likely they would come after him. Or would they? If they did, he was positive they would go straight to number 413. But number 413 was the last place Skul intended to seek refuge.

The elevator stopped on the second floor and the doors opened.

Debbie Miles never got to pull her Heckler and Koch P7-M8 pistol. Philip the Plumber's huge left hand closed tightly over her wrist and jerked her hand from the bag. Savagely, he bent Debbie's right arm to one side and jerked her to her feet with such force that she winced.

"You're not going to shoot nobody, bitch," he snarled. "You're not going anywhere, either, except with us." He turned and looked at the overhead pointer of the elevator that Skul had taken. The pointer had stopped on two. Phil looked hard at Sam Bianco who had picked up Debbie's bag and pulled out her H&K P7-M8 pistol.

"One of you guys take this broad out to the van and get her out of here," he said impatiently. "The rest of us will go after that son-of-a-bitch Sinclair. See where the elevator stopped? On the second floor! He's not fooling anybody! He'll take the stairs from the second and go up to the apartment on the fourth."

"Look, Phil!" began Big Nose Sam Bianco nervously.

"I'll take an elevator to the fourth floor," Phil the Plumber said excitedly, a wild glint in his eyes. "Two of you guys take the steps and go up to the fourth floor, that way he won't be able to get past us if he tries to pull a fast one."

"Phil—" Bianco began.

"Get going!" roared the Plumber.

Carlo Oddo, who had come into the lobby behind Bianco and Grosbinarger, shoved a 9mm Star PK pistol into Debbie's stomach, the ice cold muzzle of the noise suppressor pressed into her flesh just above her navel.

"Don't give me no trouble, slut, or I'll kill you right here," he warned her. Oddo shoved her roughly toward the metal door that opened to the maintenance hall which led to the rear of the building. "Move, bitch. We're going to the alley!" He giggled. "That's where your limousine is waiting!"

Debbie remained silent. She didn't have the least doubt that the slime-ball meant what he said. One wrong move on her part and he would kill her.

The door was locked. The silencer on Oddo's Star PK pistol went *phyyyyt* twice and two slugs blew the lock apart.

"Get the fuck in there!" By the time Oddo shoved Debbie through the opening, Phil the Plumber was in an elevator and punching the number 4 button.

Big Nose Sam Bianco and Max-Emil Grosbinarger shot apart the electric lock on the door to the general stairs and started to the second floor. They had no intention of going all the way to the fourth floor. Phil was nuts! He had flipped his lid and had let the desire to avenge the whack out of his brother overpower common sense. If he hadn't, he would have realized that the intelligent thing to do was get the hell out of the building before the police arrived. Anyhow, where in fuck did he come off giving orders? He didn't have the authority. He was only a button man. Joey Gags had been in charge, but he had been snuffed and was a cold cut. Let The Plumber shoot it out with the Blue-coats, the dumb *buco del culo!*

Bianco and Grosbinarger had supposedly complied with Phil Sirignano's orders for only one reason: they knew that reasoning with him was not possible, and they didn't want to have to shoot him, possibly in self-defense. Besides, the kidnap job had been half a success. Deborah Miles had been taken.

Big Nose Sam and Grosbinarger intended to go to the second floor, turn right around, race back down the steps, cross the lobby and leave the building by means of the maintenance hall. The hell with Phil the Plumber.

"Evidently, Mr. Sirignano has a death wish," Gros-binarger remarked casually as he and Sam neared the top of the stairs. "It's possible that he's even psychotic and should be committed."

Bianco, a Colt 9mm stainless steel automatic in his right hand, only grunted. He knew Grosbinarger was educated, half the time you didn't know what the fucking kraut-head was talking about!

"Let's cut the gabbing and watch it," Bianco said, his tone guarded. "We don't know for sure that Sinclair ain't hanging around on this floor—and he's fast. He's very fast."

"We also know he's not stupid," Grosbinarger said calmly. "Sirignano was right. No doubt Sinclair did go back to the apartment on the fourth floor. He would feel safe there. Hopefully, he and Phillie boy will kill each other.''

They paused at the top of the stairs, then walked ahead into the center of the heavily carpeted hall that stretched from south to north. Fifteen feet to the right were the doors to the elevators. Bianco and Grosbinarger noticed the pointer of the center elevator had stopped on four. Just beyond the third door was the intersecting hall whose direction was east and west.

Jon Skul waited 6 feet from the doors of the last elevator, standing by the southwest corner of the east-west hall, his back against the south wall.

Jon had reasoned that the second floor would be the last place the hoods would expect him to be. They knew he couldn't go to the roof. But it was logical to expect him to retreat back to the apartment on the fourth floor; and they would want to cut him off from escape through the lobby. He had been proved right the first time when one of the elevators had risen to the fourth floor; and right the second time when the two hoods had come up the stairs. Yet because of Debbie, he didn't feel any joy of victory, only a bleak emptiness when he heard Big Nose Sam say, ''He ain't around here. Let's get back down to the lobby and get the hell out of here.''

Still thinking of Debbie, Skul was going to derive an extra measure of pleasure from his next move. Just as Bianco and Grosbinarger turned to go back down the steps, Skul raised his fully reloaded Pachmayr Modular, stepped out from the corner of the hall and said in a loud voice, ''Hey, you two *cagacazzos*!''

The last thing that Big Nose Sam had expected was for the target to pop up and call him a ''cocksucker!'' He froze in surprise for a milli-second before turning around. Not so the clever Grosbinarger, who had a different set of mental reflexes. Although he didn't know the meaning of *cagacazzos*, he did realize that he and Big Nose Sam had been suckered. Very fast, he spun and raised the Steyr pistol and its silencer. He was a tenth of a second too slow.

The Pachmayr Modular roared, the Hydra-Shok bullet stabbing into Grosbinarger's left rib cage when he had halfway completed the swing-around. The tremendously powerful bullet bored a tunnel all the way through his torso and rocketed out his right side, leaving behind a butchered heart and lungs and 3 broken ribs. Grosbinarger was 100 per cent dead before the impact had time to knock him back.

The second roar of the Pachmayr Modular was so close to the echoes of the first shot that the two blended together as they bounced off the walls and rolled down the halls.

Skul's second slug slammed into Big Nose Sam Bianco's right hip. The man-stopper projectile shattered the pelvic bone, ripped through the main artery and turned Sam into an instant dead man. The impact knocked him back as though he were a ball of cotton caught in a tornado.

Skul stared in satisfaction at the crumpled body of Grosbinarger, blood spilling from the corpse.

Stupid! Never eat at a place called "Mom's," never play cards with a man named "Doc," and never—but never!—underestimate your enemy!

Skul stiffened at the sound of breakers clicking and closing circuits. An elevator was in motion. He stepped around the corner of the hall, rushed to the 3 elevators and saw that the center elevator was coming down. It was the same elevator that had gone to the fourth floor. Skul glanced up at the pointer. Two . . . 3 . . . Whoever had gone to the fourth floor was coming down—*To this floor? They must have heard the last 2 shots. Then again, they could be going to the lobby.*

Skul didn't wait to find out. The instant the elevator began to go past the second floor, he fired rapidly, deliberately spacing the projectiles—2 halfway up to the left, 2 to the right and one in the center, the TNT slugs tearing through the metal of the doors as though they had been made of balsa wood. Then the elevator was gone.

Skul raced up the flight of steps to the third floor. He was moving up the stairs to the fourth floor when he heard guns roaring from the lobby. Three minutes later, he was on the fourth floor and unlocking the door to apartment 416, the one next to number 413. He was certain it would be safe to hole up in number 416 until the police had made their investigation. Rightly, they would conclude that whoever had terminated the hoods had escaped.

Skul reasoned that was less than one per cent chance of the police even knocking on the doors of 413 and 416, much less searching the 2 apartments. COBRA owned the apartment house through a Swiss front named Bel-Jove, Limited. All rents were channelled through a New York bank which sent the money on to a numbered account in a Switzerland bank.

Another plus for Skul's side was that Jerrold Rhodes, the manager of the building, was a retired CIA agent and knew the 2 apartments were used by U.S. Intelligence, even though he had never heard of COBRA. No one had ever come out and told him, but Rhodes had been led to believe he was still working for the CIA, and had never suspected otherwise.

As part of the cover, Rhodes kept fake records of the rentals of the 2 apartments. Thirty-two days ago, Skeeter Ronson had called on Rhodes and told him that the 2 apartments would be in use, and that he should list number 413 as being rented by a Miss Ramona L. Bynnes. Rhodes had turned over the keys for numbers 413 and 416 to Ronson. Even mail had been delivered to 413's box in the lobby, just in case anyone should engage the local mailman in friendly conversation and "innocently" ask about 413.

Skul was not worried about Rhodes; he would know how to handle the police. He would give only the proper answers.

Closing and locking the door, Skul reflected that there wouldn't be a problem with the tenants, either, most of whom were elderly and retired. Right now, all of them no doubt had their heads under the bed. None of them had seen him and Debbie and Almaine and Holbrook. Skul and his people had not met any of the tenants in the hall; none had seen them enter or leave the apartment. There wasn't any way that the police could tie Almaine and Holbrook to apartment 413 or 416, or to any place in New York City. They carried false identification listing them as stationery salesmen from Los Angeles, both their business and their home addressess fictitious. Fingerprints would not help the police either. The prints of both men had vanished from FBI files. All the prints of COBRA agents had mysteriously disappeared from FBI central files. Should Debbie Miles be a corpse in the lobby, it would be the same for her. Her ID, too, was as false as the promise of a politician.

Skul walked over to the small bar, opened a fifth of bourbon, took a long drink and sat down on the couch. There was one irony in the shoot-out. Unit-1 had not used the two apartments as a base because Jonas Barron and Skul had not wanted to risk the apartments being discovered by the other side. The incongruity had risen when the use of an apartment had become necessary in the blackmail attempt of Alexandr Yasakev. It was obvious: the two apartments had outlived their usefulness. COBRA would sell the building and buy another one in the New York City area.

Taking another deep swallow of bourbon, Skul settled back on the couch. It would be hours before he could leave the building and return to The Farm in Mount Vernon. Fortunately, he did not have a car to worry about becoming over-parked or towed away. Arden and Hayes had driven him and the others to the north end of Central Park.

From there, each member had taken a taxi to Payson Avenue. He thought again of Debbie. Was she dead or alive? It might be better for the Unit—and for Debbie—if she were dead. He was sure those KGB bastards would really put the screws to her. Skul's mind raced back through Debbie's dossier searching for some reassurance she would have the strength to endure the torture she was sure to be delivered by those masochistic pigs. *Damned broads—they had no place in this business. She could really fuck us all up—blow COBRA; compromise all of us. Even though she doesn't know all the details, just letting those bastards know we exist is enough.*

Now he was totally flying blind. He would have no way—absolutely no way—of knowing if the KGB had cracked Debbie, until it was too late.

He went over to the telephone, picked up the receiver and dialed the unlisted number of The Farm. He recognized the cautious voice of Ann Brandon who answered and said, "Demmler's Oyster Bar?"

"This is Fred," Skul said. "I've had trouble. Two shipments have spoiled beyond repair. I'm not certain about the third shipment. I'll be very late in getting back. Possibly not until tomorrow. In the meanwhile, not to worry . . ."

Detective First Grade Lewis Journey looked at the corpse of Joey Gags Maselli. Norbert Delbowski was drawing a line around the body with marking chalk. "Why should the Underboss of the Tuccinardo mob, of all people, take the chance of going on a hit with ordinary 'soldiers?' That's all the others were—button men, trigger pullers!"

"Except for Grosbinarger." Tim Hurt pushed back his hat and looked around at the other bodies on the floor. "I'm damned sure the creep upstairs is the Dutchman. The hit must have been very important for the mob to have called him in."

"Yeah. If it is the Dutchman." Journey shifted his cigar to the other side of his mouth. "And did you see the size of the bullet holes in those two? And in Gags? They were knocked off by special slugs, that's for sure."

Norbert Delbowski, finished outlining the corpse of Maselli, stood up and indicated the dead meat of Phil the Plumber with the chalk. Butchered by slugs, the corpse of Phil Sirignano lay sprawled out on its back in the elevator. The Plumber had not been killed by Skul. Phil, coming down in the elevator, had heard the shots on the second floor and had guessed that something had seriously gone wrong. Suspecting that "Sinclair" had tricked him and might try something, the Plumber had flattened his body to one of the side walls of the elevator. Every one of Skul's Hydra-Shok bullets had missed. But the Plumber had saved himself from Purgatory only to jump into Hell. Four uniformed cops, Winchester pistol grip security shotguns in their hands, had just entered the lobby. When the elevator doors opened and they saw Phil the Plumber with his Llama .45, they fired, the barrage of 12-gauge shot blowing Sirignano apart. The entire floor of the elevator was covered with congealing blood. The suit coat, shirt and upper part of his pants hung in bloody tatters, ripped into shreds by the shotgun blasts.

"Speaking of special slugs," Delbowski said. "Look at the 5 bullet holes in the rear of the elevator. The same number of holes are in the doors, indicating someone fired through the doors in an effort to ace out Sirignano. It was probably the same guy who killed Bianco and the Dutchman."

"Only Sirignano wasn't in the elevator at the time," Tim Hurt said.

Journey shifted the cigar again. Switching to cigars hadn't helped; he still wanted a cigarette. "Un huh. You're saying that whoever it was tried to knock off Phil the Plumber, then killed Bianco and the Dutchman. I suppose you think he next came back down here, shot off the lock of the door to the maintenance hall and took off?''

"It could have happened that way," Delbowski said. "I have a feeling we're going to find a lot of screwy things about this case, like why was Joe Maselli in on a hit—*if* it was a hit. We don't really have any evidence—not yet we don't—that it was a hit. We're only assuming.''

"Your theory is as good as any, Norbert," Tim Hurt said. "But it doesn't explain the two other bodies." With a tilt of his shaggy head, he indicated the bodies of Almaine and Holbrook whom Delbowski had already chalked. "Those two might have knocked off Macaterri and Maselli. It will take the lab boys to tell us what kind of slugs killed these birds down here, as well as the other two.''

Two uniforms pushed open the maintenance door in the northwest corner of the lobby and walked over to Journey, Hurt, and Delbowski.

"We didn't find a thing out back," one of the cops said. "Everything in the basement is also normal. If anyone did skip out through the back, he's long gone by now.''

Lewis Journey nodded and glanced over at another uniformed patrolman coming through one of the front doors of the lobby. Behind him was a man in a white coat and white pants. The meat wagon from the coroner's office had arrived.

The cop said, "Reporters want to know if they can come in here and talk to you guys and take pictures.''

Journey looked at the cop's name plate and saw that his name was Joseph D. Bodds.

"What the hell is wrong with you, Bodds?" Journey said in an easy voice. "The lab boys aren't even here. Keep everybody out of here, and don't let anyone get by the ropes—particularly reporters. I don't give a damn who they are.''

"Yes, sir." Bodds said, looking self-conscious. As he

turned to leave the man in the white coat and pants shook his head back and forth in disgust.

"You mean to say we have to wait around here for these stiffs?" The man glared at Journey and the other two Homicide detectives. "How long you fellas gonna play with this garbage? What's keeping the lab boys? Me and the other guys aren't crazy about hanging around here after five."

"Bullshit," Journey said drily. "You're already thinking of the overtime you'll get. Now get out of here. We'll let you know when you can have the bodies."

"I wish to hell these goddamn hoods would knock each other at a decent hour." With another glare, the man turned and left the lobby.

Tim Hurt and Norbert Delbowski walked around the corpses and began reading the names on the mailboxes in the north wall. They and Lewis Journey turned when they heard the first elevator coming down from the second floor. The doors opened and a sixtyish man, with short gray-white air and a pleasant face stepped out. He was wearing a red poplin jumpsuit belted at the waist.

"Gentlemen, I know you have a job to do, but I have a responsibility to my tenants," said Jerry Rhodes. "How long will it be before they can leave by this entrance."

"At least another few hours," Hurt said carelessly. "We're sorry, but that's how things are."

"Well, you do have a rear entrance," Lewis Journey said, "other than the maintenance entrance. Your tenants can use it." His eyes went up and down Rhodes. He thought the building manager looked stupid in a jumpsuit. Hell, a man should look his age.

"We have the emergency fire door," admitted Rhodes. "However, the steps are narrow, and some of the tenants are elderly. Fact is, most of them are."

Journey shrugged. "What can we tell you?"

"Would it be possible for you to have some of your uniformed men help the tenants down the stairs?"

Hurt and Delbowski turned away, amused smiles on their faces.

"I'd like to, but we don't have any men to spare," Journey said very seriously. "Your tenants will have to do the best they can. By the way, we might want to talk to some of them again."

"You already have," Rhodes said. "They've already told you they didn't see anyone. Neither did my wife and I. We heard the shots, but we weren't stupid enough to go out into the halls or come down here and see who was doing the shooting. As for helping the tenants—surely you have officers stationed in back who could give them a hand?"

"No, we don't," Journey said, becoming impatient. "Like I said, your people will have to do the best they can. We'll let you know when they can use the lobby entrance."

Rhodes eyes roamed over the dead men on the floor. "Tch, tch, tch. It's a disgrace! People killing each other all over the place. I tell you, people have to get back to God. That's what's wrong with the world. People have forgotten the Almighty."

"Yes, sir, if you say so," Journey agreed, tonelessly. He watched Rhodes get in the elevator and the doors close. "I'll bet he listens to the *700-Club* every day."

"Here come the lab boys," Norbert Delbowski said.

A soft, satisfied smile was on Rhodes' face as he walked to the manager's apartment on the second floor. Whoever the man was in number 416, he would be happy to hear that there weren't any police in the rear of the building.

CHAPTER NINE

COLONEL Mikhail Borsirev turned off the television set and sat down on the couch in the living room of the spacious apartment he shared with his wife and 3 children. *Nyet!* The project had not worked out exactly as he had planned; yet half a loaf was better than none at all. There were numerous problems, although none of them directly involved him and the KGB *Apparat* in New York City.

The six o'clock news had just given a full report on the "apparent gangland shooting in the apartment building— *. . . the police believe that a major war is about to break out between the former Carlo Gambino Mafia family and the Salvatore Tuccinardo family."* The only thing that confused the police was who had been trying to kill whom and why Joey "Gags" Maseli, the underboss of the Tuccinardo mob, had been a member of a party that was composed of ordinary trigger-men. *". . . Police are questioning Salvatore Tuccinardo and other alleged members of the Tuccinardo family."* The FBI? No comment. *"More tonight on the eleven o'clock news . . ."*

"Comrade Vorontsov, continue with your report," Borsirev said. He motioned for his wife not to come into the room when she appeared in the archway. "And speak English, Comrade."

"We didn't have any trouble at all, Comrade Colonel," Vorontsov said quietly, with self-assurance. "One of the mobsters brought the woman out the back of the building. We gave her a shot of melasine in the arm and put her to sleep at once."

"And the transfer to the ship went well—obviously it did," said Borsirev with a slight, foxy smile.

"Exactly as planned. Paul and I dressed the woman in men's clothes, pinned up her hair, and put a watch cap on her head. The gangsters drove the van to within several blocks of the dock area. In the meanwhile, Comrade Kichabalarus and I changed into sailors' clothing. To anyone who might be watching, it appeared that 3 sailors were returning to their ship, one so drunk he had passed out. We supported the woman between us. Once the 3 of us were on board the *Boris Gudinov*, we turned her over to First Officer Mostinik."

"Naturally, you made it clear to him that he was not to question the woman and that she was not to be harmed in any way?" Borsirev said in a sibilant voice, studying Pytor Vorontsov. There was a deadly, quiet assurance about everything he did: the way he spoke, the way he moved, even the way he sipped his tea. This was normal with a man like Vorontsov. He was used to dealing in intrigue and violence, and had a lethal capability and an expertise that was always waiting inside his polished self-control. Vorontsov was a specialist, a KGB "hitman," who always functioned as a *Mokryye Dela*—blood wet—operative. His business was kidnapping and assassination—murder.

"I made it clear to Comrade Mostinik that you personally wanted to question the woman, and that you would be coming to the ship in a few days," Vorontsov said. "He wished you well in the name of the Motherland and said he was looking forward to seeing you. I might add, he was worried about transferring the heroin from the ship to the warehouse.''

Mikhail Borsirev's sharp-featured face did not register surprise. Neither Pytor Vorontsov or Paul Kichabalarus had been made privy to the plan to use divers to transfer the heroin from the *Boris Gudinov* to the warehouse owned by Salvatore Tuccinardo, and Colonel Borsirev wasn't happy about Mostinik's letting them in on the secret. Whether or not to tell Mostinik that he had broken security was another matter. Borsirev didn't know the rank held by Mostinik. He could not have been higher than a colonel—if even that high—or he would not be on board the *Boris Gudinov*. Even so, the man could have powerful friends in *Moskova*, the KGB main office, or even in the Central Committee of the Communist Party. After all, one did not advance by making enemies.

Pytor Vorontsov picked up his cup, took a sip of tea, then returned the cup to the saucer. His manner was polite, his big hands holding the cup and the saucer with a gentleness that gave no hint of the ruthlessness of the man. Somehow, it seemed terribly inconsistent to Borsirev that a professional killer like Vorontsov should also possess a knowledge of etiquette.

Borsirev lighted a Lucky Strike cigarette, crossed his legs, made himself more comfortable on the camel back sofa and looked across at Pytor Vorontsov who was sitting in a matching occasional chair.

"Comrade, there is still one thing that bothers me," began Borsirev in his soft voice. "There were 2 men with Sinclair and Miles. Yet when you phoned . . ."

"At the time we didn't know about the other 2 men," Vorontsov cut in very quickly. "Until the mobster Oddo returned to the van and told us about the 2 men, Comrade Kichabalarus and I didn't know they existed. Even Sinclair and Miles entered the building singly."

"Oddo saw what happened?" probed Borsirev.

"After Oddo returned to the van with the woman, he told Comrade Kichabalarus and me and the other American gangster that Sinclair and the 2 men with him had killed Joseph Maselli and Dominic Macaterri, and that Jarvis Sinclair had escaped by ducking into an elevator."

Vorontsov showed interest for the first time. "What's the difference who shot who? It's over. We have Deborah Miles and the network is in the clear. She can tell us everything we need to know."

"There isn't any such thing as having too many facts," Borsirev said quietly, taking another drag on his cigarette. "Since the 2 men with Sinclair were killed and the woman was a captive, it follows that it must have been Sinclair who killed the 3 American gangsters, the one in the elevator and the 2 on the steps."

"A logical assumption," Vorontsov commented approvingly. "Let's assume that Sinclair did kill them. What does that have to do with us now? He doesn't know where the woman is. Even if he did, what could he do about it?"

Borsirev's reply was quick and blunt. "Whoever Sinclair is, he's a very worthy and extremely dangerous opponent. He is also unpredictable. I dislike any enemy whose future actions cannot be predicated on his past performances."

"It's the final result that counts, Comrade Colonel," Vorontsov said curtly. "Sinclair is no doubt a contract agent for the Central Intelligence Agency. I have encountered such surrogates all over the world, especially in the Middle East and in Central America. They are always men who fight only for money. I think we have seen the last of Sinclair. He has been neutralized."

"Perhaps." Borsirev tapped his cigarette and watched ash fall into the round red ceramic ashtray on the glass-top end table. He considered Pytor Vorontsov a fool. The man was too quick to make snap-judgements, too quick to let speculation become fact. Worse, he did not realize that often a little experience could upset almost any theory, and experience is what you get when you're anticipating something else.

Abruptly, Pytor Vorontsov changed the subject. "Colonel, what orders do you have now for me and Comrade Kichabalarus. The CIA now knows that I am connected with Soviet Intelligence. They have to be watching everyone who comes into this apartment house. They will trail me when I leave."

"Exactly," agreed Borsirev, a solemn note to his low voice. "Because of the CIA and the FBI, you will remain here at The Armatage until you go with me to the ship several days from now. In the meanwhile—"

"We will have to use a very circumspect route from here to the *Boris Gudinov*," Vorontsov said, frowning deeply, "or the FBI and the CIA will be right behind us, unless you want American Intelligence to know the vessel is involved with our network in some way."

Crushing out his cigarette, Borsirev was quick to shake his head. "It's nothing like that. But don't concern yourself with our being followed to the *Boris Gudinov*. When the time comes, you'll see how we elude anyone who might be following us. In the meanwhile, we'll get a message to Comrade Kichabalarus by means of the drop in Morningside Park." Borsirev got to his feet. "Come, I'll show you to your quarters. It's an apartment on the third floor. Tomorrow, we'll arrange a new wardrobe for you."

On the way to the stairs, Colonel Borsirev speculated over the meeting he would have with Salvatore Tuccinardo on board the *Boris Gudinov*. He had not discussed the situation with Vorontsov because the *Mokryye Dela* agent was not involved in higher strategic planning. What he had not revealed to Vorontsov was that, while the KGB had succeeded in kidnaping Deborah Miles, the plan had failed in another way: hoodlums belonging to the Tuccinardo family had been killed, bringing not only a lot of attention from the media, but also from the police. The FBI would now bring in more racketeering specialists in an effort to indict Don Salvatore.

Colonel Borsirev had concluded that to give the heroin to Tuccinardo would be far too dangerous. Earlier that day, after learning about the gun battle, he had sent a long report—by radio—to the KGB Otdel at the Soviet Embassy in Washington, D.C. The embassy's powerful transmitters would send his recommendation to the Center in Moscow. Within 24 hours, the Center would give its decision.

Colonel Borsirev felt certain he knew what that reply would be: a confirmation of his plan to terminate Don Salvatore Tuccinardo.

CHAPTER TEN_____

ICEPICKS stabbing inside her head, Debbie opened her eyes. Memory flooded her consciousness, and intuitively she knew that the intense headache and the extraordinary dryness in her mouth were the side effects of the drug the mobsters had shot into her arm. Lying on her back, she was suddenly aware that she was dressed in a man's shirt and pants, which had been put on over her shorts and halter—*But why? Why should they do that?* And she was on a bed in a room that was almost dark. No, she was on a lower bunk; the room appeared to be dark only because the upper bunk shut off some light.

Debbie gave herself a closer inspection. The faded blue cotton pants and shirt were clean, and they almost fit her. Whoever had chosen them for her had done so with an eye toward her measurements. Her feet were bare, but when she cautiously swung her legs off the bunk and stood up, she saw a pair of work shoes. Out of curiosity, she tried them on; they were only a bit too large.

By the electric lamp mounted to the wall, she saw that she was obviously in a cabin on board a ship. *The New York docks—where else? The Jersey City or Newark docks—that's where else.* Knowing it was an exercise in futility,

119

she turned the handle on the door. Locked. She went over to the porthole and saw that it, too, was locked and in a special manner. A hole had been drilled in the extra-large handle of the latch, and a stainless steel lock had been inserted through the hole. The U-section of the lock was also in an eye-ring which had been welded to the steel wall. She could see light through the porthole glass, light through rounded openings—*Lights from the port windows of another ship! I've been blackbagged and am aboard a ship!*

She inspected the furnishings in the cabin. There was a small metal desk bolted to the floor. Its drawer was empty. The surface of a table, hinged to the wall, was so dusty that Debbie could have written her name on it. She gave a lopsided grin. *Jon would go berserk if he saw all this dust*.

Another door was between the desk and the table—narrow and made of wood. She opened the door. Beyond was a shower and a toilet stool. Debbie closed the door and went over to the lavatory at the end of the bunks against the outside wall. The bowl was surprisingly clean; so was the waterglass turned upside down on the holder. She looked at the two knobs of the faucets. Both were marked with words she could not read: respectively: *KAPKA and XOJIOÚHO.* Russian! She assumed the words meant "hot" and "cold."

I've been shanghaied to a Soviet ship!

Feeling her breath catch in her throat, she rinsed the glass, filled it to the brim and slowly drank the water, enjoying the way the dryness left her mouth. All the while, she considered her precarious position, the pieces of the puzzle rapidly falling into place. Skul had been wrong. Maybe the KGB had not gone to the apartment house, but mobsters had—and they had to belong to the Don Salvatore family. To do what? They—mobsters and the Russians—hadn't wanted her dead, or the hoods would have killed her in the lobby. Their plan had been to kidnap her and kill anyone who happened to be with her, and that is why Almaine and Holbrook were dead. Skul had escaped. She had seen him dart into an elevator after offing one of the gunmen. Knowing Skul the way she did, Debbie felt that he was alive and well—*And he's furious! God help the Russians!* Even so, Jon and the other members of Unit-1 would have no idea where she was and would never be able to find her—*Not until he invades The Armatage and obtains the information. But will he and the others think it was the mob or the KGB who grabbed me? Jon will know it was the KGB. Who else but the KGB could have known about the apartment that I and Alexander Yasakev used? The KGB had the mob do its dirty work. The mob staked out the apartment and waited. But how could they have known what I looked like?*

The pants and shirt she had on smelled of strong soap, Debbie took them off and tossed them on the floor, after which she went over to the mirror, above the lavatory, and looked at herself. Her hair was a mess, and it felt gritty. The floor of the van had been none too clean.

She sat down on the lower bunk and automatically raised her left arm. Her wristwatch was gone. It figured. Jon always said the Russians were thieves as well as liars.

She pondered again how the mobsters could have recognized her. Yasakev had never taken a photograph of her. There was one possible explanation: the KGB had followed her from the offices of the Date Right Escort Service. If that was the way it had happened, then the KGB had to have tailed her to the apartment on West 23rd Street. If so, the KGB had learned that she was living there under the name of "Mavis Sinclair" and posing as the wife of "Jarvis Sinclair"—Jon Skul. That was it! The blackbag job had been scheduled to take place at the 23rd Street apartment. Then Unit-1 had secretly moved, leaving the mob boys with an empty apartment. On the chance that she would reappear at the "love nest" apartment, the

KGB had had Don Salvatore's boys keep an eye on Payson building. Either way—*They got me!*

Her head still throbbing, Debbie took her shorts and halter off, then stepped out of her bikini underpants, dropping them in a heap on the lower bunk. She stepped into the shower, relishing the sharp needles of hot water as they eased the kinks out of her neck and soothed her troubled mind. At least she would be clean. The soap they had provided was harsh and strong smelling, but provided a rich lather. She scrubbed her skin, removing the grit and grime she had picked up in the van. As she bathed, her mind drifted and she wondered if Skul thought she was still alive. *Oh God, Jon, please look for me! Please find me!*

She dried herself with the rough towel, its raspy feel against her delicate skin raising an invigorating blush. Carefully, she dressed then sat on the lower bunk—waiting.

Debbie estimated that several hours had become history when she heard a key turn in the lock and saw the door to the cabin open. A man entered the room carrying a tray with a white cloth over it—a young man dressed in seaman's clothes. Behind him came a man in his middle thirties. He was dressed in an officer's blue uniform, wore a peaked cap, and had a pleasant face. He waited by the door as the seaman put the tray on the table. Regarding the 2 Russians with a calm, unruffled expression, she watched as the seaman turned, left the cabin, and the officer locked the door from the inside. The key was on a ring with other keys, and he dropped the ring into the left pocket of his uniform coat, then stepped farther into the room and smiled down at her.

"It's your dinner, Miss Miles," he said in well-modulated English. "I can assure you that the food is not poisoned."

Debbie was hungry, and she knew she wouldn't prove anything by not eating. She got up from the bunk, went over to the tray and removed the cloth. On a plate was a small steak and a pile of fried potatoes. A green salad was in a side dish. There was a mug filled with hot tea. Packets of sugar and powdered milk. A knife, fork, and spoon.

"I assume the tea has been spiked with some mind altering drug?" she said sweetly, looking at the officer, "such as haloperidol or aminazin? Or perhaps a dash of motiden-depo?"

"Shame on you!" the Russian said with mock seriousness and shook a finger at her. "You were supposed to protest and say we grabbed the wrong person—and you should have threatened to inform the police and demand that we release you. How could you know about drugs the KGB uses unless you were an American intelligence agent?"

"Sorry, I'll try to do better next time," Debbie said drily, not failing to notice how his brown eyes devoured her breasts, smooth stomach and long legs. Politely, he pulled the chair from the table and helped her seat herself. He then moved over to the desk and sat down on one corner, saying, "Actually, there aren't any drugs in the food. They will come later, in a few days when you're questioned."

Picking up the knife and fork, Debbie smiled. "I don't suppose you would be good enough to get me a cab after I finish my dinner?"

The officer laughed, "Oh, that's rich! That is a good one, my dear. That's what I like about you Americans—your sense of humor. I must confess it is a quality we Russians lack. I'm afraid I can't permit you to do anything. Your destination is the Soviet Union. You're quite a prize. It isn't every day that we bag ourselves an agent of the CIA—right in the heart of New York City!"

"Well, I have always wanted to see the Soviet Union," Debbie said cheerfully, cutting into her steak (*Play on his ego!*). "I don't suppose you can tell me very much, since you're only an officer of this ship and not an intelligence officer yourself. I should think the secret police would at least permit you to give your name.''

Once more the officer laughed. ''My name is Vadom Mostinik, and I think you've been reading too many of your cheap American paperback novels. I am also an officer in the *Komitet Gosudarstvennoy Bezopasnosti,* or, if you prefer the American acronym—KGB.''

''How long will it be before this vessel leaves New York—or can't you tell me?''

''We leave in 6 days,'' Mostinik said, ''but it will be several weeks before we dock in Leningrad. Once we're on the open sea, you'll be permitted on deck for several hours each day. Of course, you will have to wear clothes that are more appropriate. I'm afraid that shorts and halter will not be suitable.''

Debbie let her fork pause over the salad. She turned to him and said in an accusatory tone, ''One of your people stole my wristwatch. I would like it returned.'' She added the lie, ''It was a gift from my father.''

''Borrowed, not stolen,'' Mostinik corrected her. ''We had to check it to make sure it was only a wristwatch. After all, you Americans are very good with micro-electronics. I'll see that your watch is returned to you tomorrow.''

With a slight laugh, Debbie returned her attention to her salad.

''I suppose I should tell you that the nail of my left big toe is a sub-miniature shortwave radio.''

If Vadom Mostinik was amused at her remark, he didn't show it. He only said, ''We are both professionals, Miss Miles. There isn't anything personal in this. Your side wins some. My side wins some. If there is anything I can get to make your stay here more pleasant, let me know. I—uh—I know you will need female things.''

''My hair is a mess; I'll need a comb and a hairbrush. I'll also need a mild soap, your brand is too strong,''

Debbie said casually. "And if the Soviet Union can afford it, a couple of cartons of Virginia Slims. Oh yes, and a box of tampons."

Mostinik thought for a moment, the thumb and the forefinger of his right hand rubbing his ear lobe unconsciously. "These tampons, they are a product strictly for women?"

"They're like sanitary napkins, a woman needs them during her time of the month," Debbie said flat out. "Do you understand?"

"Yes, we have such products in the Soviet Union for our women," Mostinik said, a note of embarrassment in his voice.

Debbie enjoyed the meal. As she ate, she could feel his eyes moving up and down her body. Still, she sensed that his was only normal male interest and that he was only doing what comes naturally to any healthy male who sees a young and shapely woman in tight short-shorts and a scanty halter. It was only a hunch, yet she also felt that underneath Vadom Mostinik's friendliness and gentlemanly manner, he was a cold ruthless individual playing "good guy."

Her main concern was when they did inject her with neuroleptic psychomotor drugs. She would be powerless to resist and would tell them anything they wanted to know, everything she knew. She could not tell them very much about COBRA because she did not have much information. She wasn't even positive that COBRA was an independent intelligence agency. Only operatives like Skul, with a high G-rating, knew the full story. She didn't have to have all the facts. Even if she mentioned the word COBRA, and said that the word stood for *Counter-Subversion Operations Bureau of Resistance and Action*—that would be more than enough to trigger full scale interest by the KGB and by the GRU, Soviet military intelligence.

The secret would be out. Then it would only be a matter of time before COBRA was exposed.

In a way, the joke was on the KGB. They should have kidnaped Jon Skul. It was Jon who had all the data! He was also Debbie's only source of hope, her only salvation.

Jon Skul! You had better find me—and soon!

CHAPTER ELEVEN_____

WITH a shower and a shave and a breakfast of sausage, eggs, V-8 juice and a half of a pint of bourbon behind him, Jon Skul leaned over the old-fashioned round dining room table and studied the diagram of the sewer system.

Skul looked up and across at Christopher Shinns, who was still in pajamas and sitting on the couch. Shinns, a late sleeper by nature, was drinking coffee and still trying to get his mind in gear.

"Chris, are you sure this diagram is accurate," Skul asked. "Tell me again about the cover story you gave to the street department people."

Barry Arden, standing at the table with Skul, remarked, "If this map is correct and the information we received from Barron is on the mark, we wouldn't have much trouble once we're inside. Six feet in diameter is big enough. The problem would be carbon monoxide and maybe rats."

"It was easy," Shinns said with a yawn. "I even talked to one of the Commissioners. I showed him my credentials from the *National Geographic*— told him we were thinking of doing a special story on the New York sewer system. He gave the order and his stooges fell all over each other pulling out dusty maps from old filing cabinets. But how am I supposed to know if they're accurate?''

"Well, you did ask, didn't you?" Skul's tone was as hard as armor plate.

"Of course I did. The people in charge assured me the maps were,'' Shinn snapped, wondering how Skul and Arden and Davy Wickewire could be so wide awake at six o'clock in the morning. Jesus Christ! It was still the middle of the friggin' night!

"We have to work on the premise that the diagrams are accurate,'' Skul said to Arden. "On that basis, we can assume that a part of the old sewer system runs directly underneath The Armatage, and''—he tapped a blue square on the layout—"right here is the opening where we would come up, in the basement of The Armatage. Barron swears the opening is in a small storage room in the center of the floor.''

Shinns called out in a cranky voice, "Now you can get on the shortwave and ask Barron if his information is correct!''

"Touché, touché,'' Skul said good-naturedly. "We will have to believe that his information is accurate. It's like life. We have to have faith.'' He pulled a half-full pint bottle of bourbon from the left rear pocket of his gray Chino pants. Uncapping the bottle, he paused and looked at the various colored lines of the sewer system.

"Right here,'' Arden said quickly, as if he had read Skul's mind. He looked at Skul, then gave a distasteful glance at the bottle and jammed a finger down on a large green X. "Here on 58th Street is where we would go in. It's a full block from the Armatage on East 59th. We can use the regular sewer opening, go down, and about 100 feet in, break into the sewer that's been sealed for 66 years. And while we're at it, we'd better get this settled before you get juiced.''

"Have you ever seen me drunk, I mean really gassed?'' There was a cold, deadly quality to Skul's voice.

Arden admitted that he had not.

"Until you do—butt out." Skul finished uncapping the bottle, tilted it to his lips and took a long drink. When Arden saw him look at the red rectangle marked *Apartment-House-Hotel,* he said:

"Al and I checked out the place while you were in upper Manhattan shooting the piss out of the Don's cousins. You know the area around East 59th and 58th. Swank, expensive. Just the same, the real estate company that owns the apartment-hotel is so tight it makes the buffalo on a nickel weep. The 4 night guards are old duffers who—."

"Old retired cops have had a lot of experience with firearms," cut in Skul, "and they have a lot of know-how. They're not easily fooled."

Barry Arden's weather-lined face broke into a small grin. "That's the beauty of it, Jon. These guys aren't retired cops. We can tap on the front doors of the lobby, flash FBI badges, and those 4 would open up without any hesitation, never suspecting a thing."

"We even checked out the sewer opening in the hotel. We posed as building inspectors. The sewer-grid is in a small maintenance room off the heating-plant section. The grid is loose, All we'll have to do is lift it up. But we'll need a ladder. It's about 10 feet down to the main sewer."

"Hmmmmm, only 4 guards," Skul said thoughtfully, studying the layout on the table.

"We could dart those 4 with a mertex." Arden fell back on the cool manner which always stood him in good stead. "At 3 in the morning, it isn't likely they would be discovered by anyone."

"We can't assume that," Skul said quietly. "Not every cop has a coop at night or is shacking up with his favorite waitress. A couple of uniforms could stop by to kill time and drink coffee with those 4 watchmen. Not that the cops would know what happened. A few 100 mills of telfrosene will keep those 4 in slumberland for 3 to 4 hours, and none of the emergency procedures would be able to wake them up."

"Even if someone showed up and found them drugged, it wouldn't interfere with us," Bates said without hesitation. "Once we go down the opening and are inside, we can replace the grid over us. No will would even know we'd been there." He stopped and thought for a moment. "But would we come out the same way we went in?"

"Negative. We couldn't risk going out that way," Skul said flatly. "We'll go right out the front entrance of The Armatage. That's why we need the 3 getaway cars."

Looking slightly abashed, Bates didn't comment. Always a natty dresser, he wore a black and white striped Italian Savoia shirt and gray Teramo wool slacks.

"I'd like to know why New York is criss-crossed with hundreds of sewers that haven't been filled in. The underground of Manhattan must look like one gigantic swiss cheese!" Ann Brandon said. She sat crosslegged on the rug.

Karsten Hayes put down the grocery list he was making out. "It's the nature of government," he explained, "and goes back to the days of Tammany Hall rule. The politicians were so crooked they were always undertaking projects to skim off money. Building sewers was one way of doing it. You could always say New York needed sewers. Tell the taxpayers a new system would cost 10 million dollars when the work that was actually done would cost 10 million. Net profit: 2 million dollars. The sewers we're going to use were built back in 1920, under Boss Charles Murphy."

"I never heard of him," Brandon said. Dressed only in white nylon pajamas with lace edging, she didn't seem to mind that her nipples could be seen through the thin material and that her V-shaped bush, at the apex of her thighs, stood out with more than a hint of shadow.

"Few people today have," Hayes said. "But there are people in my generation who recall one of his proteges—Al

Smith. Smith became the Governor of New York and the first Catholic to run for President of the United States.''

"What about La Guardia?'' Shins was genuinely interested. "Was he a Tammany Hall man?''

Hayes was horrified. "Good heavens, no! The 'Little Flower'—that's what 'Fiorello' means—was a determined anti-Tammany man. He did a lot of good, but after he died, the city went to pot. La Guardia broke Tammany Hall rule; yet patronage is still an essential element of New York City government. The appointment of judges, district attorneys, high officials of all kinds come into the patronage system. I say, New York is almost as crooked as Chicago.''

"Getting back to business,'' Skul said emphatically, "The real danger is at The Armatage, from the instant we reach the top of the perpendicular sewer.''

"The floor over the opening is brick,'' Barry Arden said in a business like tone. "We'll go through that old brick in 10 minutes flat.''

"And very, very carefully,'' Skul was quick to say. "Don't forget the 3 Russians on duty in the basement.''

"Plus the 3 in the lobby and the 2 just inside the rear service entrance,'' Davy Wickewire said morosely in his deep baritone. "The only solution to dealing effectively with the 8 is to kill them instantly.''

The circle of men closed tighter around the map as they refined their plan. No one had discussed the details of the uptown shoot-out much less mentioned Debbie's fate. She wasn't a part of this plan so she didn't enter their immediate thoughts.

Ann Brandon jumped to her feet and put her hands on her hips, her black eyes filled with anger and frustration.

"Jon, why don't you and everyone else say it the way it is? Are you afraid to mention Debbie?'' She stared at the faces around her, her gaze devastatingly ruthless. "What the hell is wrong with you people. Those damned Russians might have killed her by now, or worse, tortured her. And

all we're doing is planning how to blackbag a KGB chief!''
Then, she almost spit out the words at Chris Shinns and
Henry Kowitt. ''And quit staring at what you're never
going to get any of—you perverts.''

Shinns, the bashful type, reddened and looked away.
Kowitt was made of sterner stuff. ''Sister, if you'd put on
some clothes, we wouldn't be staring at your goodies!''

''I'm not your 'Sister,' *boy*!'' she shot back, ''and I'm
not a side-show to be stared at either.''

Kowitt turned and grinned at a slightly embarrassed
David Wickewire. ''At least she didn't call me a jive-
turkey,'' he cracked.

''Go stow your cock in a meat grinder,'' snarled Ann.
Turning, she stormed from the room.

There was a heavy silence until Barry Arden said, ''Jon,
did I tell you about the queer who was asked if he had
every kissed a parrot?''

''No.'' Jon as well as the others in the big living room
were surprised since Arden, who lived his work, was a
humorless man who seldom, if ever, told an off-color joke.

''The queer said, 'I've never kissed a parrot, but I have
kissed a cockatoo.' ''

Skul chuckled for manners sake. The others laughed.

''Ann is thinking emotionally,'' Skul said prosaically,
''or she would realize that while any jackass can kick
down a barn, it takes a good carpenter to build one. She
knows that when we pull information from Borsirev or one
of his assistants, we'll also find out where Debbie is and
what they did to her.''

''She could be stashed somewhere in The Armatage,''
offered Arden. ''We can't discount the possibility.''

''We can't discount it,'' conceded Skul, ''but neither
can we count on it. With the FBI watching the Russian
apartment house day and night, I doubt if the KGB would
risk taking her there. The same goes for the AMTORG
building. It's useless to speculate where they have her
hidden. Let's face it: by now she could be dead.''

Kowitt gave a big sigh. "We have 3 choices. Borsirev and Gouzenko live on the third floor. Sergei Shumaev and his wife are on the fourth floor. They don't have any rug-rats."

Hayes turned and looked at him in surprise. "Rug-rats? What a barbarism for children."

"Yeah. Kids. Brats. Crumb-snatchers!" Kowitt got up from the armchair and headed toward Skul, who was convinced that only brainwashed masochists and Bible thumping boobs had children. Dogs and cats—any kind of pet—were cheaper to raise, far less trouble, and always more faithful.

Kowitt stopped by Arden and looked at Skul. "What I want to know is who's going with whom—inside The Armatage. We know the Russians will be armed to the eyeballs."

"Arden and either you or Little Davy, Henry," Skul said promptly. "You two can flip for it."

"Hold on a cottin' pickin' minute!" Alister Bates looked and sounded insulted. His appearance also looked odd. It was his completely bald head. He had not yet put on a wig. A young man, he should not be completely bald; therefore, everyone always assumed his head was shaved. "None of you have my knowledge of locks and security systems. I'm not blowing my own horn, I'm stating a fact. What are you going to do if you run into a tricky lock situation and I'm not there?"

Skul regarded the defiant Bates with an expression of sympathy. Never tell a lie when the truth will do as well. "Al, you don't have the experience in violence. You're a technician. If we run up against something and you were there, you wouldn't have the time to help us. If we come up against a locked door, we'll either shoot off the lock or blow it off."

Accepting Skul's explanation and knowing he was correct, Bates nodded, after which he got up and left the room.

Chris Shinns said, "Jon, you mentioned 3 get-cars. I suppose I'm elected to steal them? If we're going to invade The Armatage tomorrow, I'll need help in lifting those cars today. Look, if we grab them in Manhattan, even after I put on fake plates, by the time—"

"Forget the cars, that is forget 2 of them," Skul said. "All we'll need is one, preferably a station wagon . . ."

"We are going to escape in the same damn car we arrive in?" exclaimed Barry Arden in an admonitory tone, an incredulous look on his big face. "Jon, where's your common sense—and don't tell me we're going to crawl back through that damned sewer!"

"Henry, have you and Davy flipped a coin yet?" A soft smile played around the corners of Skul's mouth.

Kowitt and Wickewire registered surprise. So did Chris Shinns.

"Why the rush?" Henry stared at Skul.

"Look, Jon! About the car!" Arden pursued doggedly.

"Go ahead—flip," said Skul. His eyes went to a worried Arden. "I'll tell you the score in a moment." He moved from the table, walked to the couch and sat down.

A puzzled expression in his eyes, Henry Kowitt reached into his pocket, took out a dime, flipped it and slapped it on the back of his right hand. "Call it,' he said to Wickewire.

"Heads."

Kowitt uncovered the coin. Tails was face up. "You lose. I go. You stay."

"I suppose I'll have to sit in a car or do whatever," Wickewire said.

"Like hell you will," Skul said calmly. "According to your file, you're about the best there is with a helicopter. We're going to make use of your talent as a chopper pilot."

"Hot diddle damn!" Whooped Arden, guessing at once what Skul had in mind. He slammed his right fist into the palm of his left hand. "We're going to fly off the roof of The Armatage!"

"Wrong! *Lift off!*" corrected Skul. "We don't have a choice. To try to escape in downtown New York at 4 in the morning would be insanity. A chopper is a sure bet!"

"Hold on!" Wickewire said roughly in a loud voice. He stood up, looking so tall he could have been a miniature, but black, Empire State Building. "This isn't Viet Nam! We're pulling off this raid at 3 o'clock in the morning. What the fuck do you expect me to do, go to some airport at 2 in the morning and rent a chopper? That's crazy! There's the matter of timing. Or maybe we could rent the bird this afternoon and I could fly it around Manhattan for 10 or 12 hours!"

"We have all sorts of expertly forged credentials, including pilots licenses, ratings, and all that jazz," Skul said tentatively. "I'll tell you what I have in mind, Davy. This afternoon, you and Ann and Chris can drive over to the Newark International Airport, rent a 5 passenger chopper and—"

"And fly the damn thing to—to where?" demanded Wickewire impatiently.

"To here! To The Farm!" Skul was curt. "We have 20 acres and a small patch of woods. Who's to notice your landing here? Choppers are always flying all over the place—air ambulance services, traffic guys and what have you. The odds are way in our favor."

Wickewire looked at Skul as if he were an executioner in a black hood carrying a headman's ax! "I don't think you comprehend the problems involved!" he said significantly. "There's the matter of communications, although that's not really a problem. But how in hell do you expect me to find the roof of The Armatage? Have you ever seen New York City from the air—and at night? Man, there are 10 thousand rooftops! There's no way I could find that particular roof, not without a radio-guidance beam. Some helicopters are equipped with that type of receiver, but we'd still need a special type transmitter.''

"We have both the transmitter and the receiver," Skul said in a lofty tone. "Why do you think I got up so early this morning? I wanted to check all our equipment in the special room. There are some things we'll still have to buy, such as rubber suits and some other equipment. But we do have the transmitter and the receiver you'll need for the chopper. They're small, and the range is only 5 miles. From The Farm to The Armatage is less than 18 miles. Once you're in the midtown area, you'll get the signal loud and clear.''

Wickewire, who had digested Skul's breezy explanation, was still not satisfied. "Listen, a big Black dude renting a chopper will sure as hell be remembered! What about disguises—and don't tell me you can chop a foot and a half off my height and change the color of my skin!''

"Professor, that's your department. What can you do for him and Ann—and don't forget Chris?" Skul said.

Hayes studied Wickewire's large face and considered for several moments. "A dark wig with longer hair partially gray," he said at length. "The same with a mustache— and some paste-on colliten wrinkles, maybe a short beard. I can add 20 years to his age, and to Ann and Chris, enough years so that they won't be recognized after their police artist sketches are released, and their descriptions circulated.''

Wickewire dropped his big frame into an easy chair. "Well, I can tell the people at Newark International that I want to show some friends the entire New York area by air. I'll have to give a satisfactory reason for wanting to rent the bird for—how many hours?''

"Twenty hours should be about right," said Skul. "In theory, you have to return the craft at a decent hour, if you take it back, which is not very likely.''

"They will want to know where I'm going to fly it to.''

Wickewire said. "I can't give them the location of this place. I'd suggest some address in New Rochelle."

"We'll get to the address momentarily." Skul turned his attention to Hayes. "Give Davy at least 5 thousand. The insurance alone for the bird will be high."

"Jon, the rubber suits you mentioned, they're for the sewer?" asked Barry Arden, who pulled out a chair and sat down at the round table.

"We can't come up from the sewer looking and smelling as though we've been rolling in a garbage dump," commented Skul. "What is known as ALB Turn-Out-Clothing for Firemen will do nicely. We can buy them at any industrial supply store. We'll get them in extra-large to cover our other clothing and weapons."

"We'll need air tanks and face masks to defeat the carbon monoxide," Arden said equably. "Firemen's SCBA gear will do nicely. We can also buy them from an industrial supply house, in the safety section."

An expression of slight puzzlement crossed Skul's face. "Maybe I misunderstood you. Or did you mean 'SCUBA?' "

"*S-C-B-A* stands for Self-Contained Breathing Apparatus," explained Arden. "Three tanks and masks will be expensive, about 2 thousand dollars each."

"The cost is not important," Skul said. He stood up. "Let's get organized and start making a tight schedule. We have a lot of work to do this day."

Arden got to his feet, enthusiasm spreading over his face. "I've a feeling it's all going to go down exactly as we want it to."

Hayes remained silent. His opinion of the world and of other human beings was colored by self-knowledge, and he stood by his conviction that man was but a finely tuned, ingenious machine fit only to turn red wine into urine.

CHAPTER TWELVE_____

DON Salvatore Tuccinardo was too much of a realist to believe in justice or think that God or the Devil was responsible for whatever happened in the world. All people ever got was good or bad luck. Lately, all his luck had been bad, right up to the point of being the worst it could get. Joey Gags had been killed. Some of Don Salvatore's best triggermen had joined Joey in hell. If ever a job had been botched, it had been the kidnap attempt. The entire mess had exploded into unwanted nationwide publicity. There had even been "special features" on television, with "experts" discussing "organized crime" and the Mafia!

Damn it. The Outfit in Chicago must be laughing its head off. Even thinking about Anthony Marcado made a knot grow in Don Salvatore's stomach. He and Tough Tony had hated each other for 35 years. Marcado, as elder statesman of the Chicago mob, had done everything in his power to keep Sal from becoming a member of the Commission. Tough Tony had failed, his failure only increasing his hatred. Marcado wasn't all that much of a threat, for he knew that just as gentleness in politics saps virility, ruthlessness can make an enemy even stronger. Marcado was content to play a waiting game. He couldn't start a shooting war without the consent of the Commission. To start a war on his own, without the consent of the Commission, would make him an enemy of all the families, and Tough Tony was far too clever for that. He would wait very patiently, hoping sooner or later the FBI would trap Don Salvatore. The Feds were getting closer.

As a result of the slaughter in Upper Manhattan, a dozen agents of the FBI had descended on Don Salvatore's estate and had attempted to question him about Joey Gags and the other dead men. All they had received was silence and a stony stare from Don Salvatore, and threats of legal action for "harassment" from 3 of the best criminal lawyers in the business. In very polite language, the attorneys told the FBI to get the hell out of Don Salvatore's home, or ". . . arrest Mr. Tuccinardo and charge him."

To add to Salvatore's worries, there was the mystery of who had snuffed Paul Castellano. The other Dons swore they had not ordered the whack-out. Who had—if they were telling the truth. Don Salvatore was convinced that Castellano's own mob had offed him, but he couldn't prove it. Yet something had to be done; the murderers had to be found and punished—executed. To do nothing about a member of the Commission being hit could set a dangerous precedent and give the Young Turks very dangerous ideas.

And whom to appoint as *sottocapo*, to replace Joey Gags? There wasn't anyone available, at least no one Don Salvatore could fully trust. There was a lack of talent in the ranks, due to the younger generation's being so independent. Sons did not want to follow in their fathers' footsteps, Salvatore thought bitterly. His youngest son Vincent was a gynecologist, with offices on Park Avenue. What a terrible way for a grown man to make a living— sticking his hands up a woman's *fica!* And look at Pete's son Victor! A real estate developer in Arizona! Living out west with sand and desert and stinking red-ass savages. That was the whole trouble. Children no longer had any respect for their elders. God should punish them! Children no longer wanted to grow up and be members of the Honored Society.

At the moment, his most pressing problem was the Russians. They were still insisting that Don Salvatore come to the *Boris Gudinov*.

"Sal, all you have to do is refuse to go to the ship," Peter Dellacrote said. No one else was present in the meeting room, and Pete was free to use the name he had called his friend since childhood. "My advice is to forget the heroin. With the FBI intensifying its efforts, the risk isn't worth it."

"You have given this matter much thought?" mused Don Salvatore. "There are no doubts in your mind?"

"None." Dellacrote was firm. "We make jokes about the FBI, but we know that Uncle Sugar's boys are very effective. Simply tell the Russians that the deal is off and that you're not going to meet with them on the ship. There really isn't anything they could do about it. They have as much to lose as us, maybe even more."

A sneer skipped across Don Salvatore's round face. "The damned FBI has always been a cancer in our lives. But their storming into the house the other day didn't mean nothing. Those *cogliones* was only on a fishing expedition. We know what's sticking in the throat of Uncle Sugar. With that son of a bitch Castellano dead, the Government's case against the other members of the Commission will be weakened. That idiot Castellano should have been killed for being *stupido!* He was so damn dumb that the feds were able to bug his office and home and make tapes of conversations he had."

Dellacrote put down his wine glass and dabbed at his lips with a white silk handkerchief. "The problem of Castellano and the Russians is a dual one. I must also point out that the government has other tapes to help its case against Massereri and the other Dons. Castellano wasn't that important. With him dead and out of the way, the tapes the feds made of his conversation will be inadmissible in court. But like I said, Uncle Sam's prosecutors don't need them. They have 62 tapes made of conversations by the other Dons.''

"I warned them!" Don Salvatore smirked. "I told them: never talk on the telephone; have experts and their equipment make a sweep every day for hidden Government transmitters. Check every day for bugs. That's why Uncle Suger couldn't indict us. All the feds have is tapes of the other families. Castellano and the other idiots mentioned our names, but that's not evidence. It's only hear-say.''

"I don't think Mikhail Borsirev is interested in our troubles with the FBI," Dellacrote said carefully, He picked up the glass and stared into the red depths of the wine. "He is only dealing with us because we are of value to him and his scheme. I still advise you to forget the arrangement. Remember what I said about the FBI. Sooner or later the feds will get lucky.''

Don Salvatore dismissed Dellacrote's warning with a wave of his hand, and his close friend and *consigliere* subsided. Tuccinardo respected Dellacrote's ability, but he was still his own man and always made the final decision.

Introspectively, Salvatore looked through the windows of the meeting room at the woods beyond the walls of his estate. Many of the leaves had already fallen, and those that remained on the trees were a deep red, or a gold, although some were a deep brown . . . dead, and about ready to fall to the ground.

He returned his attention to Peter Dellacrote. "For almost 3 years we've been handling heroin from the Russians," he said stoutly, "and all that time the FBI has been snooping and poking and doing its best to put us behind bars. Not once have the feds suspected that we've been receiving drugs from Borsirev and his AMTORG hoods.''

Delloacrote kept his expression neutral. ''Then you are going to meet with him tomorrow night?''

''Why not? After we've come this far, throwing away millions of dollars would be ridiculous,'' Don Salvatore said. ''Even if we sold the 2 tons at only 10 million, it would all be clear profit, every cent.'' He leaned forward and smiled like a fox. ''We could make 3 times more profit if we dealt ourselves with the middle men across the nation and sold the horse in parcels of 20 kilos each.''

Dellacrote didn't show his anger and frustration. ''Such a method will only increase our chances of being discovered by the DEA. The longer the chain, the more chances of a weak link.'' He knew it was useless. Sal usually made the right decisions, but there were those times when his major weakness steered him into tempestuous waters, when his greed forced him to ignore very real dangers or to minimize them.

''Perhaps, perhaps,'' admitted Don Salvatore, his eyes challenging Dellacrote. ''Peter, tell me. What did you mean when you said the problem of the Russians and Castellano was a dual one?''

''The FBI is watching us and all Soviet nationals in New York,'' Dellacrote sounded almost belligerent. ''The longer we deal with that slick bastard Borsirev, the greater the risk for us. Sal, I tell you, don't go to the ship. Send word that the deal is off. Borsirev will let it go at that. He won't like it. Who gives a damn? What can he do?''

Don Salvatore replied with a self-assured smile. ''Peter, right now only you and me know we are meeting with the Russians,'' he said, his tone noticeably condescending. ''When we send a button man to the park with a message, he doesn't know what the message means or who gets it. Our boys pick up the shipments of H—they don't know where it's coming from—*corretto?*''

"Yes," conceded Dellacrote, becoming more worried.

"Most of the people who belong to Our Thing believe in Democracy and love this country," said Don Salvatore. Abruptly, he chuckled. "Without the free enterprise system in this country, how could we prosper? And if the stupid liberals of this country hadn't succeeded in changing the criminal justice system in our favor, we'd be serving a dozen sentences of a hundred years each—consecutively!"

"Sal, tell me in plain words what you mean?" Dellacrote forced himself to remain mild and patient.

"The other New York families wouldn't stand by and do nothing if they knew we were dealing with the secret police of the Soviet Union, the number one enemy of this country. All the families in the United States would be against us! You know I'm right."

Dellacrote adjusted his eyeglasses. "I see. You're saying that Borsirev and his people would tip off the other families, in revenge for our pulling out."

"The possibility exists. For that reason, we must handle those damned Godless savages from the Soviet Union with delicate care, the way a chef prepares *fettuccine* or *minestrone*. Can you disagree?"

Dellacrote couldn't. Or Sal would know he was lying.

CHAPTER THIRTEEN⎯⎯⎯⎯⎯

THE nights were always long for the watchmen at the Kings Royal apartment house on 58th Street. Their shift was from 6PM to 6AM, and during those 12 hours, the 4 watchmen made rounds with clocks which were special devices into which round charts had been inserted. When any watchman inserted the key of a certain station into the clock and turned it, the time was registered on the clock, proving to the insurance company that the watchman was doing his job and making his rounds on schedule.

For purposes of management, the Kings Royal was divided into Building-West and Building-East. Every hour the 4 watchmen took turns making rounds, a watchman to each building. The other 2 stayed at the central station. After 6 PM, a desk was always moved from a side room into the lobby in front of the 2 inner doors of the weather entrance. These doors, as well as the street doors of the weather entrance, were always kept locked, from 10 at night until 7 the next morning. Residents who came home after 10 o'clock at night had to be admitted by the watchmen.

Benny Sutliff was eating a corned beef sandwich and Tim Lindsey was looking through the latest issue of *Penthouse* and wishing he were 35 years younger when they first saw the headlights of the car that pulled up at the curb in front of the building. Tim and Benny couldn't be sure, but the vehicle looked like a four-door Ford Taurus.

"I wonder who they are?" said Sutliff, who was a former employee of the New York subway system. "Whoever they are, they're getting out."

Lindsey, a retired warehouse foreman, put down his magazine and watched as 2 men got out of the car, one from the front and one from the rear, and walked to the sidewalk doors of the weather entrance.

"Whoever they are, they had better be on the up and up," Sutliff said from the side of his mouth. He put down his sandwich, and unsnapped the leather strap across the top of his .38 regulation police revolver. Then he started toward the doors, leaving behind him an amused Tim Lindsey. Benny was always talking tough and mouthing off how he'd "blow up" any burglar who tried anything "funny" in the Kings Royal. Poor Benny. Lindsey doubted if he had ever fired his revolver.

By the time Sutliff unlocked the inner doors and was approaching the doors to the sidewalk, he saw that one of the men had opened a badge case and was pointing the beam of a penlight at it. The man and his partner wore hats and were dressed in light topcoats. While the days were still warm, the temperature at night was often in the lower forties or upper thirties.

Sutliff stared out through the glass of one of the doors. The man with the badge case now shoved it against the glass and pointed impatiently at Sutliff's flashlight in its holder on his belt, indicating he should use it to look at the identification. Sutliff turned on the flashlight and, in its glow, saw that the card in the leather folding case identified the bearer as John Howard Phillips, an agent of—my God!—the FBI. There was Philipps' photograph, his thumbprint and the words *Federal Bureau of Investigation*. The badge was gold, an eagle on top with its wings spread, and the words *Department of Justice, Federal Bureau of Investigation*. Sutliff was startled. What could FBI men want?

John Howard Phillips began tapping on the door, an angry, impatient look on his good looking face.

Nervously, Sutliff unclipped the big ring of keys from his Sam Browne belt and unlocked the door. He then stood to one side as Phillips and the other agent entered. Hardfaced, the two men waited as Sutliff relocked the door, then strode through the inner doors into the lobby, Sutliff trailing after them. By the time he had followed them into the lobby, Phillips had announced his name, was thrusting his badge into the face of Tim Lindsey and saying, "And this is Special Agent Frank Fullerton." The other man promptly pulled his badgecase from his topcoat, flipped it open and showed it to Lindsey and Sutliff, both of whom felt self-conscious and were wondering why the FBI had come to the Kings Royal—at 2:15 in the morning!

"We're here on special business," said Phillips, his voice low and ringing with authority. He had blond hair, a saggy blond mustache and a large blemish—it could have been a birthmark—on his left cheek. The other man, not as muscular, had black hair and a small black mustache.

"You men love God and your country? Isn't that right?" Fullerton asked in a solemn voice.

Lindsey and Sutliff, their excitement and sense of intrigue mounting, hastily assured him that they did.

"Good! You're fine Americans," Fullerton said, revealing that two of his upper teeth were gold-capped.

"We must swear you to secrecy," Phillips said in a whisper. "We're here on a stakeout. We're not at liberty to reveal what it's about. I will tell you this: it's very important to the security of the United States and its people." Skul's eyes went to the walkie talkie on Lindsey's belt. "How many of you are on duty?"

"Uh . . . 4 of us, sir," Lindsey said, trying to act

casual. "The other 2 are making their rounds. They'll be back in about 15 minutes."

"Use your walkie talkie and get them down here on the double," Phillips ordered. "We can't lose any time. Every minute counts." *And that's the truth!*

"Yes, sir." Lindsey pulled the transceiver from its case on his belt, and turned it on. As he called the other 2 watchmen, Special Agent Fullerton asked Benny Sutliff, "Is there a small empty room close by, some place where we can set up our monitoring equipment?"

Sutliff's eyes went wide. "Aren't you going to watch through windows with binoculars?"

"Please answer the question."

"There's a room just off the lobby." He pointed with a finger. "Over there. It's where the night guard desk is kept during the day. You could use it."

Fullerton nodded. "Good. It will do fine."

Presently, one of the elevators descended and David DeDolph stepped out and walked over to the group, his curiosity changing to awe when Lindsey indicated Skul and Barry Arden and said, "Dave, these gentlemen are Agents Phillips and Fullerton of the FBI. We have to help them with a stakeout." He lowered his voice to a whisper. "It has to do with national security."

Rodney Whimms, the fourth watchman, arrived a few minutes later, carrying his timeclock and its leather shoulder strap in his hand. All he got to ask was "What's going on?" He never received an answer. Skul and Arden reached underneath their top coats, pulled out 2 strange looking weapons and calmly began to pull the triggers. Twice each Mertex Dart Gun made a *shuuuuuuu* sound. Electrically powered by a tiny battery, each M.D.G. fired a half-inch long special dart that, once it penetrated flesh, broke and released either poison, a tranquilizer, or some other kind of drug. Twenty darts could be fired as fast as one could pull the trigger.

Astonished looks popped out on the faces of the 4 watchmen. Their knees folded, and they went down, 360 milligrams of telfrosene coursing through their veins.

Like well rehearsed actors, Skul and Arden went to work. Skul bent down and unclipped the keys from the belt of Dave DeDolph, after which he turned and hurried toward the outside doors of the weather entrance. Arden picked up Benny Sutliff by his armpits, placed him in the chair behind the desk and gently pushed him over and cradled his head in his arms. He took the keys from Tim Lindsey, then dragged the man by his ankles to the door of the room that Sutliff had pointed out. By the time he had unlocked the door, dragged Lindsey into the room, gone back to the desk area and was pulling Whimms across the lobby floor, Jon Skul and Henry Kowitt were coming through the inner doors into the lobby, each carrying a footlocker by its side handle, the weight of each case evident by Skul and Kowitt's breathing.

"Hold the fort, Henry." Skul walked over to DeDolph, bent, grabbed the man by the front of his Sam Browne and started to pull him across the floor. A few minutes more and DeDolph had joined the 3 other unconscious watchman, and Barry Arden took the master keys from Whimms. After locking the door to the small room, Arden followed Skul back to the desk.

"Bates said to take the hall to the left, then to the right." Skul said and picked up one of the footlockers. "Barry, if we should meet anyone—dart 'em."

Weighed down by the footlockers, they walked as fast as they could past the elevators, came to the hall and turned, their feet soundless on the thick rug. Fifty feet more and they came to the horizontal hall. They turned right. They found the lighted sign half down the hall— *Freight Elevator*. Skul pressed the button. In no time at all, they were inside the elevator and Skul was pressing the

B button. Twenty-two seconds later, they were in the basement and moving to the right.

"There's the heating plant," remarked Kowitt.

"We go this way, unless I have Bates' directions mixed up."

"You haven't," confirmed Arden. "The room we want is on the other side."

The room was, and upon entering, they saw that it was a general repair and maintenance area. There was a long work bench and numerous spare parts for the gas furnace and the 6 water tanks. More importantly, toward the center of the room was the sewer cover, a metal grid 30 inches in diameter.

"One of you close the door," said Skull. He started to open one of the footlockers. "I know there's no one down here, but I'll feel better with the door closed, but don't latch it."

"We know. You're the nervous type," joked Arden. He walked over to the door and pushed it shut.

"You bet! Any kind of violence sends me hiding under the bed."

The 3 COBRA agents went to work. Using a short pry bar, Skul lifted the heavy sewer cover and pushed it to one side. SCBA tanks and their full face-masks were taken out of the footlockers. There were numerous other pieces of equipment—UZI submachine guns with noise suppressors attached; pointed scrapers for digging into crumbling mortar; flashlights; three Aerotron PAC-1 walkie talkies which operated on a frequency of 450 to 470MHz; range: 4.3 miles. Finally, there was the closed-signal transceiver that would broadcast its beam to Davy Wickewire. The transmitter was packed in a case lined with a double layer of DuPont Kevlar.

Skul and his 2 partners climbed into the ALB fire fighters suits—pants and long coats made of Neoprene—

and made sure they could reach their weapons in shoulder holsters under their suit coats.

As Skul checked to make sure the lickpick kit and the very special laser projector were secure in his coat pockets, Kowitt extended the aluminum ladder and pushed the bottom end through the sewer opening. Since the ladder was 12 feet long and it was only 7 feet to the bottom of the rounded sewer, once the ladder was in place, 5 feet extended through the sewer opening.

"Lower the footlockers first," Skul said. "I'll put the other stuff on top of them. We don't want to get anything wet in that mess below."

He climbed down the ladder, stepped off and found himself ankle-deep in brown, stinking liquid that flowed north. Ahead and behind him was darkness.

It took only minutes for Kowitt and Arden to lower the equipment to Skul, who carefully placed each item on the footlockers. The last thing that Arden and Kowitt did before going down the ladder was to inspect the floor, very carefully, to make sure they hadn't left any telltale evidence. After they had climbed down the ladder and were in the sewer, Skul, who had put on a pair of rubber gloves to keep the liquid mess off his hands, folded the 2 bottom sections of the ladder.

Henry Kowitt opened and closed his hands several times. "The feslitone spray makes the skin feel tight, doesn't it?"

"Yes, but the spray is more convenient than gloves, and with it on, there isn't any danger of leaving finger or palm prints." Skul said. "All right, Barry. Hold your side of the ladder."

With the 2 bottom sections folded, the ladder was now only 6 feet high. With Skul holding one side with both hands, and Arden's firm on the other side, Kowitt climbed the ladder, stopping when he was in a position by which he could reach up and grasp the rounded side of the sewer cover.

"Hold the ladder steady," Kowitt said. Twisting himself slightly on the wobbly ladder, he began to pull the cover into place, a difficult task since it weighed 160 pounds. At length he succeeded and the cover was snug across the opening. He climbed back down the ladder, and Skul immediately folded the upper 2 sections.

It was easier to wear the air tanks and the face masks than to carry them. After strapping the air tanks to their backs and putting on the face masks, they adjusted the air flow and started down the sewer in a north direction. Skul carried the folded length of the ladder. The ladder was a precaution, for if Skul and his 2 men missed the sealed sewer, if they failed to find it, or, even if they did find it, failed to break through the floor in the basement of The Armatage, they would have to continue in the regular system and come up through some manhole in one of the nearby streets.

Skul flashed the beam of a 6 volt industrial lantern from side to side, and now and then down into the dirty water. He, Arden and Kowitt proceeded forward at a steady pace, even at a rapid clip, considering how they were weighed down. Arden carried a bag containing the 3 walkie talkies and a larger canvas satchel filled with engineers' hammers and masons' chisels. Kowitt carried the special beam transmitter. Over his shoulders were the straps of the three UZI SMGS, plus the canvas straps of the pouches containing the magazines for the deadly little submachine guns.

It did not take long to walk the 100 feet. There it was, to the right: a rounded portion of the main sewer that had once been open but had been sealed over with bricks. Several blows with the engineers' hammers sent half a dozen bricks flying inward.

"It's going to be easier than we thought," Skul said, his voice sounding tinny through the voicemitter of the SCBA masks. With Kowitt standing by, holding the ladder, the bag of tools and the walkie talkies, Skul and Arden went to work removing the bricks that had sealed the sewer for over half a century, a job that required only 10 minutes.

Skul flashed the beam of the lantern up and down and from side to side. The rounded sides of the sewer were surprisingly clean, and there was little water in the bottom. They could only imagine the stale, dead smell because the SCBA gear enclosed them in a self-contained breathing environment.

"Open the tool bag, Henry," Skul said. Kowitt did and Skul took out a large metal spool on which had been wound 1,218 feet of fishing line—the distance from the opening of the sealed sewer to the cover in the floor of the room in the basement of The Armatage.

Skul tied the end of the thin fishline to the end of one of the bricks sticking outward from the side of the sewer. First he made certain the brick was solidly placed.

"Barron had better be right," Arden said. "If he's not, we've done a lot of work for nothing. I wonder how he develops such information?"

Skul began turning the spool and unwinding the fishline. "By patience and by spreading a lot of money in the right direction and to the right people."

Now, Kowitt carried the lantern. Movement in the formerly sealed off sewer became more difficult, especially for Skul who had to walk backward as he played out the fishline. When he came to the end of the line, he put down the spool and looked up at the rounded top of the sewer. "It should be right above us," he said, "but it isn't."

Kowitt began flashing the beam of the lantern over the top of the sewer, moving slowly forward. At length, after moving 20 feet, he called out, "I've found it. It looks like it's been sealed with concrete."

Skul hurried ahead, reached up and tapped the gray-looking material. Bits and pieces, from where the hammer had struck, fell downward. "It's plaster of Paris," Skul said, relieved.

The aluminum ladder was unfolded, and, with Arden and Kowitt holding it steady, Skul climbed and went to work. Using a rubber mallet and a wood chisel, he soon had cut large chunks of plaster of Paris from the sealed opening in the floor above. It was reinforced by number 6 chicken wire; nonetheless, Skul, by working rapidly, had soon smashed out an opening large enough for a man to crawl through—a man without an air tank on his back.

"I wish we hadn't left our hats and topcoats in one of the footlockers," Arden said slowly. "If we have to crash out onto the street—"

"If we do, it won't make any difference," said Skul, who was removing his face mask. "Topcoats would only get in the way."

He sniffed the stale air, which reminded him of the inside of a tomb. There could be methane gas in the sewer, but Skul doubted it. With one end of the sewer open, and air coming from the room above, the gas would not be dangerous for short periods, even if it were present.

After taking off his mask, air tank and firefighter clothing, Skul went up the ladder, thrust his head and shoulders through the ragged hole, arced the beam of a flashlight into the room and looked around. Empty wooden boxes and half a dozen old trunks stared back at him.

He went back down the ladder and whispered, "This is it. Get rid of everything we don't need."

The door of the room looked out of place. For one thing, it was covered with sheet steel bolted into place, the heads of the bolts ground down so that a wrench could not be fitted over them. The door was also equipped with 2 Yale locks with extra-long dead bolts.

As Skul took out his lockpick kit, Kowitt and Arden checked their Uzis. The weapons were not the usual 9mm or .45 caliber full-size SMG, or even the later mini-Uzi. The weapons were micro-Uzis—awesome firepower in just under 4 pounds, in a 9.5 inch overall package. The smallest submachine gun in the world, the micro-Uzi could fire 12 rounds per minute. This meant that on full automatic, it could empty the 32 round magazine in only 1.6 seconds of fire. The micro-Uzi could be fired on either full or semi-auto. The weapon could be held in one hand and fired like a pistol, although the 8 inch silencer attached it was top heavy. No matter. In the hands of an expert, the micro-Uzi was pure murder. And Skul, Arden and Kowitt were 3 of the best.

It took Skul 17 minutes to open the two locks. He tried the handle of the door. It turned. The door was open. Skul nodded at his 3 companions. They reached into their coat pockets and pulled out soft rubber masks that fitted entirely over the head. Skul became President Nixon. Arden became the Wolfman while Kowitt was changed into Adolf Hitler.

"Ready?" asked Skul.

Both men nodded.

CHAPTER FOURTEEN_____

FOR the third time, Colonel Borsirev read the message that the Soviet Embassy in Washington, D.C. had sent by shortwave—double-scrambled and frequency-hopped—to the AMTORG building. Decoded, the message read.

Your request is denied. Proceed with delivery as scheduled. We do not want any delays.

"Reading it again is not going to change its contents," muttered Major Andrei Gouzenko, who was slumped in a chair to one side of the desk. Like Borsirev, he, too, was sleepy. "The Center in Moscow has made up its mind, and there isn't anything we can do about it."

Borsirev, who needed a shave, crushed out his Lucky Strike, then methodically tore the paper into small bits and dropped them through the top slot of the square container close to his swivel chair. The container was filled with a powerful corrosive; within minutes the bits of paper would be dissolved into nothingness.

When Borsirev had sent the message to the Embassy, to be relayed to the KGB Center in Moscow, he had expected an answer within 24 hours. Not only was the reply days late, but it was not the answer he had expected. *Nyet.* The reply was not really "late." The only "lateness" existed in his own mind. Colonel Zivestrev, the Resident at the Embassy station, disliked him, but Zivestrev would not deliberately withhold a reply after he received it. He wouldn't dare. He was too cautious. The reply had taken so long because Moscow had not been able to make up its mind. Well, the *nachal stvo*—The Bosses—had sure as hell made the wrong decision. Deliver the heroin to that damned gangster on schedule. It was insanity!

"This has been some day," complained Gouzenko, hunching his shoulders. "I tell you, we could learn a thing or two from these Americans. "We have too much red tape. We're too rigid. Why couldn't Moscow have sent the message to the Embassy in the afternoon. Instead, The Center orders the Embassy to have us stand by. That was 3:15 yesterday afternoon!"

"Yes, yes, I know. We had no choice," Borsirev said irritably. "At least I didn't. I had to stay. You could have gone home."

"I preferred to remain here rather than have dinner with Glavatsky and his wife," Gouzenko said distastefully. "He tells the same stale stories over and over. I'm so sick of hearing how his grandfather knew Lenin personally. I told Raya not to invite them. She went against my wishes and invited them anyhow."

Frowning, Borsirev pushed back his swivel chair. "Your cover with TASS comes in handy. I suppose you gave the excuse that you had to interview some American statesman or some other diplomat?"

Gouzenko nodded. "At the United Nations. She didn't believe me. She never believes anything I tell her."

Borsirev got to his feet and reached for his suit coat hanging on the back of the swivel chair. "It's none of my business, but I feel you should learn to control your wife."

"She is too independent and believes all that nonsense about the 'modern Soviet woman,'" Gouzenko replied sheepishly. "I'd rid myself of her if our Home Office didn't frown on divorce."

Borsirev glanced at the clock on the wall. "Let's go home. It's past three-thirty. We both need the peace of a good night's sleep."

CHAPTER FIFTEEN _____

QUICK death could be anywhere. Jon Skul cracked the door open and looked out. Beyond was partial darkness, the only light the side illumination coming through the open door of a room to the west. There was only one sound: the *chug-chug-chug* of a sump pump, and an occasional loud gurgle from the water storage tanks. The warm air smelled of rubber, metal that had been heated, and disinfectant.

Skul and his 2 men had to continue to believe that the diagram Barron had sent was accurate. On that basis, the unused storage room—through the floor of which they had just emerged—was in the southeast corner of the basement. To the north were the gas-heating units. Toward the center of the basement were the 4 freight elevators and the single passenger elevator that went all they way down to the basement. The other 5 passenger elevators only went to the ground floor. Northwest were the water tanks and the water purification system. Storage and repair were against the west wall.

Directly west of the empty storage room was a 2 room apartment that, at one time, had been occupied by the furnace man, years earlier when the building had been heated by coal. The CIA was convinced that the apartment had been soundproofed, and was now being used for intensive interrogation by the KGB—reserved for dangerous enemies of the Soviet Union who would vanish from New York streets and end up in the basement apartment of The Armatage.

West of the row of elevators was the room where the Russians—the 3 always on duty in the basement—killed time, playing cards, etc.

Skul pushed open the door and stepped out. Barry Arden and Henry Kowitt followed, Arden gently closing the door.

"Our targets are to the west," Skul whispered. "At this hour of the night, they might be dozing. But watch yourselves. They could be anywhere. This basement is their turf. They're familiar with it."

Making sure his Uzi SMG was on SAFE, he shouldered the weapon by means of its narrow strap, and pulled a Bernardelli semi-automatic pistol from a pancake holster between his belt and his shirt. He stooped, pulled up his left pant leg, took a silencer from an ankle pouch and screwed it onto the extra long barrel of the autoloader. It would not be wise to terminate the three Russians with the Uzis. The .45 Hydra-Shok slugs were too powerful. They could go all the way through a body and hit some of the machinery in the basement. In turn, this could cause warning bells and other alarms to go off and, awakening the entire complex, preventing Skul and his men from reaching the upper floors.

Skul took the lead, Kowitt and Arden fanning out on either side of him. To the west, 50 feet in front of them, they could see bright light coming through an open door, and knew this is where the targets were. And maybe not. Nothing was certain. The 3 men did not have to be inside. Or suppose only 2 were there, and the third one upstairs? Nor did Skul know who might be in the 2 room apartment.

There was another danger, a very real danger: Debbie Miles could have talked and told the KGB everything she knew. Miles did not know the details, but she did know that a plan to attack The Armatage was in the works. It was possible that the KGB was waiting and had prepared a clever trap. In truth, it was difficult to decide what the KGB might do should they have the knowledge of the apartment house invasion. They wouldn't inform the New York Police Department or the FBI. They would handle the matter themselves and try to do it as quietly as possible. The KGB could be very clever and act with a high degree of planning and intelligence. At other times, the KGB could be incredibly stupid. KGB disinformation experts often made mistakes that were silly and inexcusable, such as using translation of Russian terms that didn't have any meaning in American usage. One supposedly internal U.S. memo—a very excellent forgery—had referred to the CIA not as ''The Company'' as some Americans do, but as ''Competent Bodies,'' which is the Soviet term for their secret services. In another document, supposedly taken from Israeli files, KGB disinformation experts had spelled the name of Israeli military intelligence as AMEN. The correct spelling was *Aman*. Dumb mistakes; stupid mistakes.

They closed in quickly on the room in which a light burned. Soon they could hear voices speaking in Russian. A man laughed. Another man commented, and there were more laughs.

Skul motioned for Arden to remain outside the room and act as rear guard, and for Kowitt, who nodded. Both men moved into the light and stepped through the door into the room.

There were 3 Russians sitting at a card table, one drinking coffee and watching the other 2 play cards. All 3 had only seconds to live, and those brief moments would be filled with total astonishment.

The 3 Russians looked up and saw Richard Nixon and

Adolf Hitler, weapons in their hands, walkie talkies belted around their waists—and Nixon had something belted to his back. The 3 Russians didn't have time to act; they were still staring, their mouths open, when Skul began firing the silenced Bernardelli. *Phyyyt.* The first .380 bullet struck one Russian in the chest and knocked him off the wooden folding chair. The second man was trying to pull a 9mm Makarov pistol from a belt holster as—*phyyyt!*—a projectile hit him in the right side of the neck, just underneath the jaw. The third man had half risen when Skul's slug thudded into his stomach, doubled him over and made him fall on the card table, his head crashing down next to the walkie talkie.

Skul walked quickly to the fallen men and calmly fired 2 more times, giving head shots to 2 of the men. The man who had been shot in the side of the neck did not need a second slug. He was obviously dead, lying in a pool of blood, his legs twitching reflexively.

In spite of the gravity of the moment, Kowitt went into his act. "Like man! Dig the walkie-talkie on the table!" he drawled. "If the dudes upstairs call down here . . . like man, us cats'll be in deep shit."

Skul smiled beneath the rubber of his Richard Nixon caricature mask. "Bro, I believe you're right. We'll get our butts upstairs as soon as I test our communications. These modified PACs had better work or we might as well pack up and go to the nearest rib joint."

It was a matter of getting a message to David Wickewire at The Farm. Little Davy could fly the helicopter from The Farm to the roof of The Armatage in less then 10 minutes, once he was airborne, but he had to know when to leave, when to lift off from the patch of woods.

The range of an Aerotron PAC-1 was 4.3 miles. Therefore, any message sent to Wickewire would have to be by relay. As part of the relay-line, Skeeter Ronson had checked into the St. Regis Sheraton Hotel at 8:15 the previous evening. The St. Regis Sheraton was on the corner of East 55th Street and Fifth Avenue, only a few blocks from The Armatage. Ronson had brought with him, in a large suitcase, a PRC-10 portable FM receiver-transmitter. The set had a power of 10 watts, a range of 30 miles, and operated on a frequency of 6.3MHz. The set could be operated by either voice or code key.

At 2 AM, Ronson had stretched a long-wire antenna across his room and tested the PRC-10 by tapping out 6 *Ms* in Morse code. Immediately The Farm replied, and *M M M M M M* came through Ronson's head-phones.

Ronson had then begun the wait with his PAC-1 walkie talkie.

Skul's contact signal came through at 3:44AM—a brief series of *bzts, bzts.* Skul had first pressed the signal button, then had sent the signals by pushing the talk-button, opening and closing the channel and using the open/close as a telegraph. There were 4 *bzts,* a pause, then 6 *bzts,* in rapid succession, another pause, then 3 slow *bzts.*

Ronson promptly pressed his own call button, and when he got the open channel, he replied with an identical series of signals, indicating that he had received Skul's signals and understood.

"If I were a religious man, I'd say 'Thank God' " Kowitt said.

Skul shut off his PAC-1, hoping that none of the signals had been accidentally picked up on walkie talkies by KGB guards inside The Armatage. It was not likely. All four PACS—Ronson's and the 3 carried by Skul and his 2 men—had been modified with transdiodes to give quadrature sensitivity and, coupled with r-transducers, to lock the channels to a single setting. But if there had been a freak crossover and one of the KGB walkie talkies buzzed, even if only briefly, a cautious Russian might suspect that another transmission had been sent from somewhere inside the building.

Skul finished reloading the Bernardelli auto-pistol. "Now to get upstairs and take care of the guards in Receiving and in the lobby."

"We could take one of the elevators down here right up to the third floor," suggested Barry Arden. "It would save us a good deal of time. But would the sound of a elevator warn the KGB?"

Henry Kowitt snorted. "Why should the sound of an elevator warn them? There are 6 floors here. Are people going to use only stairs and ignore the elevators?"

"At almost 4 o'clock in the morning?" amended Skul. "We're not going to take the chance. We're going to put to sleep the 5 on the first floor."

There were 3 sets of steps from the basement to the ground floor of The Armatage. There were narrow, metal steps not far from the freight elevators. Another set was in the north center section of the basement, close to the valves that maintained the pressure in the overhead sprinkler system throughout The Armatage. The third set of stairs was located in the west central section, the top of the steps opening into a hall.

Skul, Arden and Kowitt crept up the west-central stairs and were not surprised when they found the metal door, disguised as wood, locked by an ordinary Yale lock. Three minutes later, the ordinary Yale lock was unlocked, and Skul was returning the lockpick kit to his pocket.

They found themselves in a long hall lighted by a soft blue glow from small bulbs set in decorative holders fixed to the walls. COBRA headquarters had not been able to develop any information on the number of occupied apartments on the first floor. Who cared? The only thing that mattered to Skul was that the hall led north, made a turn to the east for 20 feet, then moved north again, cutting across an east-west hall. Thirty feet north of the east-west hall, there were 2 doors. These opened to the Receiving Room which handled deliveries from the rear, usually large items such as furniture.

In a few minutes, Skul and his 2 men were standing in front of the 2 doors, both of which opened by pushing down on a horizontal bar. He had put away the Bernardelli, and now held the silenced micro-Uzi in his right hand.

There was only one way to effect the terminations: go in and do it. Skul looked at Arden and Kowitt. They both nodded. He pushed down on the bar of the door to the left, Arden on the bar to the right side door. Together, they rushed into the room, Kowitt behind them—all 3 in a crouch, their fingers lightly resting against the triggers.

There weren't any targets. The half-dark room was empty.

"They were here," whispered Arden. With his Uzi, he indicated a table ahead on which a gooseneck lamp was burning. On the table were several magazines and a newspaper.

"Henry, watch the door," said Skul. He moved farther into the room, wary of a trap. He saw a machine for X-raying packages and letters. There were hand-trucks and rows of metal shelves, packages on some. He didn't, however, see any door that opened to a toilet. Anyhow, the 2 men would not be inside the toilet at the same time.

"The chances are, the 2 jokers who should be in here are with the others in the lobby," he said. "Let's go."

There were 2 routes to the lobby: Skul and his helpers could use the east-west hall. The problem was that after it turned to the south, it ended in the center of a wall facing the lobby. This meant that any KGB guard in the lobby could see them coming the last 60 feet.

The second way was a hall to the south. Slightly past the center of the building, it stretched from east to west. There was still a chance that a KGB guard might spot them, but the risk was less than by the other route.

Skul, Kowitt and Arden retraced their steps. Running soundlessly over the thick carpet—it was a sickly shade of green—they moved past the door to the basement steps, sprinted another 30 feet and came to the hall they wanted. They turned, hurried east, and were soon at the end of the corridor. Twenty feet to their left— to the north—was the lobby.

Kowitt watched the rear. Arden kept both eyes to the south. Skul looked around the corner. The lobby was empty. Not a single Russian dumbo was in sight. Conclusion: either Barron had made some serious mistakes—*That's not too likely!*—or else the KGB guards were in a room close to the lobby. The only way to find out was to go forward and investigate.

Barry Arden made a face, but neither Skul nor Kowitt could see it beneath his Wolfman's mask. "I don't like any operation that has a lot of variables," he said. "Too much can happen; too much can go wrong."

The 3 men crept along the west side wall. They came to the corner of the bank of 6 passenger elevators, paused, and listened. The lobby, lighted by only 2 tall column lamps, was very quiet. They moved forward another 6 feet, going along the front of the elevators. And that's when they saw the light coming through the small rectangular window of a door that faced north. The door was to a room on the south side of the lobby, in that smaller section between the 4 inner doors and the 4 sidewalk doors of the weather entrance. Skul and his men had not been able to see the light and the door from the hall because they had been too far to the south.

Quickly, they moved in on the room. They carefully opened one of the inner doors, crept into the weather section of the lobby and closed in. The danger now was that a passerby from the street might see them. Again, this was not very likely, considering the early hour.

Very carefully Skul put his hand on the silver-colored door knob. He turned it, pushed open the door and moved inside. Behind him were Arden and Kowitt.

It took only 9 seconds. Five startled faces looked toward the door, the faces of 4 men sitting at a table eating. The fifth man was standing and pouring a cup of coffee from a coffee maker resting on a black filing cabinet.

There were only 2 series of *phyyyyt* from Skul and Kowitt's silenced Uzis, some short groans of agony, and the *thud-thud-thud* of bodies hitting the table and the floor. There were also the louder sounds of chairs overturning and half a dozen loud *ping-ping-pings* as the .45 Hydra-Shok slugs zipped right through the bodies of the Russians and hit metal objects on the far side of the room. Then there was silence, and drifting blue-gray smoke from the fired cartridges—the odor of gunpowder, and the peculiar sweet smell of death.

"Perfect," said Arden happily. "We don't have to worry about our rear when we go upstairs."

Skul inspected the corpses. The large .45 projectiles had butchered the 5 KGB agents, who lay grotesquely in pools of their own blood. It would take a lot of *S.O.S.* or *Mr. Clean* to put the floor in shape.

Skul smiled beneath the hot rubber mask of Richard Nixon. "Now gentlemen, we can take an elevator to the third floor and pay our respects to Mr. Borsirev and his family." Chuckling, he turned to Kowitt. "Like man-you know-we're right on schedule."

"Like Bro, do we ring the bell?" cracked Kowitt.

The cream colored doors came together behind them and the elevator began its descent to the lobby. Skul, Arden and Kowitt looked at the numbers of the doors—318, 317, 316. The number they wanted was 327.

"We go this way," Skul said. He turned and started down the wall heading west. While he held a mini-Uzi, Arden and Kowitt had shouldered their SMG's and held Mertex Dart Guns in their hands. Why terminate innocent people, even if they were Russians?

They turned a corner, walked another 50 feet and came to the target door. There it was, number *327*. Below the number was the card in the brass holder: *Mr. and Mrs. M.P. Borsirev*.

Skul took out his lockpick kit and whispered, "Once we're inside, you know what to do. Borsirev has 2 teenage sons; they may or may not share the same bedroom."

"Hurry with the lock," urged Arden, looking up and down the quiet hall.

In a few minutes, they were inside the apartment. Skul carefully closed the door, making sure he heard the lock click. They saw they were in a tiny foyer. To one side was a large living room; beyond it the dining area. The kitchen was to the rear. Directly ahead of the foyer was a narrow hall, and Skul assumed it led to the bedrooms. He assumed right. They saw 3 doors along the hall. Two were on the left, indicating smaller bedrooms than the one on the right, which had to be the master bedroom. From it came soft snoring.

Barry Arden and Henry Kowitt moved toward the bedrooms on the left. Skul shouldered his Uzi, and pulled the Mertex Dart Gun from its holster on the left side of his belt he had buckled over his suit coat. Ever so gently, he turned the knob, pushed the door inward, and stepped into the bedroom. He paused, adjusting his eyes to the darkness, although the bedroom was not pitch black. Background light was coming in through the 2 windows, one of which was partially open. There was the usual furniture—a long dresser, a smaller chest of drawers. The door to the bathroom was to the left; closets with fold-out doors to the right.

Creeping toward the kingsize bed, Skul suddenly felt as if he had been slapped in the face with a wet towel wrapped in barbed wire. The bed had only one occupant, and, getting closer, Skul saw that the person was a woman. She lay on her right side, one arm high on the pillow.

It's his wife! And if Borsirev isn't here, then perhaps Gouzenko and Shumaev aren't in the building either!

Skul had to find out what was going on. Now by the bed, he moved quickly. He sat on the edge of the bed, put his left hand over the woman's mouth, jammed the stubby barrel of the Mertex Dart Gun against the back of her neck and waited. He had only to wait a few seconds. The woman awakened, gave a muffled cry and began struggling.

"Stop it!" hissed Skul. "I'm not going to hurt you, and I'm not here to rape you. I want information. I'll take my hand away from your mouth, but only if you promise not to scream. I warn you: if you scream, I'll kill you. Your sons will also die. My people are with them now. Nod your head if you agree not to scream."

Larissa Fedorovna Borsirev moved her head as best as she could and nodded. Skul removed his hand, and, all the while keeping the Mertex Dart Gun trained on her, leaned back, reach out and pulled down the shade. He turned on the bedside lamp on the night table.

Larissa Borsirev sat up and, holding the light blue cover tightly to her breasts, stared at Skul as though he were some monstrous alien from a galaxy far, far away.

If Skul in his Richard Nixon mask horrified her, she surprised him. She didn't look Russian. There was none of that potatoes and cabbage beefiness about her, none of that muscular mannish look so common with ordinary Russian women. To the contrary, Larissa Borsirev was a pretty woman, her features well-formed and almost delicate. She was small boned, her skin clear and without blemishes, her hair long, black and shiny. In a way, she reminded Skul of an innocent child; then again, she made him think of a high priced French *Marie-couche-toi-là* who, for a price, would perform any kind of sexual act—but would never kiss you on the lips.

"Where is your husband—and don't lie to me!" Skul said in a low, threatening voice.

"He . . . he is n-not here," Larissa Borsirev said timidly, her frightened eyes roaming over Skul. Trying to control her voice, she remembered what she and the other wives had been told regarding terrorists: cooperate, don't make them angry, be polite, try to act natural.

"Why isn't he here? Where is he?"

"H-He phoned during the afternoon and said he had to work late at AMTORG," she said, her English excellent.

"Is Andrei Gouzinko at home?" Skul quickly added, "I warn you: think before you answer. Your own life, as well as the lives of your sons, hangs in the balance. Lie to me just once, and the 3 of you will die. I suppose you're going to tell me that Mr. Gouzenko isn't home, either?"

He could see alarm and panic rise in her eyes, and knew at once that Gouzenko was not in his apartment. He also sensed that Larissa Borsirev was caught in an emotional whirlpool, trapped between telling the truth, yet afraid that if she did he wouldn't believe her, and afraid that if she lied and he found out, he would kill her and her sons. She decided that it would be safer for her to tell the truth.

"But . . . b-but Mr. Gouzenko isn't home!" she said in desperation, tears forming in her eyes. "Fainna—she is his wife—dropped by earlier this evening, and she said that her husband had to interview some dignitary at the United Nations. He is a correspondent with TASS. She w-was angry. She said she knows he was lying. She said that if some famous person had to be interviewed, she would know about it. The husband of a good friend of hers—and a good friend of mine—works for *Izvestia,* and he did not have to go on an interview."

"Do you mean Sergei Shumaev?" Skul watched her carefully for a reaction, and sensed—from experience—that she was telling the truth when she nodded and said, "Yes, I m-mean Mr. Shumaev."

"Is he at home?"

She looked confused. "I-I don't know. I suppose he

is.'' She drew back in greater fear when she saw Adolf Hitler and The Wolfman creep into the bedroom, Mertex Dart Guns in their hands. Neither Kowitt nor Arden said anything, letting Skul carry the ball.

"I think you're lying, Mrs. Brosirev," Skul said.

"I've told you the truth," she sobbed; starting to lose control, she began to tremble.

Skul believed her, but he didn't say so. He only pulled the trigger of the Mertex Dart Gun. The dart zipped through the blue cotton blanket and her nightgown and struck her in the left breast. Her eyes went wide, and her mouth flew open, for a scream that never came. The 360 milligrams of telfrosene worked instantly. Her eyes closed, her mouth went slack, and she fell sideways. She would have fallen off the bed if Skul had not caught her. He eased her head down to the pillow and pulled the blanket up to her neck.

"Well, she won't wake up until the sun is high in the sky," Arden said, fuming in impatience. "So where is Borsirev?"

"We darted both the kids," Kowitt said. "No trouble there. But it looks like we've scored zero here."

Skul explained what Larissa Borsirev had told him. "And I believe her. She was too frightened to lie."

"That leaves us with only Sergei Shumaev," Arden said menacingly.

"So what are we doing standing here?" Skul turned and headed for the bedroom door.

They left the apartment and headed for the fourth floor stairs, Jon Skul thinking of the things that could go wrong, even after they bagged Shumaev. A circuit could blow in one of the walkie talkies, or something could go wrong with the PRC-10. Highly improbable, but nonetheless possible. And suppose Ann and Chris weren't waiting in the park? *The hell with it! The first thing I want to know is where they have Debbie hidden?*

They found apartment number 431, and Skul had soon

picked the lock. Like silent shadows, they crept into the apartment, Skul and Kowitt moving toward the master bedroom, Arden on his way to check out the spare bedroom.

Skul and Kowitt entered the bedroom and crept toward the double bed. Skul moved in on Sergei Shumaev as Kowitt leaned down, put his hand over the mouth of Lydia Shumaev and shoved the muzzle of his Mertex Dart Gun under her chin.

Across from Kowitt and Lydia Shumaev, Skul pushed the end of the silencer on the Bernardelli pistol and said, "Wake up, stupid. It's talk and tell time. Try anything cute and I'll scramble your brains with a bullet."

After Skul turned on the lamp on the nightstand between the beds, Sergei and Lydia sat up, and while she was afraid and showed it, he regarded Skul and Kowitt was calm eyes, his mouth a tight line, nor did he flinch when Arden came into the room and announced the rest of the apartment was clear.

"Tie the woman's hands and gag her." Skul said to Kowitt.

A short, dumpy woman with a peasant's face, Lydia Shumaev did not resist when Kowitt tied a handkerchief tightly around her mouth, then secured her hands with thin closthesline rope.

"We want answers, 'Comrade,' " Skul said, looking down at Sergei Shumaev. "We either get them or we'll kill you both faster than you can blink."

"I'm only a newspaper man. I'm a correspondent for *Izvestia*," Shumaev said with quiet conviction. "I don't have any information of importance."

"You're an officer in the KGB," Skul said, his tone even and mechanical. "Furthermore, you're an aide to Colonel Mikhail Borsirev. That's why you know where Deborah Miles is stashed—or have you sons-of-a-bitches killed her?"

Shumaev feigned ignorance. "I have never even heard the name before now."

Skul turned and pulled the trigger of the Bernardeli pistol with such speed that he surprised even Arden and Kowitt. There was a *phyyyyt,* and a muffled cry from Lydia Shumaev as her body jerked violently. The .380 bullet had cut across the upper outside of her right arm and had buried itself in the mattress. Only a fifth of an inch deep, the wound was not serious, but with blood pouring out of it, it looked worse than it actually was.

Surprise and hatred flashed over Sergei Shumaev's face, and for a moment it looked as if he might try help his wife—or attempt to grab Skul! He began to breath heavier when Skul shoved the muzzle of the silenced Bernardelli into his face.

"That was only a warning," Skul said savagely. "The next time, I'll blow off one of her kneecaps. 'Adolf,' " he said to Kowitt. "Pull the blanket off. I don't want to miss."

Shumaev's expression turned to fear as he watched Kowitt jerk the blanket from his wife's body. Blood from the gash on her arm had soaked part of the pillow and the sheet on the mattress, and she was whimpering in terror. Skul was counting on the human element, on emotion being stronger than a sense of duty and obligation to one's country. His intuition was correct.

"Wait!" The word popped out of Shumaev when he saw Skul shift aim of the silenced pistol toward his wife. "I'll tell you where the woman is. I'll tell you anything you want to know."

Colonel Borsirev and Major Gouzenko parked their individual cars in the lot adjoining The Armatage and hurried toward the front entrance. Both men were chilly from the early morning air and anxious to get to bed. Borsirev opened the box to the right of the doors and pushed the button. Three times he pressed the button. None of the guards appeared.

"Something is wrong," Borsirev said nervously. "Petrov and the others are very efficient."

"But . . . but what? It's impossible to get inside the building!" replied Andrei Gouzenko, trying to reassure himself as well as Borsirev.

Borsirev took out his own master key and unlocked one of the doors. Both men stepped inside, and Borsirev relocked the door and pulled an American made Detonics .45 semi-automatic pistol from an inside coat pocket. Gouzenko pulled a 9mm Soviet Makarov autopistol.

"Careful," warned Borsirev. Together, they approached the guard room on the south side of the weather entrance. What they found inside the room filled them with rage and fear. They knew that the impossible had happened and they knew who was responsible—the same mysterious group that had terminated Dynamite Jackson and Salvatore Tuccinardo's best gunmen. The enemy was looking for information; the enemy was searching for Deborah Miles. With a sharp stab of realization, Borsirev and Gouzenko became acutely aware that they were the targets, they and Captain Sergei Shumaev. The enemy knew!

"Mikhail, do you think our families—" began Gouzenko.

"Don't think about it! We won't know until we get upstairs," Borsirev snapped angrily as he stared at the carnage in the small room. "We have to take what life throws at us."

"My God, if we notify the police, they'll be all over this building," Gouzenko said hoarsely. "When The Center back home hears about this—"

"Eventually, the New York police will be running around in here," Borsirev reminded him. "This is neither an embassy nor a consulate, and none of the people here have diplomatic immunity, including you, me and Sergei. If the enemy is still in the building, that is where he will be, in Sergei's apartment.''

''We can't be sure,'' began Gouzenklo. ''And there are only the 2 of us.''

''Go get the machine pistols from the filing cabinet.'' Borsirev sounded grim. ''We're not alone. I'm going to phone Vorontsov, and Khomenko and Tsygasov on the second floor. If the enemy agents are still in the building, there's a good chance we can trap them.''

Borsirev picked up the receiver and began to dial.

Moving to a filing cabinet, and stepping around a pool of blood, Gouzenko secretly hoped that the enemy gunmen were miles away.

CHAPTER SIXTEEN_____

JON Skul evaluated the information Sergei Shumaev
had just given him. Little beads of glistening sweat had
popped out on the KGB officer's forehead and upper lip.
The Russian turned his head, looked at his bloody wife,
who was trembling, then stared up at Richard Nixon.

"And you still maintain that Miss Miles is aboard the
Soviet freighter named the *Boris Gudinov,* and that the
ship has 2 tons of heroin on it!" Skull sneered, cleverly
faking his disbelief. "Do you actually think we'd believe
such garbage?"

"Don't forget, Don Salvatore is scheduled to go aboard
about eight tomorrow night—eight tonight, rather!" inter-
posed The Wolfman. "Our Russian comrade does have a
vivid imagination, doesn't he?"

Shumaev's face underwent a series of contortions, the
rapid and changing expressions of a man imprisoned by
despair. "The vessel is there at the docks," he said in
desperation. "The woman is on the ship. The heroin is on
the ship. What more can I tell you?"

"Nothing more, comrade," conceded Skul with a slight
smile. He raised the Bernardelli and squeezed the trigger.
The silencer whispered—*phyyyt.* Shumaev's head gave a

175

jerk, the impact of the bullet pushed his body against the headboard. There was a dark hole an inch above the bridge of his nose, the slug freezing the expression on his face. His eyes remained wide open. His mouth formed an *O*. The corpse sagged to its right and would have tumbled off the bed, to the right, if Barry Arden hadn't caught it by the arm, and pulled the torso forward so that it hung, head down, blood dripping from the hole above the nose.

A muffled scream came from Lydia Shumaev, and she began to struggle. It was a pathetic effort in protest against horror, in protest against death; and it was a useless effort. The silencer went *phyyyyt* again. Her body gave a jerk and went limp. The .380 piece of metal had entered her head through the right temple and killed her instantly.

"Well gee, golly-gosh!" muttered Henry Kowitt. He pushed the dead woman forward and let her head fall to the bed. "I thought the idea was to take them with us."

"A changing situation calls for a change in strategy," Skul explained. He put the pistol on the side of the bed, and pulled the PAC-1 walkie talkie from the case on his belt. "We found out what we wanted to know. He told us the truth. No one could make up such a story on the spur of the moment; he was too consistent."

"I guess . . . I suppose it was the way we shot them down," Kowitt said slowly. "I mean—I don't know what I mean!"

"The way *I* killed them," Skul corrected him. "Shumaev was part of a sinister plan to wreck countless American lives—and not just the idiots who take drugs, but their victims, the people they kill to maintain their habit. We couldn't take them to the roof with us. It would have been too risky. They had to die or they would have told Borsirev what they told us. As it is, even now it might be too late to save Debbie."

"He'll suspect we made them talk," Arden said worriedly.

"But Borsirev won't know for sure. Go to the front and

crack the door. See if it's all clear in the hall. I'm going to contact Ronson.''

Arden and Kowitt left the bedroom Skul switched on the walkie talkie and pushed the signal button. When he received the 6 M reply, he pushed the talk button and left it in, opening the channel.

"This is Delta," he said. "Do you hear me, Alpha—over?"

"Affirmative, Delta—over."

"The time is now. Tell Blue Moon to come and get us. I repeat: tell Blue Moon to come and get us—over."

"Acknowledged—over."

"Out. I repeat: out." Skul shout off the walkie talkie and shoved the transceiver into its case. He picked up the Bernardelli, had a last look around the bedroom and hurried to the tiny entrance hall where Kowitt and Arden were waiting. Kowitt had the door barely open, "It's as quiet as the inside of a moron's head," he whispered. "I'm not sure, but I thought I heard an elevator."

Skul turned his back to Barry Arden. "Turn on the transmitter, and use your penlight. You have to be positive that the gain and the broadcast dials are set to full power."

"I *have* done this sort of thing before," Arden said. he turned on a penlight and opened the control panel door of the beam-transmitter.

"Yes, but this is not Africa, and you're not with Mad Mike Quinlan and his Thunderbolts," Skul said, trying to decide whether Arden was joking or a bit annoyed. "This is the middle of New York City."

It took only a few minutes for Arden to throw the necessary switches and set the dials of the transmitter. The last thing he did was close and secure the control panel door and pull up the 2 antennae to their full 15.4 inches.

Skul had put away the Bernardelli, and once more his right hand was wrapped around the straight-butt of an Uzi. "We'll take the regular stairs to the sixth floor," he whispered. "From the sixth, we'll use the steps in the fire escape well. They lead to the roof. Don't give me an argument. So far, Barron's been right."

"We can argue later, if we're alive," said Arden.

They left the apartment, looked up and down the hall, saw no one and started west. They had raced past the row of elevators and were almost to the stairs when they heard not one but 2 elevators rising. From the sounds, one was a freight elevator. Why would anyone in the building be using a freight elevator at 4:45 AM? No one would!

"It's curtain time! We've been discovered!" Skul said tersely.

The faster of the 3, Barry Arden was first to reach the steps that led to the fifth floor. The stairs were so arranged that as one was climbing to one floor, he could look up to his right (or his left, depending on the floor to which he was going) and see who might be on the steps to another floor. Conversely, the person on the upper floor could look down and see who was on the lower flight of stairs.

Arden glanced down to his right and, to his chagrin, saw a thick-set man three-fourths of the way up on the stairs that led to the fourth floor. The pig-face was raising aa Czech Vz-25 submachine gun—or a machine pistol as the Russians (and the Germans) called submachine guns.

"ON THE STEPS BELOW!" yelled Arden. He twisted to his right and threw himself backward—to the left.

During that shave of a second, Skul, too, had detected movement on the steps below. So had Henry Kowitt. He tried to sidestep to his left at the same time that Skul twisted around and began to drop to the rug.

Skul, worried about the transmitter strapped to his back, had moved very fast. Kowitt had also been quick. Yet he was a milli-moment too slow, or maybe it was only that his time to buy The Farm had come.

Pytor Vorontsov triggered the Vz-25 SMG, the chatter box roaring, the muzzle spitting out a stream of 9x19mm

Parabellum projectiles that burned air in an upward trajectory. All missed Arden and Skul, although 4 did come close to the back side of the beam transmitter strapped to Skul's back.

Most of the Para Luger projectiles missed Henry Kowitt—most, but not all. He had spun to his right and was halfway to the floor when 3 hit him. One tore off part of his left ear. Another exploded his left eyeball, tore through his brain and blew out the back of his skull. The third bullet hit him in the chin. It broke the bone, bored through his throat, came out the back of his neck and buried itself in the wall. Kowitt was stone dead before he could swallow. His long legs went out from under him, and the rest of his body slumped to the floor, blood flying slowly from his left eyesocket, but copiously from his throat.

Skul and Arden swung their Uzis in the direction of the lower steps and triggered off bursts, the projectiles popping into the far wall. They needn't have fired. An expert in wet affairs, Pytor Vorontsov realized he had only one chance to terminate the 3 men above him. Only a fool would have charged up the stairs into a tornado of slugs. An instant after Vorontsov fired, he dropped, scooted to the right side of the steps and waited.

Skul, flat on his stomach on the rug and as enraged as a junkyard dog, could see not only the top of the stairs on which Vorontsov lay, but also the length of the hall stretching east—much to the regret of Mikhail Borsirev and Safar Khomenko.

Khomenko was too anxious, too keyed up. In contrast to the careful Borsirev, the inexperienced Khomenko stepped forward a moment after the elevator doors opened. As Borsirev warned, "Wait, you fool!" Khomenko started to look around the west end of the elevator. With an automatic motion, he first thrust out part of a Czech M-61 Skorpion submachine gun, the fingers of his left hand around the magazine.

Skul, still prone on the floor, didn't wait. He fired the Uzi. Twelve .45 Hydro-Shok slugs burned air down the hallway. With the loud scream of metal striking metal, 3 of the projectiles hit the side of the SMG. A fourth slug struck the side of the barrel. Two more chopped Safar Khomenko in the left hand and tore it off at the wrist. He screamed like a banshee as the savage impact ripped the weapon from his right hand and it—and his bloodly left hand—fell to the floor.

''UHhhhhhhhh!'' wailed Khomenko. He staggered back and leaned against the back wall of the elevator. Shock had numbed the pain, but now the full horror of what had happened flooded his brain. All he could do was stare at the stump of his wrist and watch blood spurt from the ulnar and radial arteries. The shock was more than his system could stand. He slumped in a faint.

Cursing in frustration, Mikhail Borsirev pressed the button that would take the elevator to the third floor. It would be pointless to go to the fifth or the sixth floor. The enemy would only keep him bottled up in the elevator on the fifth and the sixth floors. Borsirev was sure that the enemy was in a panic and headed for the roof. Fine! He would go to the third floor, rush to the fire escape well and wait on the landing of either the well's third or fourth floor. He would have plenty of time. The enemy, once they reached the sixth floor, would have to move east, then north, to reach the fire escape well in the northeast corner of the building. Andrei and Tsygasov were already on the roof. Then there was Pytor Vorontsov. He could get lucky. Borsirev felt excited. Either way, the enemy—whoever they were—would be trapped on the roof. There could be no escape for them. He glanced at the unconscious Khomenko, who was slowly bleeding to death. Too bad. He had been an excellent code clerk.

The elevator came to the third floor. The doors opened. Borsirev stepped out.

*   *   *

Jon Skul got to his feet and, simultaneously with Barry Arden, fired another short burst at the top of the steps to the side. Just before he tore up the steps to the fifth floor, Skul sent five .45 Uzi slugs into the head of the dead Kowitt, the blast dissolving the rubber mask, the face of the corpse and the frontal, jaw, temporal and parietal bones.

His photograph will never appear in any newspaper!

Skul wasn't worried about Kowitt's fingerprints; they weren't on file anywhere. There was not a single item in his pockets that would help the police—and that included the FBI—identify him.

"The Ruskie on the fourth floor steps will follow us," panted Arden, his feet pounding close to the top of the fifth floor.

"I want him to!" Skul's words had the edge of a sharp knife. "Our only hope now is Little Davy and the W-S."

They reached the top of the stairs, turned, ran 20 feet, came to the bottom of the stairs to the sixth floor and looked toward the top. They didn't bother to stop and listen. If the KGB triggerman was following, they wouldn't be able to hear him on the thick rug.

They darted up the stairs, reached the sixth floor, and moved 15 feet to the corner in the hall that stretched from the west to the east. While Arden faced the east and watched, ready to fire should any of the elevator or apartment doors open, Skul got down flat on the floor, facing the top of the stairs. He aimed the Uzi at the top step and waited. Twenty seconds later, he got what he wanted.

Pytor Vorontsov knew that Skul and Arden couldn't go to the seventh floor. There wasn't any seventh floor. There was only the roof. The KGB hit-man also realized that they had only 2 choices: either they could go down the east-west hall, or they could take the north-south corridor directly at the top of the steps.

Down on the steps like a big slug, the Vz-25 SMG in his right had, Vorontsov crawled up the steps until the top of his head was only a foot below the level of the sixth floor. Highly experienced in the art of how to avoid quick and sudden death, he had considered the possibility of a trap, even though he didn't really expect one. The 2 enemy gunmen were too desperate, too much in a hurry. Nonetheless, he dare not take the chance. People who foolishly assumed often ended up dead.

Bracing himself with his feet, Vorontsov took out a handkerchief, placed it over the muzzle of the barrel of the SMG, and very slowly raised the weapon until it was only an inch above floor level. Nothing happened.

Skul smiled. *Keep coming, Ivan . . .*

He knew what the Russian would do next, and Pytor Vorontsov did it. Very slowly he started to raise his head, all set to jerk back down at the least sign of trouble. Skul didn't even wait until he had half the forehead of the man in the "T" sights of the Uzi. When he saw only an inch of Vorontsov's curly hair, he squeezed the trigger. The Uzi sang its song of death, an aria that was flat, since it was only a short *phyyytttt.* Three .45 Hdra-Shok projectiles exploded the top of Vorontsov's head, taking with them not only chunks of the parietal bone, but also gray matter from the top of his brain. There was only a long sigh from the dying Russian. The Vz-25 SMG slipped from his hand. His body went limp and slowly started to slide down the steps.

Satisfied, Skul got to his feet. "Let's go. I want to see if the freight elevator has gone to the roof."

Arden was perplexed. "We won't be able to see it."

"The elevator itself—no. But we'll be able to see the overflow cables beneath it and the airhose of the brakes."

Halfway down the hall, Skul stopped and peered through the windows of the doors facing the shaft of the freight elevator. There was the hose—Damn it!—and the two "U" cables hanging below the floor of the freight elevator.

"Well, that tears it!" exclaimed Arden in a bitter voice. "Some of them are up there in the air conditioning unit house, waiting for us. Or around some of the ventilators!"

"Little Davy had better be there," Skul said and started to run east. He and Arden came to the end of the hall, turned north, sprinted down the hall, and were soon in front of the door to the sixth floor fire escape well. The door was locked. Skul unlocked it with a short blast of Uzi slugs.

"They could be below and above us," Skul said scornfully, shoving a full magazine in his Uzi, then pulling back the cocking bolt.

"It's 15 feet to the top," remarked Arden. "How do you want to play it?"

Skul opened the door and looked out at the stairwell. The steel steps and handrail were one tall spiral fixed around and fastened to a central post, a central axis. From each floor the steps were accessible by an 8 foot square landing below, or lean out farther, look up and see who might be climbing the steps above.

Arden's face, underneath his Wolfman's mask, lit up like the White House Christmas tree. "Hear it! By God! That's the sound of a rotor. Little Davy's made it!'

"Barry, you shoot a blast toward the top of the stairs, at the opening in the roof," Skul said, trying to keep excitement out of his voice. "I'll slam slugs toward the bottom. Then we run for it. Ready?"

"No, but let's do it anyhow!"

They moved through the door together. Arden looked upward and, in the yellow light, saw the door of the roof's housing over the stairs. He was triggering off a long burst by the time both his feet were on the steel landing.

Skul went to the far edge of the landing, held the Uzi downward and fired off almost a full magazine of .45

cartridges, moving the weapon from side to side and listening to the loud whines of the ricochetts as slugs struck steel below.

"*Blyat-skaye dyeluh!*" snarled Mikhail Borsirev, cursing. With projectiles screaming all around him, he darted back through the door into the fourth floor hall. Now he had a new fear, for he, too, had heard the *thub-thub-thub-thub* of the helicopter's main rotor. He wanted to strike out at his own stupidity. *Nyet!* The enemy had not been in a panic. They had not rushed blindly to the roof. They had gone to the roof deliberately, to be lifted off by a helicopter. Damn it! Now it was up to Gouzenko and Tsygasov.

Skul pulled out the PAC-1 walkie talkie, switched it on and soon had made contact. "This is Delta. Can you hear me up there, Omega—over."

The reply was immediate. "This is Omega." The voice belonged to Shinns. "We're 400 feet up. We're both wearing Cylops NVGs and there are 2 guys waiting for you, unless you're already on the roof and 2 of them are part of your group. One guy is waiting behind one of the ventelators on the north center side. The other crud is by the northwest corner of the building that contains the air conditioning units. What the hell is going on, and where are you guys—over?"

Skul gave a brief report, explaining that "one of us bought The Farm," and that ". . . the two of us are in a small housing in the north-east corner. Can you get those two with the CETME? If you can't, then me and my friend are in the worst trouble of our lives—over."

"Hang on. Now that we know the score, we'll clear the opposition and come down on the roof of the air conditioning house in no time at all—out."

Vladimir Tsygasov was behind a round metal ventilator—one of seven—40 feet west of the housing enclosing Skul

and Arden. The door and the housing itself were con-
structed of thick metal, which would withstand low level
sub-gun projectiles. But they were trapped; they could not
go back down the spiral steps, and they didn't dare stick
their heads out.

Andrei Gouzenko waited by the corner of the air conditioning housing, a Czech Vz-25 SMG in his hands. Not
wanting to tip off the enemy to their position, neither he
nor Tsygasov had fired at the door of the small square
building over the fire-well steps. In fact, Gouzenko and
Tsygasov were not even certain that the enemy had come
up the stair and were on the roof. Pytor Vorontsov, or
colonel Brosirev and Khomenko might have already killed
them.

Then, there was the chopper to the northwest. All that
Gouzenko and Tsygasov knew was that it was hovering.
They knew it wasn't a police helicopter. There were no
spotlights raking the roof—and the craft was too high. In
the dark, Gouzenko and Tsygasov couldn't see any mark-
ings. Against the background light of the sky, all they
could discern was a large shadow and the blue and green
lights underneath the fuselage.

Both KGB officers looked upward in apprehension when
they heard the rotor rev and saw the bird start to move.
Wickewire lowered the chopper, then swung east of the 60
foot tower on the west side of the roof. He then turned the
bird so that its starboard side was facing the roof. It was on
the starboard side that Chris Shinns had ring-mounted, on
a swing out U-frame, an MG-82 CETME, a general purpose light machine gun that, while it weighed only 15
pounds, could fire 1,250 rounds per minute. The cartridges
were in disintergrating belt links stacked in an ammo box
attached to the MG.

Wickewire stopped the bird at 90 feet above the roof.
Shinns first sighted in on Vladimir Tsygasov, who, seeing
the chopper coming down, had decided that he had better

return to the safety of the air conditioning units. Tsygasov was halfway home when the CETME roared and 50 boat tail 5.56mm projectiles exploded his body and sent parts of him falling to the roof.

Andrei Gouzenko didn't intend to become a sacrificial victim to stupidity. He darted back inside the air conditioning housing and headed toward the open freight elevator. He almost made it. He was only 7 feet from the raised wooden gate of the elevator when a wave of 5.56mm slugs washed over the west wall and the roof, the scream of glance-offs an off-key opera of pure destruction. Solid base projectiles tore into condensers, filters, and cooling coils. Motors, pumps, and ducts were wrecked. Two of the exhaust blowers were destroyed. So was Major Andrei Dorandovitch Gouzenko. Three slugs tore off his lower left leg. Several more hit him in the buttocks, churned his intestines and bored out his belly. Two more exploded his head and sent a spray of bone, brain and blood outward in all directions—into the air already thick with released freon gas from the demolished air conditioning units.

A jubilant Shinns contacted Jon Skul on a PAC-1

"I've got 'em. You guys get to the roof. Little Davy and I are coming down."

By the time Wickewire had positioned the blue and white Westland-Sikorsky and was starting to bring the bird down to the roof of the air conditioning housing, Skul and Arden were halfway across the roof. They had climbed the iron ladder, bolted to the north side of the housing, and were climbing inside the chopper through the starboard entrance.

Wickewire, his hands light on the controls, worked the collective stick; he "pulled in pitch" and the bird rose. Expertly he turned the cyclic controls and the throttle. His feet pressed the pedals. Continuing to rise—faster and faster, the four bladed rotor a blur—the chopper shot northwest. In only seconds the roof of the Armatage was lost in darkness, which by now had changed to a very deep twilight. The mutation, however, was mostly psychological on the part of the observers. It was the kind of awareness that comes when one realizes the night is dying and dawn is being born. Far below, the street lights were pinpoints. Above, in a half-cloudy sky, a sliver of moon hung crookedly and the most distant stars were fading.

"Chris, you're supposed to be in Morningside Park. What are you doing here?" That was the first thing that Skul said to Shinns in a cold voice.

Shinns started to unbuckle the straps holding the Cylops night vision device to his face. "I traded with Bates. He doesn't like riding in a chopper. He's afraid of heights. He's in the park with Brandon." He shrugged. "What's the difference. In a few minutes, we'll all be in the park. It's less than 18 thousand feet away. Ann and Al are using an infrared flasher to single Little Davy."

The difference is that I don't like my orders disobeyed. But it was a minor point. Skul only said, "Debbie is being held on a Russian freighter called the *Boris Gudinov*. We also found out that there are 2 full tons of heroin on board. The ship's right off the West Side Highway docks—pier fifty-six!"

Shinns put down the Cylops. "When do we attack?"

Barry Arden, holding onto a handhold, looked solemnly at Skul. "How do we attack, Jon?"

Skul did not have the answer—yet.

CHAPTER SEVENTEEN_____

SOME people are born with cast-iron stomachs. Colonel Mikhail Borsirev was double-lucky. He also had an armor-plated nervous system; he could withstand a tremendous amount of pressure. A stranger to true anxiety, he never permitted failure in one direction prevent him from going in another, his mind always working constructively and pragmatically.

He was questioned extensively by the police, since it was he and Andrei Gouzenko who had discovered the murdered guards and surmised that the apartment house had been invaded by terrorists.

He knew very little, he told the police, all the while pretending great nervousness and sorrow at the loss of his friends. All he knew was that he and Mister Gouzenko had found the murdered men and had then awakened some of the other Russians, all of whom had attempted to apprehend the terrorists.

The police had not found any submachine guns. Russians, on the various floors, had managed to hide the SMGs, including the Vz-25 that Gouzenko and Tsygasov had intended to use on the roof.

The police were skeptical. Uh huh. Apprehend the terrorists—without weapons?

Borsirev shrugged. "We are a brave people," he said seriously. "We had to do what we could against the terrorists. They were no doubt American hooligans!"

The police didn't believe Borsirev any more than they believed the story of Alekseevich Diakanov, the manager of the apartment house. Diakanov didn't have to lie; the truth would do as well. He said that the first indication of trouble he had was when he heard weapons firing, that is, when he had heard the terrorists killing innocent people. He would certainly have the Soviet Embassy file a protest with the United States government. No, as far as he knew, none of the tenants had weapons. After all, the possession of handguns would be in violation of New York City law, and Soviet citizens believed in obeying all laws.

Borsirev was not worried about his wife Larissa and their 2 sons even if he did make a big production of almost having a nervous breakdown in his concern for them. All 3 were taken to a hospital, doctors as puzzled about their condition as other physicians were perplexed about the unconscious state of the 4 watchmen at the Kings Royal apartment house on 58th Street. All 7 appeared to be in a coma from which they could not be aroused; yet all their vital signs were normal.

Borsirev knew that his wife and children and the watchmen had been "darted" with special drugs and would awaken none the worse. The watchmen came to life at 7:15 A.M. and promptly told the police how they had been "shot" by 2 men posing as FBI agents.

Larissa and Steven and Gregory Borsirev awakened at 8:52 A.M. in the Medical Arts Center Hospital. Wife and sons knew that husband and father was a high officer in the KGB's First Directorate, and they acted accordingly. They told the detectives that they had not seen or heard anything—and what were they doing in a hospital?

By 10:30, the police had discovered the connection between the Kings Royal and The Armatage. They found the old sewer. Hours earlier, they had found the Westland-Sikorsky helicopter and had traced it to the Ro-Pardalis Helicopter Service at Newark International Airport. A Black man and his wife had rented the craft. So—a Black man! One of the gunmen killed at The Armatage had been a Black man. "The Russians seem to be able to perform miracles. That black dude was cut apart with slugs—and the ruskies did it without weapons."

By high noon, Colonel Mikhail Borsirev had a new problem. The terrorists had posed as FBI agents. Now the Federal Bureau of Investigation could enter the case.

Borsirev wasn't concerned about The Center in Moscow berating him for lack of security, for not knowing about the old sewer under the basement of The Armatage. Before he had been sent to the New York post, the Center itself had assured him that all routes to the building had been sealed.

Live with that which cannot be changed. A logical rule that Borsirev intended to follow. Live with it—and capitalize on it. He had no way of contacting Salvatore Tuccinardo. The mobster's phone was tapped, and there wasn't time to arrange a drop in the park. He could not inform the Mafia chief that, due to the developments that morning, the meeting should be cancelled, and that it was now far too dangerous to move the heroin from the *Boris Gudinov*. He had to work on the premise that the mobster would come aboard the ship. He also had to assume that Sergei Shumaev had been forced to tell everything he knew, in which case the American assassination specialists knew that the Miles woman was aboard. They also knew that two American tons of heroin was on the vessel.

But what could they do about it? Even if the FBI and the Drug Enforcement Agency knew about the heroin, they would be helpless. The *Boris Gudinov* was the same as

Soviet soil. The Americans could not come aboard. They could watch the vessel. They could wait—and that is all they could do. The vessel would leave port, and the woman would leave with them—maybe.

And the special group of agents, who didn't seem to care about breaking the laws of their own country? Borsirev had to admit to himself that he feared them. But what could they do? They could hardly come charging up the gangplank! Swim to the side of the vessel and walk straight up the steel hull? *Nyet!* There wasn't anything they could do.

During the late afternoon, Colonel Borsirev left the AMTORG building and took a cab to the Empire State Building at the corner of 34th Street and Fifth Avenue. Almost certain that agents of the FBI were trailing him, he left by way of the entrance on West 33rd, hailed another taxi and rode to Gimbel Brothers department store on Avenue of the Americas. He used escalators to go from floor to floor, then took an elevator from the top floor to the ground floor and left by way of the entrance on West 32nd Street. A few minutes later he was in another cab and on his way to the Collingwood Hotel on West 35th Street.

Borsirev left the hotel dressed in seaman's blues. He now sported a short brown beard, a heavy mustache and a wig of heavy brown hair. He walked a block, caught a cab and had the driver drive him to the corner of Washington and Gansevoort Streets. He walked the rest of the way to the docks, a raincoat over his right arm, concealing a 9mm Makarow pistol. It was almost dark, and this area was not exactly the safest section in the city.

Borsirev was soon aboard the *Boris Gudinov* talking with Captain Basil Kunavin and First Officer Vadom Mostinik. Both assured Colonel Borsirev that the vessel was secure. There were 6 men stationed on deck close to the end of the gangplank. Six men, all heavily armed, were at the docking cables.

"Comrade Colonel Borsirev, this is not an apartment house," Captain Kunavin said proudly. "Many members of my crew have served in the navy of the Motherland. Should any unauthorized person attempt to come aboard, he will be dealt with quickly and efficiently."

Kunavin was a barrel-chested man with a shiny face and a doorknob of a nose. He had never liked the idea of having a First Officer who was also KGB. It made him feel as if he were walking on egg shells. He also suspected that other members of the crew were either in the KGB or the GRU. Wisely, he said nothing and always pretended that everything was normal.

Borsirev, seated in a chair in the wheelhouse on the bridge deck, was not impressed with Kunavin's assurance. Over-confidence was always dangerous. Scowling slightly, he turned to Vadom Mostinik, who was smoking a cigarette and drinking coffee so heavy with cream it looked like milk. Borsirev sensed that Mostinik was a very tough person and his own man.

"The woman—Miles," said Borsirev. "Have you had any difficulty with her?"

"What trouble could she cause?" Mostinik smiled, his thick lips moving back over his teeth. "What kind of trouble could she cause? She's locked in the spare cabin on the second deck. I've seen to it that she had cigarettes and toilet articles. Her food has been from the officers mess. I have the drugs prepared, Colonel. When do you want to question her?"

Borsirev consulted his wristwatch, an American Pulsar. It was 7:30 P.M. "That damned Mafia hooligan should be here in another 20 minutes. We'll wait until after he leaves." He smiled at Captain Kunavin. "I have not had dinner. How about some food?"

CHAPTER EIGHTEEN_____

JON Skul was convinced that if he killed every man on board the *Boris Gudinov*, he would still be damned lucky if the filthy water of the harbor didn't poison him. Almost noiselessly he moved through the oily water, pulling the plastic watertight bag along with him, his course one that took him up the starboard side of a Danish freighter, across its bow and over to the next slip where a West German freighter was moored. Next to the German merchantman was the *Boris Gudinov*, a modern T-2-class Soviet cargo vessel, 23,800 ton, some 542 feet long between her perpendiculars; 6 large holds and 6 large hatches; 10 large king-post booms.

Amidships was the control center—the bridge, wheelhouse, gyro room, radio shack, chartroom, Captain's office and quarters and deck bay, galley, and engine room officer's quarters.

Skul was making a double gamble: the Sergei Shumaev had told the truth, and that Colonel Mikhail Borsirev had not been able to change his plans. Skul had only one goal: rescue Debbie Miles, terminate Colonel Borsirev and Salvatore Tuccinardo, and blow up the *Boris Gudinov*. One way or another, the Soviet stink-boat and its 2 tons of heroin would never leave the harbor.

All he had to do was get past a 100 or so Russians.

For the present there was little danger of his being discovered in the water. Not only was the entire waterline shrouded in darkness, but who would look for a man swimming around the hulls of merchant vessels? Who would even suspect he was there?

The Russians on board the *Boris Gudinov* would expect him to try to get aboard, but they would be watching the gangplank and the docking lines. They would not expect him to walk up a perpendicular hull.

He swam horizontally across the raked stem of the German ship, the *Deutschland,* the disturbed waters of his passage drowned out by water falling from the slush-mouths of the bilge pumps, and then came to the sharp prow of the *Boris Gudinov.* He swam 8 feet up the port side until he was underneath the roller chock, that long opening in the all metal railing of the forecastle deck.

Skul knew the climb would be extremely dangerous. If any Ivan happened to look down and caught him while climbing up—one slug and that would be the end of the mission—*And the end of me!*

He placed the loop of the large bag around his neck. Holding the upper part of the bag high, he unfastened the 2 compartments, reached in and took out an electromagnetic grappler, then held the device in his left had. He reached up as high as he could, pressed the grappler against the hull of the ship, and squeezed the activator button in the side of the handle. Immediately the magnetized device became "welded" to the hull, steel clinging to steel with such intensity that it would have taken explosives to separate them. Some water had splashed into the bag when he had been forced to release it, but he didn't mind. The water could not get inside the main compartment.

His hand locked tightly to the handle of the grappler, Skul pulled himself upward until only his feet were dangling at the water line. The freeboard was only 15.6

feet—but try climbing it hand over hand with almost 20 pounds of kill-equipment around your neck!

Hanging there—between the water and the stars, between heaven and hell—Skul removed the second grappler from the bag and, pulling himself as high as he could with his left hand, stretched out his right arm, placed the grappler against the hull of the ship and pressed the button, activating the device and pinning it to the steel plate of the *Boris Gudinov*.

Now, while supporting himself by hanging onto the right grappler, he pressed the button in the left grappler which, shutting off the current from the batteries, deactivated it and freed it from the hull.

The process was tortuous. Gradually, almost painfully, he pulled himself up the freeboard. His strength at low ebb, he reached the roller chock and looked through the long slot. There were only running lights on the deck, but the bright lights from the dock shone on the deck, giving him more than enough visibility.

He both saw and heard the 2 Ruskies standing on the foredeck close to the roller chock on the starboard side. Talking in low tones, their arms on the railing, the two men seemed relaxed—Skul knew they were ever alert. From each man's shoulder hung an AKR Krinkov assault rifle on a canvas sling. In spite of his present "human fly" status, Skul felt almost honored. The Soviet Union guards its merchant ships well in foreign ports. Just the same, Russian sailors do not patrol decks with commando assault rifles.

Colonel Borsirev is sure expecting me—from the dock side!

Skul didn't hear the other 2 men. He saw them. They were walking on the foredeck on the starboard side, holstered pistols belted around their waists. Skul ducked down. If they came to port and looked over the side, he would not have one single chance.

For protection against the water, which was not warm, he had worn a thin, one-piece, rubberized suit, over which he had put on dark pants. His feet were bare and he did not wear a shirt.

Hanging onto the side of the hull with his left hand around the handle of a magnetized grappler, Skul unzipped the rubberized suit in front with his right hand and pulled a .22 caliber Ruger pistol from a shoulder holster. The weapon had been manufactured with a suppressor built around the barrel. He thumbed off the safety and waited. He would have to do something very soon. His strength was rapidly diminishing. He would either have to climb over the railing onto the deck or drop back into the water—*or kill all four of the commie cruds!*

The Starcraft Montego speedboat bobbed in the dirty water of the Hudson River, west of the Southern tip of Manhattan. The distance from the New York docks to the piers across the river in Hoboken, New Jersey, was 4,500 feet. The *Little Bug* bobbed at a distance of 2,000 feet west of the Manhattan piers.

In the darkness—there were only 4 small green lights on the control panel of the speedboat—Barry Arden got into his SCUBA gear—a black rubber suit, twin air tanks and a full face mask, the breathing system closed so that no telltale air bubbles would rise to the surface when he was under water. The Vencotex communications system— earphone and mike built into the helmet— was tied in not only with a receiver on the *Little Bug*, but also with the Temco personal communicator that Skul had as part of his equipment.

"This scheme is wild," said Alister Bates, who was helping Arden with the air tanks. "It's so damned crazy, it will work—if we get out of here in time." He glanced at the tall, thin man with the wavy silver hair. "You got us here, Skeeter. I guess you can get us back up the river."

"And then some," Ronson said, looking with satisfaction around the interior of the 18 foot Montego. With its Tr-V highly responsive hull, jets from 250 to 295 hp and I/O engines of 250 hp, the *Little Bug* could do almost 65 mph on calm and glassy water, or in a chop.

"My job is easy," Arden said, finished with buckling the air tanks to his back. "All I have to do is swim to the Soviet ship, attach the 3 magnetic mines and swim back. All we do then is sit out here and wait until we get word from Jon. We zip in with the boat, pick him and Debbie up, and get the hell back up river. When we pull out, we detonate the mines. Hand me the helmet, Al. I want to check the mike and headphones before I put it on."

"Be sure of the hose couplings," advised the always cautious Ronson.

"We know Jon made it to the *Boris Gudinov*," remarked Bates. "Chris said he let him off by the docks and saw him slip into the river. Frankly, he gives me the willies."

"Chris or Jon?" Aden completed the job of fastening the backflow hose to the helmet.

"Skul, of course," said Bates, his voice so low he could have been in a church."I could never decide whether he had a death wish or is an expert of experts!"

"He's dedicated. That's all there is to it," Arden said irritably. He disliked discussing personalities. "Get the mines ready. I'll finish testing the suit and helmet."

In another 10 minutes, Arden was ready to go. He had tested the air mixture and made sure the flow was regulated to the helmet and its fullface window. He slipped into the flippers, sat down on top of the cockpit's port side solid teak trim board, and tossed himself backward into the water. He surfaced toward center port and placed a hand on top of the hull. Leaning down, Bates let the KL-mines down into the water. Each mine was attached to its neighbor by means of a two-foot chain with a metal snap on each end. The snaps were fastened to O-rings in the mines, each of which weighed 8.9 pounds and contained 4 pounds of Pentaerythritoltetranitrate, or, as it was better known, PETN. The most sensitive of all the powerful military explosives, the PETN was mixed with 2 pounds of paraffin and could be exploded by a detonator in a tiny radio receiver attached to each mine. The radio receiver was made to operate to a depth of 50 fathoms, or 300 feet. Range: 2 miles.

Watching, Bates and Ronson saw Arden disappear beneath the black water and knew he was on his way. He would swim at a depth of 15 feet, keeping his bearings by means of the compass on his right wrist. When he reached the starboard side of the *Boris Gudinov,* he would place on K1-mine against the hull at the bow. Another would be placed midships. The third mine would be clicked to the hull near the stern, against the plates of the tunnel recess of the propeller shaft tunnel.

Bates and Ronson settled down to wait. They had other equipment on board—a depth sounder, and a kit for analyzing pollution in water. They also had more than enough identification to prove they were members of Columbia University's Department of Oceanography, in case NYC Harbor Police or the U. S. Coast Guard happened along and asked them who they were and what they were doing.

Bates looked up at the sky. There was only blackness. No moon and not a single star. The wind blew through his hair; cool, almost cold, wind.

''The weather report is for rain,'' Ronson said.

The 2 men with the holstered pistols stopped, and said something to their comrades at the railing on the starboard side. One of the men by the railing laughed. Another man—one with a holstered Vitmorkin machine pistol—lighted a cigarette. He and his partner then turned from the 2 at the railing, crossed over to port in front of the huge singletree mast, and continued to walk slowly toward Skul. For 5 or 6 seconds they were lost in the darkness caused by the hood over a booby hatch. All too quickly, they reappeared. They came within 10 feet of the steel-tube railing, and would never know how close they had come to being dead. Skul would have fired if they had walked to the railing and looked down over the side. Instead, they turned and headed aft. Skul pulled himself up and saw them head toward the superstructure. In another minute, they had moved by the upper deck and were gone.

The other 2 men were still at the starboard railing. *Yeah, I'll make them spine shots.* Skul thrust the Ruger through the roller chock, sighted in and twice pulled the trigger, putting 2 ordinary .22 long-rifle slugs into the small of the back of one Ivan. The joker jerked, half turned, then fell flat on his face. The man next to him drew back, inhaled loudly in surprise and tried to free the Krinkov A-R from his shoulder. He had turned almost completely to his right when Skul fired twice, both .22 projectiles hitting the man in the chest. With a low groan, the Russian took two steps forward. His legs folded and he fell, hitting the deck on his back.

Leaving the magnetic grapplers attached to the hull of the vessel, Skul pulled himself up over the railing of the forecastle deck, a wave of relief flowing through his muscles, now that the terrible strain had been removed from his arms.

The first thing he did was race over to the Russian sailors and give them head shots. Now he was positive they were dead. Still breathing heavily from his earlier exertion, he went to the fore side of the booby hatch, got down in the darkness, removed the nylon loop from his neck and opened the bag of goodies. The Coonan .357 Magnum auto-pistol, snug in its Assault Systems ballistic nylon holster, was buckled around his waist; the pouch of extra magazines was snapped to the belt.

He reached into the bag and pulled out other equipment. There was a MAC Ingram submachine gun. With the SMG came a shoulder bag of 6 magazines, each holding 30 rounds of .45 caliber Hydra-Shok ammo.

Another piece of equipment was the Tempo Personal Communicator, which was built into a leather band that fitted around the neck of the wearer. The mike and speaker were in front, just below the chin of the wearer. There were 3 buttons in front. One was for the volume of the speaker—3 settings. Another button kept the T.P.C. on open channel, in which case the device became a kind of open speaker phone. The other button turned the T.P.C. on and off like a conventional walkie talkie.

He pulled a small canvas bag from the larger waterproof container, and slipped the strap over his shoulder and across his chest and back. The bag contained seven F-4E Israeli offensive grenades. Each was 2.5 inches in diameter, round like a baseball, and filled with 7 ounces of TNT. It was the body of the grenade that made it so extremely deadly. Instead of being composed of fiberboard or squares of conventional shrapnel, the body was made of thousands of tiny darts, each only one-third of an inch long. Glued together, the darts flew in all directions when the grenade exploded.

Skul handled the last item very carefully, a pouch in which were two half-pound blocks of COMP-C, a combination of nitrostarch and tetrytol, which was more powerful than nitroglycerin. In the bag were also a length of wire and the blasting machine, no larger than a pocket watch. He attached the pouch of explosives, along with the blaster, to the back of his belt, letting it all rest high against his right hip.

First things first. He turned on the Tempo Personal Communicator.

"One, two, three, four, five," he whispered.

"Six, seven, eight, nine, ten," Skeeter Ronson replied— then, "He's on his way."

"Out," Skul whispered. Satisfied, he switched off the T.P.C.

Ok. Ronson and Bates were waiting. Barry was on his way to the *Boris Gudinov. All I have to do is find Debbie, plant the explosive, and get us both off this tub!*

Feeling like a telephone lineman, with all the junk around his middle, he crawled to the left and looked around the side of the booby hatch. No problem as far as the patrolling Ivans were concerned. When they returned along the starboard side, he'd blow their heads off with the suppressed Ruger, then cross the foredeck to the super-structure. It stood to reason that the KGB would have Debbie stashed somewhere in the mid-housing, perhaps close to the captain's cabin.

Fate had her own plans. There was a walk-down man-hatch starboard, 6 feet from the booby hatch and several feet to its stern. Before Skul could duck back, the small door opened suddenly, a Russian stepped out, looked at Skul, and instantly started to shout a warning to the other men below on the second deck. Skul didn't bother to pull the Ruger; the damage was done. He raised the MAC SMG and touched his finger to the trigger. The music-box chattered. Four .45 Hydra-Shok slugs exploded the Rus-sian's chest and pitched him backward in a shower of blood.

Skul didn't hesitate. The damned Russian had yelled loud enough to be heard all the way back home in Mos-cow! Skul took out a grenade, pulled the pin, jerked open the door of the walk-down man-hatch, and pitched the grenade down the stairs. Four seconds later, the grenade exploded with a God-awful roar.

At the rate I'm going, I'm never going to get to be captain of the steamboat or president of the bank!

Jumping up, Skul began a zigzag course toward the superstructure that contained the nerve center of the *Boris Gudinov.*

*   *   *

Debbie Miles had sensed something was happening when Vadom Mostinik did not bring her supper at the usual time. It had been 7:50 PM when the door was unlocked and a man, carrying a tray, entered. For a moment he stood in the doorway and looked at her. Well built, he was of medium height, had almost wavy blond hair, a slightly ruddy complexion, intense gray eyes, and an air of total confidence. She knew he wasn't a sailor. For one thing, he wore blue slacks and a light blue shirt, open to his waist. For another, he had a Makarov pistol in a pancake holster tucked inside his belt, to the left.

Debbie regarded him with calm, even eyes. His own eyes never leaving her, Paul Kichabalarus had placed the tray on the desk and without a word, had backed to the door. He backed out, closed the door and locked it.

Debbie had eaten in silence, her mind racing in desperation. This was the first time that only one man had brought her meal. Was it possible? Would her plan work? Even if she failed, she wouldn't be any worse off. If she failed, he might beat the hell out of her and rape her for good measure. But doesn't God help those who help themselves? Anything was better than being taken to the Soviet Union. She had to try. She did have one thing in her favor: the Russian's total disdain, his total sense of superiority over her, a mere woman.

She ate the liver, potatoes and cabbage, but she poured the coffee and the milk down the drain of the lavatory, afraid they might be drugged. Then she sat down and waited, glancing every now and then at her wristwatch, which Vadom Mostinik had returned to her.

It was 8:13 when Paul Kichabalarus unlocked the door and came into the cabin. Debbie got to her feet, picked up the tray and started toward the KGB officer, saying cheerfully, "I enjoyed the liver. I've always loved liver."

Kichabalarus stopped, and for a split second acted as if

he might become angry. As Debbie held out the tray to him, she could almost see the little wheels of his mind turning and concluding that she was being only helpful and was not a threat.

Just as Kichabalarus reached for the tray, Debbie pretended that she was about to drop it and gave a little cry of alarm. She had to catch him off guard, and she did. Kichabalarus stepped forward and, with an automatic action, reached out to catch the tray he thought was about to crash to the floor. At the same time that he reached for the tray and Debbie jerked it back, she brought up her right knee and slammed it as hard as she could between his legs. Her aim was accurate. Her knee caught him in the testicles and smashed them against the pubic bones. All she needed was a few seconds and she got them.

Helpless, Kichabalarus let out a hoarse cry of rage and agony and started to double over. Debbie stepped back and letting the plastic dishes fall to the floor, darted to her left and started to raise the tray.

Enraged at how Debbie had tricked him, Kichabalarus reached out with his right hand and, in spite of the horrible crucifixion in his groin, tried to get his fingers around her throat. All he succeeded in doing was crooking several fingers over the narrow center of her bra, pulling it off as she jerked away.

Holding the steel tray with both hands, Debbie took another step, got behind him, and brought the edge down on the back of his neck, swinging with all the strength she could muster. The edge of the tray hit that part of the neck known—technically—as the *third intervertebral space,* the target of a hatchet or a machete or a Karate chop.

The rounding edge of the tray not only broke several vertebrae, but caused such trauma to the spinal cord that Kichabalarus was killed instantly. Without a sound, he fell to the floor. Just to be on the safe side, Debbie slammed him again with the edge of the tray, this time to left side of his neck. Seeing that his eyes were open, but seeing only the endless stretch of eternity, Debbie rolled the corpse over on its back and pulled the 9-millimeter Makarov from its pancake holster. Then she pulled the ripped bra from his right hand. It was useless; the clasp had been ripped from the material. Highly elated—she knew that all she had to do was get to the deck and jump overboard—Debbie checked the pistol. The Makarov had a full magazine and a cartridge in the chamber. She shoved the clip back into the butt, switched off the safety and went to the door. She opened it slightly and listened. She jumped when she heard the furious chattering of a submachine gun. She couldn't be sure, but—*I'm almost certain it was an Ingram— toward the bow!*

She was debating what to do when she heard shouts— below decks, in the very corridor in which the cabin was located.

BLAMMMMMM! Then came the explosion.

Every nerve in her half naked body quivered.

Jon, what took you so long?

Salvatore Tuccinardo and Peter Dellacrote wished they were somewhere else, preferably back at Don Salvatore's estate near Glen Cove on Long Island. The two mobsters had gone to the trouble of coming into Manhattan, eluding the FBI in Little Italy, and then making their way to the *Boris Gudinov* disguised as Soviet seamen, should anyone be watching in the distance.

After Mikhail Borsirev, Captain Kunavin, and Vadom Mostinik had welcomed them in the officers mess, in the upper deck, Borsirev had come directly to the point. He told them that there could not be any further transfers of heroin to the warehouse, including the 2 tons below decks, in hold number 6 because ". . . of what happened this morning at The Armatage. The FBI had even entered the case."

"We heard the news on television and read about it in the paper," Tuccinardo said heavily. He concealed his disappointment and thought about the millions of dollars his family would lose.

"It was impossible for us to get word to you," explained Borsirev, who was seated at one end of the table. "We couldn't phone. We could not send anyone to your home. We hoped that you and your people would analyze the overall situation and decide not to come aboard this evening."

"But you need not worry, gentlemen," interjected Vadom Mostinik. "There isn't any connection between The Armatage and this vessel. However, as you both know, the FBI always keeps an eye on Soviet vessels. We have fooled them all these years, and there is not any reason to suppose that we aren't still making fools of them."

Don Salvatore tugged at the collar of the black turtleneck sweater he was wearing. He had always hated anything tight around his throat. It always reminded him of his great great grandfather who had been hanged in Catania, Sicily.

"We of the Honored Society always keep our appointments," Salvatore said for effect, knowing fully well that if he had known earlier what he knew now, he and Pete would never have come to Manhattan.

"Don Salvatore, we can still get back to Mulberry Street by 10 o'clock," Dellacrote said in his low and hoarse voice. "We can be on Long Island before midnight."

Don Salvatore glanced speculatively at Dellacrote—still another reason why he abhorred anything tight around his throat. Pete's would-be assassins had come very close to strangling him to death.

"Gentlemen, at least have a drink with us before you leave," Borsirev said smoothly. He looked toward Mostinik, who had gone to the side of the messhall and was returning with glasses and a tall bottle of wine.

"I'm sure you Italian gentlemen will enjoy our wine," Borsirev said cordially. "Much of our wine from the Ukraine is similar to—"

The snarling of a submachine gun cut him off in mid-sentence.

Captain Basil Kunavin pushed back his chair, jumped to his feet, and said savagely in Russian, "The enemy agents have gotten board! Damn it, Colonel, you said—"

Ignoring him, Borsirev yelled out for the 2 messmen, who were across the corridor in the cooks and messman section. Both had been standing by in case of serious trouble; both were KGB.

"It was a machine pistol firing from toward the bow!" gasped Mostinik. His tone was incredulous as he placed the tray, with its bottle of wine and glasses, on the table. "But how—"

The next thing the men heard was the explosion of a hand grenade—again from the bow and on the second deck.

By now, Don Salvatore and Peter Dellacrote, who had got to their feet, were deeply afraid, the Don snarling, "We must get off this damned ship. We can't stay here."

The 2 Mafia gangsters were now a dangerous liability to Colonel Borsirev. Neither had any knowledge of Soviet intelligence activities, nor were aware of the action that had been carried out by the mysterious group of American agents—but the 2 damned pieces of trash knew all about the heroin operation.

"Neither of you can leave the ship," Borsirev told them in a cold voice. "That racket will surely bring the police, and if the FBI is watching, they will close in and wait on the pier. They'll grab the 2 of you. How will you explain being on board this ship?"

"But the police don't dare come aboard," Mostinik reassured the mobsters. "This vessel is the same as territory of the Soviet Union."

Tuccinardo and Dellacrote, remaining silent, looked trapped.

Georgi Suplichny and Viktor Vermenko, the two KGB officers, hurried into the officers mess from the cooks and messman section, and Borsirev began to bark orders. "Captain, the terrorists are below decks. Give orders to the crew to watch all the outside hatches. We'll keep the Americans below decks."

As Captain Kunavin turned and started up the steps to the boat deck, Borsirev's chinless face turned to Vadom Mostinik. "You and Comrade Suplichny"—he indicated one of the messmen with a wave of his Vitmorkin machine pistol—"go below to the second deck and kill the woman. They'll never get their hands on her." He looked at the other KGB officer who had been using the cover of messman. "Comrade Vermenko, you remain here and watch our guests. Should they try to leave, kill them."

"What are you going to do?" asked Mostinik, accepting the AKR Krinkov assault rifle from the broad-chested Georgi Suplichny.

Borsirev ignored the looks of helpless rage on the faces of Tuccinardo and Dellacrote. "I'm going to take 5 of the crew and try to come in behind them from the bow. I'll use the same walk-down hatch they used. Comrades! Do your duty. We have the damned *chernozhopy* trapped. They will never leave this ship alive." He swung on the 2 Mafia gangsters. "And neither will you if you try to get past Comrade Vermenko."

Jon Skul was not about to underestimate the sailors of the *Boris Gudinov*. Now that the grenade had exploded, the sailors would arm themselves within minutes—and come looking for him. He thought of making a wild dash up the foredeck and charging the midship housing by going in through the upper deck. Debbie would almost have to be somewhere in the superstructure, and so would

Colonel Borsirev. But an instant's development forced him
to change his mind—the two guards on patrol. Hearing
the MAC Ingram firing and then the grenade exploding,
the 2 men had rushed up alongside the starboard, and
spotted Skul. Only he spotted them first—and fired, his
chain of deadly .45 projectiles cutting them down with
bloody ferocity.

The entire scheme was falling apart, and Skul had momentarily forgotten about the deck officer on bridge watch.
He remembered a few seconds later when the officer in the
wheelhouse switched on the spotlights, bathing the entire
foredeck in white light. Skul had been caught with his
pants down.

He had no choice. He could either go over the side into
the water—and forget Debbie—or else take his chance
with the walk-in hatch he had blasted with a grenade.
Choosing the hatch, he turned and was soon charging
down the steps.

He found that the grenade had killed 3 Soviet seamen.
They lay cluttered around the bottom of the steps, the
entire front of the corpses bloody from the thousands of
rocketing darts released by the F-4E offensive grenade.

He looked up the length of the main passage of the
second deck, toward the stern. The deck was clear. In a
half-crouch, he pulled the Coonan Magnum from its holster, at the same time thinking he had heard someone call
his first name. He didn't have time to decide whether his
mind was playing tricks on him. That's when he saw
Vadom Mostinik and Georgi Suplichny come from a port
to starboard corridor to the main passageway of the second
deck, Krinkov assault rifles in their hands. They stopped
as if they had run into a brick wall when they spotted the
barefooted invader in the black rubber wet-suit and pants.
Very fast, each man threw himself to the side of the
passage, raised his Krinkov and fired.

Skul had time only to drop flat in the middle of the

corridor, and raise the MAC-Ingram in his right hand the Coonan Magnum autoloader in his left hand as he went down and several dozen solid base spitzer-shaped projectiles cut through the air above him with a 100 times the force of angry hornets, some slugs striking the stairs up to the hatch-door and ricocheting with high-pitched shrieks.

Skul had 2 seconds lag-time. He spot-aimed and fired, the MAC-Ingram snarling, the big Coonan booming twice. Georgi Suplichny never felt any pain or even had time to know he was dropping into the Silent Land of the Pale People. Nine .45 Hydra-Shok projectiles from the MAC-SMG rained all over him and blew him up. He fell with some of his intestines and his left lung exposed, the momentum of his fall leaving a spray of red in the air.

A .357 Mag bullet hit Vadom Mostinik high in the front of his left leg. The big bullet nicked the main artery, shattered the femur and left the limb hanging by only tendons and muscle. The impact knocked him to the left so that as his back slammed against the wall, Skul's second .357 bullet hit him in the right side of his neck, tore out his throat and made his head sag at a weird angle.

Skul got to his feet, ducked over to the wall to his right and reloaded the hot Ingram. He was pulling back the cocking bolt when he heard a whispered, *"Jon!"* Auditory hallucination hell! He had heard his name. Then again, low but very clear—*"Jon!"* From 20 feet ahead, to the right. He was positive when he saw the door to a cabin cracked an inch or so. It couldn't be a KGB trick. Any Russian would have fired and have been done with it.

Skul swung the MAC-Ingram toward the door. "Come out of there—now!"

The door swung open, and out stepped Debbie Miles, her bare breasts bouncing like half-weighed balloons. Skul's mouth fell open. For once, he was speechless.

"Damn it Jon! Haven't you ever seen a pair of bare

breasts before?'' Debbie snapped, slightly embarrassed. "Don't tell me you're a virgin!''

"What were you doing in there, and where's your halter?'' he croaked, feeling a flush spreading over his face.

Debbie rapidly explained that she had been in another cabin—"Over there, on the other side!''—and how she had tricked the Russian and killed him with a tray, losing her top in the process.

"There were other men up at this end after you tossed the grenade. They left and ran toward the stern. I went into the empty cabin to wait for you. I called you so you wouldn't get trigger-happy and maybe fire before you knew it was me—I mean if I just stepped out unexpectedly.''

Skul looked again at her breasts, then shook his head. "Let's get the hell out of here while we can. We have work to do!''

They ran sternward, stopping only long enough for Skul to shoulder his MAC-Ingram and pick up the Krinkov assault rifle that Georgi Suplichny had dropped. Debbie scooped up the AKR that Vadom Mostinik had carried.

"Do you know how to use that weapon?'' Skul asked. He glanced toward the intersecting corridor.

Out of breath, Debbie nodded, wishing he had been wearing a shirt. She could have put it on and covered her breasts. Strange! In front of Skul, she always felt naked, even with all her clothes on.

Colonel Borsirev and his group of 5 were approaching the walk-down hatch close to the booby hatch on the stern when the heard the submachine guns roaring—and the booming cracks of the Coonan. A cautious man, Borsirev and his men raced back to the midship superstructure and crept down to the second deck by way of the stairs in front of the officers mess in the upper deck. He and his men soon came to the bloody, butchered corpses of Vadom Mostinik and Georgi Suplichny. One of the sailors turned to the wall and vomited. Several others gagged. So did Borsirev. He couldn't stand the sight of vomitus.

There were no signs of the American agent or agents.

A Vitmorkin machine pistol in each hand, Borsirev, had another look around, then moved rapidly to the cabin where Debbie Miles had been held prisoner. There on the floor was Paul Kichabalarus.

"Those clever bastards," muttered Borsirev, feeling half rage and half admiration for the *Amerikanska*.

"Comrade, they have be be still on board," Ladislav Pistrok said emphatically. Pistrok, an oiler, was an agent of the GRU, Soviet military intelligence. Borsirev suspected that he was. The man was too intelligent to be just an oiler.

Mastik Aluboz said, "It's possible that the others will find them before we do. Comrade Karelin and his group went into the sixth hold from the stern."

Dressed in a blue uniform, the fat-faced Aluboz was the first assistant engineer. He had so many hairs in his nose they resembled an ingrown mustache.

Borsirev nodded. "We'll use this deck to go to the first hold and work our way toward the stern. It's possible that we might trap the enemy between us."

The destination of Skul and Debbie Miles was the engine room space in the center of the cargo vessel. One section of the engine room contained the fuel oil settle tank for the big diesels. The oil would provide a lot of fuel for fire. Skul had chosen the engine room in which to plant the explosives he carried. He had modified his original plan. Instead of using 2 blocks of COMP-C, he would use only one half-pound block, which was more than ample to do the job. He rather suspected that he and Debbie might need the other half-pound to escape from the vessel.

Bravery does not mean acting like a daredevil. Skul was not about to hot dog it down directly to the engine room from the second deck. The vessel was in port. There should be few men in the engine room, only the men needed to keep an eye on the pumps and generator.

On the other hand, now that the *Boris Gudinov* had been invaded, Colonel Borsirev might have sent more men to the engine room. If the bridge was the heart of the ship, the engine room were the lungs, stomach and liver.

Skul and Debbie took a side corridor from the main deck and used the steps that led down to Hold No. 3. He had logically concluded that while Borisrev would post guards at all the hatches that opened to the main deck, he wouldn't have ordered the floor-doors at the bulk-heads, between the holds, automatically sealed. Sealed bulkheads would prevent the Russians from going hold to hold in their search.

They reached the deck of the third hold and began to move sternward between crates of cargo wired and braced in position. They were only 30 feet from the bulkhead that opened to the engine room when the oval-shaped door of the bulkhead opened and 2 Russians sailors stepped into the hold. Both spotted Skul and Debbie behind a long crate filled with Smith-Corona electric typewriters.

Skul and Debbie could have easily blown up the 2 Ivans. They hadn't fired because they hoped to reach the engine room without discovery, without the roaring of gunfire giving away their position to the entire vessel. A .22 slug from the suppressed Ruger might leave the victim conscious and still let him get off a few rounds from his own piece. Skul reasoned that if he could get to the engine room and plant the COMP-C without a lot of racket, he and Debbie would have a better chance of reaching the main deck, and he wouldn't have to blow a hole in the port or the starboard hull to effect escape. Now the damage was done. They would have to make a fight of it.

As Skul and Debbie pulled back behind the crate, one of the Ivans got off a brief burst with his AKR Krinkov, one of the projectiles coming so close to Skul's right rib cage that it cut into his rubberized underwear.

Skul let out a loud cry of fake but very realistic agony, then quickly turned and whispered to a horrified Debbie, who thought he had been wounded, "I'm all right. I only hope they fall for it! They'll try to surround us and come in from the sides and if possible, from behind us. Watch your side and stay down. I'm going to use grenades."

Up ahead, the 2 sailors ducked behind crates, one yelling in Russian to Anatoli Karelin and the other 6 men in the engine room, *"THEY'RE IN HERE. YULIN WOUNDED ONE!"*

Skul pulled three F-4E Israeli offensive grenades. He knew that the rest of the Russians would now storm into the hold. It was the only thing they could do.

Skul warned Debbie, "Stay down after I go out there."

COBRA's ace operative had been right. Karelin and the rest of the Ivans stormed through the bulkhead, scattered, and were moving toward crates when the first grenade arced across the area, hit the floor and exploded, peppering the crates and the Russians with steel darts, each of which cut through the air with the speed of a bullet.

Karelin and 3 other men were killed. Two others were still screaming when the second grenade exploded with a bright flash of red and speared its darts in all directions. There were more screams. Blinded by darts that had struck his eyes from sideways angle, Yulin Dzyuba screamed loudest of all.

BLAMMMMMM! The third grenade exploded and killed 2 more men. There was now only one man alive—Dmitrevich Traviskov. It was he and Yulin Dzyuba who had first entered the hold. Traviskov had been down behind a crate to starboard and had not received as much as a scratch. He would have lived and remained healthy if he had stayed down and out of sight. But he let panic slip in. Logic fled, and so did Traviskov. Or rather he tried to dash back to the

engine room. he was half successful; he was halfway to
the bulkhead when Skul's .357 Magnum bullet smacked
him in the left hip and slammed him to the deck.

Skul moved forward, looked around at the corpses,
turned and motioned for Debbie.

"Watch our rear," he said and moved toward the open
bulkhead. He turned to port and for a time studied half of a
large fuel tank that projected into the hold from the engine
room. The tank was 12 feet in diameter and 2 feet long.
But how much fuel oil did it contain?

Carefully, the fully loaded MAC-Ingram in one hand
and Coonan autopistol in the other hand, he stepped through
the bulkhead into the engine room. He could hear several
pumps and smell metal, oil, and gunpowder fumes. There
weren't any Russians.

"Come ahead," he called to Debbie, "and close the
door."

He moved 10 feet more inside the engine room and
looked up at the flight of steps that moved up to the second
deck. There was a flight to the left, then a landing, the
another flight to the right and another landing. Finally, the
third flight of steps, to the left, led to the second deck.

As soon as Debbie stepped through the oval opening of
the bulkhead, Skul picked up an oil can with a long spout,
went over to the door that she had closed and spun the
wheel to the right, locking it. It could be opened from the
other side by anyone turning to lock-wheel to the left, in
which case the lock-wheel inside the engine room would
turn to the left. Skul placed the oil can in the center on the
top rim of the round lock-wheel.

"Not bad," commented Debbie. "If anyone turns the
wheel on the other side, the oil can will fall and warn us."

"We're like the Boy Scouts." Skul grinned and tried to
keep his eyes from her naked breasts with their pointy
nipples. "Keep an eye on the steps to the second deck,
and watch the bulkhead to the sixth hold."

Skul pulled out a half-pound block of COMP-C and an electrictimerdetonator. He- jammed the 3 prongs of the timer through the brown paper into the putty-like explosive and looked around the engine room. His eyes finally settled on the system of 8 valves on top of the outflow pipes of the large fuel tank. Under number 4 valve was a wooden box filled with rags. The box and rags had been placed there to catch an occasional drop of diesel oil that dripped from the valve, which had not yet been replaced.

He would have preferred to use a remote-controlled detonator. But he had used all he had brought with him to the New York City area. The electric timer would have to do the job. It could be set from one minute to 30 minutes.

Skul made a quick decision. In less than 3 minutes, he and Debbie could race up the 3 flights of steel steps and be on the second deck. Should they be caught on the steps when the COMP-C detonated, they wouldn't necessarily be ripped apart, but the concussion would turn their brains into mush.

Skul turned the timer to 5 minutes, then placed the explosive underneath the rags in the wooden box.

"Let's get to the second deck, kid," Skul said and picked up the Soviet Krinkov assault rifle.

Debbie didn't appreciate his calling her "kid." But she didn't complain as she ran with Skul to the first flight of steps. You had to take the good with the bad and weigh one against the other.

They raced up the steps, reached the first landing, and started up the second flight. The peremptory metallic clank, of the oil's can hitting deck, was an unwelcome interruption which forced them to turn around and look down at the bulkhead. The oil can had indeed fallen, and they saw the lock-wheel on the engine room side turning to the left.

"We're too close together. Get to the second landing and watch the door at the top," Skul ordered Debbie. "Don't argue—do it!"

Debbie ran up the steps. Skul waited until the bulkhead had been pulled open from the side of the cargo hold and he saw 2 men step through the opening into the engine room. He felt if would be several moments before they glanced upward. They would first inspect the engine room at eye-level. A third ruskie stepped through the bulkhead, and Skul fired. The chain of 5.45mm metal almost cut one man in two. So many projectiles ripped into Ladislav Pistrok that they came close to exploding him and turning his body into a crowd! The third man stitched along his right side, fell back through the bulkhead door.

Maybe 20 seconds before they try again. And only a few more minutes until the COMP goes off! Skul dropped the empty Krinkov, ran to the second landing, and pulled the MAC-Ingram from his shoulder. No sooner had his bare feet touched the serrated metal of the second landing than he spun, depressed the barrel of the Ingram and squeezed the trigger.

And Debbie fired—neither she nor Skul any too soon!

Skul's chain of .45 Hydra-Shok projectiles mashed into metal and screamed off into space, all save one which caught Oleg Diakanov in the upper left shoulder and tore off his arm—but only a shave of a second after he fired. Diakanov's stream of 5.45mms streaked close to Skul's right side and missed Debbie who was behind him and to his left. Only one slug came too close. It ripped through his pants and rubberized swim suit and cut a fourth of an inch into the skin of his right thigh, leaving a 2 inch gash from which blood began to flow.

Her face turned toward the bulkhead at the top of the third flight of steps, Debbie had fired the moment she had seen the door swing open and a figure appear. The Russian gave a choked cry and fell backward.

"Run for it!" Skul said. It was a giant risk. If there were more Russians beyond the door—*We're dead. But if we stay here, we'll be just as dead!*

Debbie went first up the last flight, Skul right behind her. They moved through the bulkhead and Skul swung the door shut and spun the lock-wheel.

Below, a disgusted colonel Mikhail Borsirev and Mastik Aluboz stepped through the bulkhead opening into the engine room, Borsirev shaking with rage and frustration.

"We will—" Those 2 words were the last Borsirev would ever speak. He and Aluboz never heard the giant explosion. Their universe became a stygian nothingness, an incomprehensible blank into which not even Time could intrude.

Skul and Debbie felt only a thunder-crashing roar, a gargantuan *BBBERRRRRUUUUMMMM* that made the *Boris Gudinov* shudder from stem to stem and rock slightly from port to starboard.

Skul glanced at a white faced Debbie Miles and turned on the Tempo Personal Communicator around his neck. "Do you hear me?"

"Yes," came back the reply.

"We—repeat—we will be going over the port side in 5 minutes. Get your putt-putt over here—fast."

"We're on our way."

Captain Basil Kunavin and his officers on the bridge had also heard the explosion and had felt the vessel give a giant shudder. To a man they sensed that the vessel was doomed and would never leave port. Their fear became fact when the indicator lights on the fire board began to flash. The engine room was burning, and it was a fire they could not put out.

To complicate Kunavin's troubles, the American authorities had arrived. Several dozen police cars were on the pier, their top lights flashing and spinning, the officers grouped around the vehicles, ready with automatic weapons and assault shotguns.

The police had demanded to come aboard and Kunavin had refused, speaking to them through an electric bullhorn from an open window on the starboard side of the bridge: "YOU CANNOT COME ABOARD THIS VESSEL. TO DO SO WOULD BE A VIOLATION OF INTERNATIONAL LAW. THIS VESSEL IS THE TERRITORY OF THE SOVIET UNION!"

At the top of the steps of the gangway from the ship to the pier, a group of sailors waited nervously. Their orders were to keep the Americans off the ship—but suppose the Americans opened fire?

Valantin Dumokisk, the second officer, turned to Kunavin, his voice shaking with emotion, "Captain, what are we going to do? We can't keep the Americans from coming aboard, not with a fire below decks. International law says that when a vessel is endangering another vessel in port, the authorities have a right— "

"I know what International Law says," snapped Kunavin.

Salvatore Tuccinardo and Peter Dellacrote were not burdened by the least bit of indecision. All this time, they had sat at the table in the officers mess in the upper deck, Viktor Vermenko, a Stechkin machine pistol in his hand, sitting across from them.

It was only a few seconds after the explosion below decks that Tuccinardo and Dellacrote knew they had to act—and fast. Or sit there like damned fools and let the police find them.

Dellacrote suddenly pressed both hands to his chest, gave a choked cry and muttered in a weak voice, "M-My heart p-pills! I—" He let himself fall sideways from the chair to the floor.

"Do something!" demanded Tuccinardo in pretended anger, getting to his feet. "He had a weak heart. He could die."

The suspicious Vermenko could not see Dellacrote on

the floor, and he couldn't look underneath the table without taking his eyes off Don Salvatore whom he trusted the least. Carefully, he got up, walked around the end of the table and looked down at Dellacrote—and at the small muzzle of a Seecamp II .25 pistol, which Dellacrote had pulled from a left ankle holster. Dellacrote fired 4 times, the crack of the small auto-pistol ringing in the long room.

With four .25 slugs in his chest, Vermenko dropped and finished dying. Dellacrote jumped to his feet, then walked over and picked up the Stechkin machine pistol.

"We sure as hell can't use the gangplank!" Don Salvatore was in a rage. "There must be 1000 cops waiting on the dock!"

Dellacrote jerked his head to port. "That way. We'll go that way and jump over the side. We can both swim. We're strong and in good condition in spite of our age."

Don Salvatore drew back, his expression becoming even more angry.

"Sal, it's our only chance," Dellacrote told him ruthlessly. "It's a slim chance, I admit. But it's all we've got."

Jon Skul and Debbie Miles were almost positive that they would have to waste more Russians before they reached the main deck and were able to jump portside into the water. And maybe not. They could smell smoke and the stink of burning metal and oil. The entire engine room must be a mass of flames. The Russians could be abandoning the vessel.

Debbie had used all the ammo in her borrowed Soviet Krinkov assault rifle and was weaponless. Skul gave her the now fully loaded Uzi. Her hands were too small for the big Coonan magnum pistol. He could have let her use the suppressed Ruger, but if she had to buy The Farm, let her die with a proper weapon in her hands.

They went up the corridor, turned and found themselves facing the stairs that led to the upper deck—the same steps that had been used by Vadom Mostinik and Georgi Suplichny on their mission to whack out Debbie.

Skul paused and looked up the steps. "These steps should lead to the upper deck. Careful. Fire the instant you see anyone."

Skul's right thigh burned like liquid fire, and the outside of his leg, from the thigh down, was bloody. The blood had even dripped to his right foot.

The steps did lead to the upper deck. Very quickly, Skul and Debbie had emerged and were in front of the officers mess. Their eyes watching all approaches, they moved to port, to the corridor that would take them past the port side of the officers mess to the stern door that opened to the main deck.

Only Karma could have planned it. Just as Skul and Debbie turned the corner and were in the corridor facing the stern, Don Salvatore and Pete Dellacrote come out the door on the port side of the officers mess.

On both sides, there was only a flashing montage. Salvatore and Pete glimpsed a tall, barefooted man with a large pistol in one hand and a smaller, thick-barrelled autoloader in his other hand. His chest and upper arms encased in skin-tight black rubber. A belted holster. Shoulder bags. A leather collar around his throat. And his face! The face of a hunter, of a man who would never admit defeat. The face of a killing expert!

Skul and Debbie were as thunderstruck as the 2 Mafia gang leaders. In the brief half a second, they recognized the faces that all crime watchers knew by heart. There before them, only 20 feet away, were Salvatore Tuccinardo and Peter Dellacrote.

Debbie's .45 Hydra-Shok slugs ripped into Don Salvatore's chest, the impact knocking him back with such force that he might as well have been picked up and slammed to the desk. Stone-dead he lay with his right leg doubled under him, his chest one big, gaping hole filled with blood.

Skul's Coonan boomed once, twice! The second bullet was a waste of time and U. S. Government money, since the first .357 Magnum projectile had struck Peter Dellacrote in the upper lip and exploded his head, the TNT impact sending a cascade of skin, bone and blood splattering against both walls.

Skul and Debbie only glanced at the 2 corpses as they sprinted down the corridor and moved onto the main deck. The stern deck was empty, except for a group of Russian ordinary seamen clustered around the paint room and deck lockers. None of the sailors were armed, and at the sight of Skul and Debbie—their hands full of weapons—they quickly moved to the starboard side of the lockers. Skul and Debbie also saw the thick, black smoke boiling from four of the stern deck's ventilators.

Hurrying toward port, they heard the voice coming from the bullhorn on the starboard side of the bridge: "AMERICAN AUTHORITIES. THIS IS CAPTAIN KUNAVIN. I GIVE YOU PERMISSION TO COME ABOARD THIS VESSEL. WE ASK YOUR HELP. WE HAVE A SERIOUS FIRE BELOW DECKS!"

Skul and Debbie also saw a dozen spotlights from the starboard side of the *Deutschland* raking the main deck and criss-crossing the hull of the *Boris Gudinov*. Skul slipped a hand inside the black suit and made sure the penlight was in place.

They came to the portside railing, and he said to Debbie, "Jump feet first and bend your knees slightly. Once I'm in the water, we'll swim between these two tubs."

He helped her to the top of the railing. For a moment she paused, then she jumped, her feet striking the water moments later.

Skul unbuckled his gun belt and let it fall to the deck. Off came the shoulder bags. He shoved the Coonan and the

Ruger next to his skin beneath the rubber suit and fastened the snaps. The police must not find the professionally silenced Ruger.

He climbed to the top of the railing and was caught for a moment in the bright glare of a spotlight from the *Deutschland*. Then he was over the side, holding his breath. His feet struck the water which closed over his head. He twisted around, swam upward and reached the surface.

"Over here," he heard Debbie call out. Keeping his legs moving and spitting out dirty water, Skul pulled out the penlight, turned it on, held it up, and flashed it on 4 times, pointing the light-end west. From 800 feet away, he saw the red return signals, then heard the engines of *Little Bug* start to increase their revs per minute.

Spotlights from the *Deutschland* continued to rake the side of the *Boris Gudinov* and the narrow stretch of water between the Soviet vessel and the West German merchantman. Two of the beams caught Skul and remained with him, for he and Debbie had not been the only ones to jump. Five Russian sailors had also jumped port side and were paddling around in the water.

Suddenly, there was the loud tinkling of glass and shouts of anger from German sailors on the *Deutschland*. Every spotlight had been shot out. There had not even been a whisper of gunfire. Barry Arden had used a suppressed Colt-CAR submachine gun.

In only minutes, Skul and Debbie were being pulled aboard *Little Bug*. Skeeter Ronson turned the craft and headed west.

"Blow that commie ship!" Skul said to Barry Arden, who had turned on the remote control detonating station and was holding it in his left hand. Smiling in the darkness, Arden pushed the red button.

BBBEEERRRRBBLLLLAAAAMMMMMMMMMMMM! The 12 pounds of PETN in the 3 K1 magnetic mines exploded with a fulminating roar that many people would hear in Midtown Manhattan.

Skul and his people in *Little Bug* could not see what was happening. If they had been closer, they would have seen the demolished *Boris Gudinov*—almost all of her port hull ripped open—list heavily and throw Soviet sailors and American cops to port. Some even fell into the water between the doomed vessel and the *Deutschland*, for the tilt-over had been so great that the top sections of the *Boris Gudinov's* cargo booms were now over the *Deutschland*. Some of the booms of each ship had become entangled with each other. The water helped to put out the fire which had spread to the fifth hold. The inrushing water flowed over redhot metal (and 2 tons of heroin in the sixth hold), and created clouds of steam so that the distance between the 2 ships became filled with fog—It was chaos—there were several men in the water yelling for help.

Skeeter had turned the *Little Bug*, and was moving the speedboat north up the Hudson at full throttle.

"We killed Don Salvatore and his chief goon Dellacrote," Skul said. "Whether we scratched Colonel Gouzinko" —he shrugged—"who knows."

He accepted the pint of brandy from Alister Bates and watched Debbie slip into a shirt that Arden had given her.

"All we have to do now is get back to base, clear it out, and steal silently out of the New York area," Bates said smugly.

Opening the brandy bottle, Skul did not reply. At the moment, his only goal was getting Debbie Miles into bed, without making a fool of himself.